Julie was born in Bovey Tracey, Devon, and grew up in the South Hams near Kingsbridge.

This is her second novel in the *Moorland Forensic* crime series set in and around Salcombe and Dartmoor.

Julie is a classically trained flautist, proficient horse rider and journalist.

This book is dedicated to my husband, Terence, and all the other law enforcement personnel who worked for the Australian Federal Narcotics Bureau.

This book is in memory of Christopher Robin (son of AA Milne), a family friend who read to me when I was a young child. His love of books inspired so many.

Julie D. Jones

MOORLAND FORENSICS
DEVIL'S REALM

AUSTIN MACAULEY PUBLISHERS™
LONDON • CAMBRIDGE • NEW YORK • SHARJAH

A CIP catalogue record for this title is available from the British Library.

ISBN 9781528913461 (Paperback)
ISBN 9781528913478 (Hardback)
ISBN 9781528913485 (Kindle e-book)
ISBN 9781528960489 (ePub e-book)

www.austinmacauley.com

First Published (2019)
Austin Macauley Publishers Ltd
25 Canada Square
Canary Wharf
London
E14 5LQ

A special thank you to my children, Alexander (Zander) and Tamsin.

To the team at Austin Macauley, friends and family in the UK and Australia.

Preface
July 12th, 2013

Mill Bay Beach, South Devon presented a hive of activity. Tourists and locals revelled in a rare burst of warm summer weather, truly welcome following a long drawn out winter. The sun danced on pristine waters creating a mystic vista; scattered strato-cirrus clouds hung motionless, suspended kilometres above in a hazy sky.

A small passenger launch hummed rhythmically on its short journey across the shallow waters from Salcombe, its impertinent two-stroke beat echoing along the green-blue divide.

Sonia Mercer scanned the beach for her son, anxious to locate him amongst the hedonistic throng. Her eyes swept the stark, foreboding cliffs on this stretch of coastline, embedded in folklore for their entrapment of the unwary.

For a fleeting moment an alien sensation rippled over her, the ominous crash of thunder sounded far out to sea; a portent of predictable late afternoon storms brewing down Channel.

At first upon hearing the scream, everyone thought the young lad was having fun until they saw him plunge from the cliff face on to the jagged rocks below. A few people watched in horror, others looked away. It occurred in the blink of an eye; yet, rolled out like a slow-motion replay.

That day on the East Portlemouth beaches was one artist Lois St John would never forget. As events unfolded instinct prompted her to keep her finger pressed firmly on the auto shutter of her Leica. She captured the event on film and eventually one of those photographs became a celebrated painting "Falling Memories".

Chapter One

'I've always liked Salcombe,' James remarked, negotiating his old Land Rover through the main street, no more than a narrow passageway, scarcely allowing room for one vehicle to pass.

'Yes, it's an attractive little town,' his sister replied, happily soaking up the bubbling atmosphere, 'I rarely come here in summer, too many sightseers.'

It was now late July. Hordes of holidaymakers strolled along the narrow Fore street not seeming to care that a car was only inches from running over sandaled feet. The scene was one of relaxation and enjoyment, a picture postcard day in glorious Devon.

James located the car park on his left-hand side near the Victoria Pub, his keen vision searching frantically for a parking spot. After a frustrating ten minutes of watching and waiting he finally secured a place, backing up to the water's edge. 'We need to turn left, head up the road where a small ferry will take us across to Portlemouth,' he informed Fiona, jumping out of the Land Rover to consult his note book.

Although, barely a hundred-yard stroll to the jetty they attracted many glances striding along clad conspicuously in their white forensic overalls.

'They must be filming one of those detective shows.' James heard one lady say to another. 'I do like a good murder mystery. It's fun to guess who the murderer is. They must get through a fair amount of tomato sauce.'

James smiled inwardly. If only it were that simple, sadly, real life forensics was not quite so theatrical.

A young constable stood sentinel at the top of the ferry steps preventing all access to the waterfront and ferry except for authorised personnel. He stepped aside as James and Fiona approached.

'We've been told to ask for Ralph Morris who will escort us to the scene,' James informed the young officer, producing his ID card.

'Yes of course, sir,' the constable acknowledged, 'wait here. I'll let Detective Inspector Morris know you've arrived.'

Without delay, a burly-looking chap appeared, sweating profusely from the combined effects of a scorching sun and an inappropriate dark grey suit. 'That didn't take you long,' Morris said, clapping James firmly on the back, 'I've already got some of my guys doing the preliminaries, but now you're here you can take over. The ferry is waiting if you'd like to follow me. Watch your footing, these cobbles can throw you off balance if you're not careful.'

By "ferry" he was referring to a wooden, half cabin dory about fifteen feet long with a small outboard motor hanging off the back. Despite not being state of the art water transport it did the trick, within ten minutes all three were standing on the white, silky sands of Mill Bay Beach.

With forensics already underway a large section of the beach had been sectioned off to prevent the gathering crowd encroaching on the deceased. A few jostled for vantage points stepping in the way of James as he tried to manoeuvre himself under the police tape.

'There's nothing to see folks,' James snapped. 'If you could kindly move back and let us do our job it would be greatly appreciated.'

Almost immediately the assembled flock began to disperse like mist rolling out to sea. James instilled authority into his voice, indicating he meant business.

As he trod the soft sand James reminisced back a few years to the early challenging days before Moorland Forensics, when he'd not always been so assured. For the first two years they'd survived hand to mouth begging forensic work from old mates at the Bristol Home Office Labs and on occasions James had undertaken casual lecturing roles for his ex-Professor at the School of Chemistry over at Exeter University. Many a time having a Ph.D. in DNA Analysis proved more hindrance than help.

Things finally changed when James convinced Katie and Fiona to throw in their inheritance share as partners enabling them to set up the private forensic practice in Bovey Tracey, on the edge of the Dartmoor National Park, a town which could trace its origins back to the late Anglo-Saxon period. His siblings being single-minded, no nonsense business women with expert qualifications in forensic pathology and psychology was the key, granting them the diversity to finally turn a profit, securing the future of Moorlands.

'This way,' Morris bellowed, jolting James back to reality, guiding them to a remote stretch of sand. 'You'll have to hurry, the tide has already turned and is coming up the bay.'

Clambering over rocks laced with wet seaweed Fiona reached out for her brother's arm as she almost lost her footing under the thick slime.

'We don't want any more accidents,' she murmured softly, moving to where the body lay in one crumpled mass screened from view and insulated from the late morning heat inside a white makeshift tent. Placing her forensic case on to the soft white sand Fiona donned a pair of gloves and knelt down near the corpse, taking hold of the dead man's arm whilst James busied himself adjusting the settings on a 35mm SLR camera.

'The deceased was found around seven this morning by one Lady Scott-Thomas whilst out walking her dog,' the DI informed them. 'She owns that big white house, visible between the oak trees,' he pointed with his stubby right hand, his other moving to shield grey eyes from the blinding glare.

'Been dead at least 6 hours,' Fiona noted after a few minutes of careful, systematic observation checking the usual physiological indicators. 'The body under the arms is still slightly warm. Rigor has set in but only moved half way down the body, therefore time of death must be greater than 3 hours, also the cornea of the eyes is milky.'

These comments were made of emotion. After a brief silence, she continued, 'Fixed livor or purple discolouration of the skin has developed but is not complete on the side of the body against the sand, indicating the body has not moved from the right lateral position since impact and death. At a quick glance it appears unlikely he committed suicide. If you look carefully you can see red strangulation marks around his neck probably caused by twine or tie. I'm assuming there was a struggle, then he either slipped or was pushed over the edge.'

Fiona shuddered, glancing upwards to survey a precipitous sixty-foot drop. There was no way anyone could survive such a fall. Death would have followed quickly.

'There's also a three-inch vertical gash on the right side of his face,' she continued, examining the body in more detail, 'I'd say this happened during the fall, he probably hit a sharp rock or something similar on descent.'

Fiona ushered James over and they both systematically searched the pockets of his worn suede jacket and blue chinos. A mobile phone, black-leather wallet and a set of car keys were extricated. The keys and phone were placed into a clear plastic bag, the wallet opened to extract a driving licence.

'Here we go,' James announced, 'we're about to discover our victim's identity.'

'Liam Derek Mercer,' James read over her shoulder, 'born on July 25th, 1979; makes him thirty-nine.'

'Thirty-nine today,' Fiona declared, as she realised today's date, 'it could be coincidental he died on his birthday, yet something to keep in mind.'

James proceeded to take photos of the body from various angles whilst Fiona scribbled notes. The tide continued to lap its way up the small inlet forcing them to work at a measured pace.

'This is interesting,' Fiona commented, carefully removing a small cream coloured envelope from underneath the deceased. 'Maybe someone got to the body before we did.'

James moved to get a better view. 'Assuming Mr Mercer was murdered it wouldn't be unusual for the killer to leave a calling card.'

The envelope went into a bag for further analysis back at the lab.

James measured the distance between the body and the bottom of the cliff taking photos of a large, barnacle-encrusted rock suspended a couple of metres over the body. Ralph Morris looked on totally absorbed in the pair's proceedings.

'What do you think, Sis? Is this the point of impact?' James asked.

'Judging by the shredded fragments of clothing, they appear to match the tears on his pants. That looks like blood and tissue on the barnacles. Better add that to the evidence samples,' Fiona concurred, 'I'll need to go over the body again.'

Moving across to where Mercer was laying Fiona gently moved the head back and forward feeling it flop around like a rag doll, as Morris stepped forward. 'Something else for the mix,' she announced, 'his neck is broken, check out the severe bruising, both atlas and axis vertebrae crushed.'

'Caused by the fall?' Morris probed.

'Probably,' Fiona replied, 'we won't know for sure until we complete the autopsy. That wraps things up for now, there's nothing more we need to do here. Body is good to go. I'll be in touch with our findings.'

Detective Inspector Morris moved away while James and Fiona stood watching the Kingsbridge District ambulance load the body onto a stretcher before making its way up the winding hill towards Portlemouth village, its wide frame brushing the thick hedgerows as it made its climb. 'I suggest we pay this Lady Scott-Thomas a visit to get her version of events,' James turned to his sister, 'she may have some valuable information to pass on.'

'Do we have to?" protested Fiona, 'I could really go a stiff brandy.'

Although an experienced forensic pathologist Fiona always had trouble with confronting death, a demon she had to continually suppress throughout her career.

Ignoring her plea, James led the way across the warm, sandy beach, negotiating the rocks towards the home of Lady Scott-Thomas. Half way up a set of stone steps he turned to take in the dramatic sweeping view of the beaches and across the estuary to Salcombe. 'Breathtaking,' he remarked, suitably impressed, 'you're not going to get much better on the South Coast.'

James recalled a recent article he came across referring to Salcombe as *Chelsea-on-Sea*: average run-of-mill properties valued at one million pounds or above. For the very wealthy Salcombe was a fashionable location to have that holiday home attracting diverse professionals desperate to escape the pressures of urban life; generating animosity from locals as house prices soared out of reach. There was a well-known gulf between newcomers and locals. Devonians, although a friendly bunch, didn't always take too kindly to city types. Generally, they preferred to keep to themselves, leading comfortable yet relatively simple lives without obvious extravagance.

The pair soon found themselves negotiating the gravel driveway of a large early 20th century property lavishly endowed with well-manicured lawns surrounded by sculptured hedges. It didn't take long for a young female to answer the door at the appropriately titled *Estuary View.*

'Can I help you?' she enquired, a frown deepening across her forehead, 'If you're here to see Lady Scott-Thomas she's not receiving visitors today. She's had a nasty shock.'

'We're part of the police forensic team,' James explained, 'we understand it was Lady Scott-Thomas who discovered the body on the beach?'

The young woman hesitated then stepped aside granting access into a cavernous entrance hall. 'Yes of course. I'll show you into the drawing room, this way please.'

They followed her into a spacious, elegantly furnished room which enjoyed a 180-degree panorama across the beach and estuary.

'Visitors for you, Madam. They're officials, here about the body on the beach.'

Lady Scott-Thomas was sitting in an armchair by the window gazing out. She turned slightly when her visitors walked in but made no attempt to get up.

'You never tire of a view like this,' she informed them, 'day or night it's mesmerising.'

'So much to take in,' Fiona agreed, coming to stand next to her. Lady Scott-Thomas looked to be in her early to mid-sixties, silver-grey hair styled to sit fashionably around the nape of her neck. Her features were soft with skin well cared for. She bore only a smattering of wrinkles, her pale sapphire-blue eyes reflecting sunlight sweeping through the room.

'Lady Scott-Thomas, we were wondering if we could ask you a few questions about the body found at the bottom of the cliff this morning,' James began, 'we're with the investigating forensic team.'

'Please, have a seat.' she instructed, her eyes not moving from the bay windows. 'Nancy, could you fetch a pot of tea for my visitors.'

'Yes Madam.'

James sat down in a chair opposite Lady Scott-Thomas. 'Can you confirm the exact hour you ventured out this morning Ma'am?'

'I take a constitutional every morning between seven and eight,' Lady Scott-Thomas replied, still with her gaze fixed on the bay.

'Did you come across other walkers?'

'Jack Longeley was out for his usual morning jaunt; he lives further up the precipice at *Sumurun*. There were also a few holiday makers about, which is not uncommon for this time of year.'

'Which path did you take, could you give us a brief description?'

'I took the long way, the path running along the back of the house towards Garra Rock. I paused to take in the view from Pipers Point for about ten minutes, before heading back along the beach.'

'And that's when you came across the body?'

'Yes. At first, I thought he was sleeping, but when Chatz, my golden Labrador, started barking madly and prancing around, I knew something was amiss.'

'Did you go straight home to alert the authorities?' Fiona asked.

Lady Scott-Thomas shook her head, 'No, I didn't need to. I have a mobile so used that to call emergency services. They asked me to wait on the main part of the beach for the police and ambulance to arrive. To be honest, I was thankful to move away from the deceased.'

'Stumbling across the body must have come as a dreadful shock,' Fiona sympathised.

'I'm just grateful there wasn't a lot of blood,' Lady Scott-Thomas continued, 'that would have upset me a lot more.'

Fiona knew exactly what Lady Scott-Thomas meant, a relatively undisturbed body was a lot easier to digest than one traumatised and distorted.

At that moment Nancy arrived with a tray of light refreshments which were placed on a nearby coffee table. They waited for her to scurry off before the conversation continued.

'How long have you lived at "Estuary View"?' James enquired, raising the teacup to his lips and checking out a large cruising ketch beating out to sea against the incoming tide.

'A little over six years,' Lady Scott-Thomas replied, 'we moved shortly after my husband retired.'

Noticing James still absorbed in the vista, she paused a few moments before continuing, 'This coast line is outstanding. We fell in love with the place the moment we set eyes on it. The Salcombe to Kingsbridge estuary is unusual because it has no large river feeding it – only small streams.'

'Yes. I had heard that,' James remarked, 'I used to do a bit of dinghy sailing from the Yacht Club in my teens. I owned a Salcombe Yawl, when you race around here you get to know the estuary well. You must have welcomed the move to such a glorious location?'

Lady Scott-Thomas sighed, leaning forward to pick up the bone china teapot. 'Our move to the South Hams was not plain sailing.'

The pun intentional or otherwise not lost on James.

'Shortly after we arrived it was marred by the death of young Daniel Mercer. Daniel was my godson who fell to his death from those very same cliffs that killed this young man today. I keep telling local authorities the sheer drops are dangerous, needing some sort of barrier, but they harp on about areas of outstanding natural beauty. A fence is anathema to them.'

'Did you say Mercer?' James asked in surprise.

'Yes why?'

James and Fiona exchanged looks but refrained from making a comment.

'Can I confirm you didn't get a good look at the body on the beach?' Fiona asked, thinking if Liam Mercer was related to Daniel Mercer why hadn't Lady Scott-Thomas picked up on that, especially as Daniel was her godson.'

'Well, I wasn't wearing my glasses dear,' she replied candidly, 'I trust I can see perfectly well without them. Besides, I'm also not in the habit of standing staring at dead bodies. Is there something you should be telling me? I find your line of questioning rather odd.'

'No, of course not, we just need to gather as many facts as possible,' Fiona mumbled, hiding behind her teacup.

'I vaguely remember the Daniel Mercer case,' James piped up. 'If my memory serves me correctly, we're going back about five years, aren't we?'

'Yes, that's right. It was Daniel's tenth birthday, the day he died,' Lady Scott-Thomas explained, 'his family held a party for him. I remember the day as if it were only yesterday. There was a light sea breeze blowing and…'

'Sorry to interrupt, but did you say it was Daniel's birthday the day he died?' Fiona asked.

'Yes, I did. Please pay attention young lady. I don't hear this young gentleman having difficulty with my explanations. Like I said, it was Daniel's birthday, which made things so much worse. Where I found the gentleman this morning, was almost an identical spot where Daniel was found. I believe the cliffs are the realm of the devil.'

For a few moments a hush descended. James finally broke the silence, 'I know you're giving a full statement to the police, but there'll be more questions we'd like to ask over the coming days. There's also a counselling service we offer.' He produced a business card belonging to his sister Katie, a forensic psychologist.

'I won't need that,' Scott-Thomas replied firmly, pushing his hand away.

'I'd like you to take it just in case,' James insisted, placing the card on the coffee table, 'by the way, is your husband around to answer a few questions? Perhaps, he noticed unusual events over the past few days, which may help our enquiries.'

Lady Scott-Thomas shook her head, 'Leicester went sailing before breakfast this morning. I'm not expecting him back until after dark.'

James rose to his feet, 'Thank you, Lady Scott-Thomas. Don't bother getting up, we'll see ourselves out.'

'Sailing on what?' Fiona remarked, watching the tide now in full flood roll relentlessly in as they headed back to the beach. 'The estuary's been mud flats since early morning. Lady Scott-Thomas must be lying about her husband's whereabouts.'

'Or maybe her husband's the one lying,' James replied, 'come on, let's grab a bite to eat, there's nothing more to be gained from hanging around here. We better make a start on our preliminary report once we get back to the lab.'

****

Moorland Forensics was in the main street of Bovey Tracey on a site previously occupied by an old bakery. With the luxury of a substantial inheritance the family renovated the hundred-year-old building and installed a state-of-the-art forensic laboratory complex in a dedicated extension including reception area and office on the ground floor: two small bedrooms, a large luxurious bathroom and storage facilities occupied the first floor. Only access was via a drive-in courtyard at the rear enclosed by a high brick wall and security gate under full CCTV coverage from the office. The premises were discreet and private. A small brass plaque "Moorland Forensic Consultants" on the courtyard wall above the intercom gave little away as to what business went on inside. Even the locals were for the most part in the dark about the site. The common opinion bandied around being 'professional psychiatric suites'; the way the siblings liked it.

James busied himself in the scientific instrument room at the back of the building changing gas bottles on the GC/Mass Spectrometer whilst waiting for professional acquaintances Nicholas Shelby and Mathew Tyler to arrive. Shelby, a Forensic Pathologist was an old friend of the family. He knew Fiona from their time at London University where both gained their specialisation. A Kiwi, he grew up in Queenstown and moved to England after gaining his Bachelor of Medicine. He now commanded a major Home Office forensic position in the West Country, sharing his time between high level administration and indulging his passion for getting involved 'hands on' in criminal investigations. Autopsy was his obsession. In ten years for the Government, Nick had worked his way up from a lowly assistant FP at Aberdeen to become one of the most respected pathologists in the UK. His dark good looks and flecked, jet-black hair belied his claim of being from 100% Scottish South Island stock. James guessed at least 25% Polynesian but had never broached the subject.

Matt by comparison was almost the complete opposite. Introverted, almost shy he worked alone, had few friends and minimal social life apart from the occasional dalliance with Katie. He was a misfit at school and rebelled against authority. Leaving before gaining exams he worked as a computer game designer, retrenched after ten years with the same company. Unable to find suitable employ and at a loose end, he almost succeeded in cracking the RAF's daily operations schedules for Iraq, "just to see if I could do it". But they didn't throw the Official Secrets Act at him. The Ministry of Defence was so impressed they gave him a computer, a desk and two staff at New Scotland Yard, with a job description so sensitive even his Chief Commander was not privy. Katie once told Fiona she thought he had succeeded in breaking into the Islamic Republic of Iran's Organisation of Atomic Energy top secret, central computer files, stored at the Uranium Enrichment and Technology Facility at Natanz.

These days he worked almost entirely for law enforcement from home on the moors, as a contract computer analyst. He had become a real asset to many local authorities. On the flip side, he also managed to create a few enemies along the way, helping to put several people behind bars from unearthing darkest secrets hidden in the depths of computer hard drives.

James had fitted out the Moorland lab with all the latest technology making the team self-sufficient in conducting an extensive range of chemical, biochemical and physical evidence testing, including the latest semi-automated DNA analysis instrumentation and procedures. The more complex testing was carried out by the Government facilities in Exeter or Bristol, but most times Moorland Forensics was independent with their contract investigations. From the start the team had ensured the lab was accredited to all relevant Government and International standards.

Although the bulk of the Lab's business derived from contracted Home Office matters, the siblings also offered their services to private clients and industry, occasionally working for the other side of the fence in criminal matters.

Not one to remain idle James reached for the envelope recovered from beneath Liam Mercer. With a pair of forceps, he carefully removed the contents: a colour photograph and a print of a portrait painting of the same photo. It depicted five people lazing on one of Devon's most pristine beaches, James instantly recognised it as East Portlemouth, near where the body of Liam Mercer had been located. He donned a pair of gloves studying the photo and portrait in more detail, unusual items to find on the deceased.

'What's that you've got?' Katie enquired, entering the lab and leaning over her brother's shoulder. Her bright-blue eyes sparkled, complimenting her fair complexion and long blonde hair. Katie was quite a stunner attracting many admirers of the opposite sex. 'Can't be one of your photos, they normally end up blurred with people's heads missing.'

James didn't rise to the bait, still focusing on the finer details to hand. 'For your information these were discovered with the deceased, Liam Mercer.'

Katie peering closer at the print gave a low whistle. 'I recognise the artist's style. I'm sure I've seen their work before. Is there a name anywhere?'

James opened the top drawer of a nearby desk producing a small, powerful magnifying glass, 'Let's look, shall we?'

They scanned the portrait carefully, eventually locating a small signature on the bottom left hand corner in black ink.

'Lois St John,' Katie read out loud. 'That's right. I remember now. I've been to a couple of her art exhibitions. She owns an up-market gallery in Salcombe. A real eccentric by all accounts who chooses to spend her spare time on board a wooden yacht moored near East Portlemouth.'

'Well that's interesting, Portlemouth is the exact location where Liam Mercer was discovered this morning,' James remarked, 'I think we need to pay Lois St John a visit. She undoubtedly can offer some insight on this picture and the people in it.'

'Count me in,' Katie pleaded, 'I love exploring the minds of bizarre types. I reckon this Lois St John could be quite a character.'

James continued to examine the print in fine detail. It was a pleasing work, expertly executed in pencil and soft shades of pastels. As he moved the magnifying glass across the top right-hand corner Katie suddenly jabbed him in the arm. 'Hone in there,' she ordered, pointing with her forefinger to the top right-hand side of the painting, 'that almost looks like someone falling from the cliff, a young child.'

Her brother obliged, 'Unless I'm very much mistaken I'd swear this is meant to represent the fall of young Daniel Mercer, who died a little over five years ago,' his excitement soared. 'Why on earth would anyone paint such a morbid depiction of a real-life tragedy?'

'Well, Picasso did it with "Guernica". Pretty successfully too in whipping up hate against Franco's Nationalists. Bizarrely he spent the war years domiciled in his studio in Paris happily co-existing with the Germans,' Katie informed, 'anyway artists can be weird and like I said, Lois St John is known for her eccentricity. If I remember correctly a lot of her work was banned from public viewing for being too controversial.'

'Yes, but painting the death of a young boy is surely taking things beyond exocentric, it borders on being sick,' Fiona remarked, entering the lab through the side entrance accompanied by Nick and Matt, 'this artist woman sounds crazy.'

'Not necessarily,' Katie continued, 'I researched this in my fine art elective at Uni. I don't think Hieronymus Bosch's grisly depictions of Hell were crazy or politically motivated. Europe had just come through the Great Plague, death and unspeakable horror were commonplace…Although, they probably did their bit in bringing about the Enlightenment. On the other hand, I've seen Gericault's "The Raft of the Medusa" in the Louvre. It's big, powerful and… unsettling. Even spooky. Easy to see the work almost brought down the French Government of the time. It will certainly be interesting to get her version of why she painted such a reactionary work.'

'Are you ready for my preliminary findings on the death of Liam Mercer?' Nick Shelby broke in, not wishing to stand around all day speculating on works of art. He made himself comfortable on a high-backed stool, smart phone at the ready.

'Fire away,' James replied, swivelling around in his chair giving Nick his undivided attention, 'I trust you've got good news.'

'Having examined the photographs taken at the crime scene, it appears highly improbable Liam Mercer accidentally fell to his death,' Nick informed the small gathering, 'it's more likely he was pushed. This is backed up by evidence of a scuffle the initial police forensic team unearthed at the top of the cliff. I've also been running a background check on Liam Mercer and his position as a sometime criminal barrister for the Crown didn't earn him a lot of friends. He's part owner of Grays Law Firm in Exeter, which I understand has earned itself quite a ruthless reputation inside the legal fraternity.'

Nick paused momentarily, before pulling out a small note book for further information, 'I can't be sure until we conduct a full post mortem and toxicology tests, but I did sight a small puncture wound under Liam's collar bone which complicates things. It appears he was injected with something, possibly lethal, which would have made pushing him off the cliff that much easier. Another interesting fact, it's almost certain nothing valuable was stolen from the deceased. As you know his wallet was found about his person along with his mobile phone and car keys. His wallet housed at least two hundred and fifty pounds in fresh notes, so I think we can rule out a motive of robbery.'

'Any noteworthy calls traced to or from his mobile?' Fiona asked.

Nick shook his head, 'Nothing outstanding, a few text messages to his accountant a Ronald Mills in Salcombe, several calls to the Exeter Courts… and, a call to the local hardware co-op in Kingsbridge. It looks as if Liam rarely used his mobile.'

'What about his car?' Fiona pressed, 'Anything unusual there?'

'I've got a team going over the slate green VW as we speak, which was parked outside the Portlemouth Arms,' Nick replied, 'So far, they've not produced anything of interest.'

'What do we know about his personal life?' Katie asked.

'Not a great deal,' Nick continued, 'he was married to Sonia Mercer, who also happens to be a lawyer working at Grays Law Firm. They had a son Daniel who died five years ago, falling from the same cliffs where we found Liam.'

A few moments of silence, and several eyebrows raised before Matt spoke. 'I've begun pulling apart Liam's personal flip mini-computer signed over to me by DI Morris, but so far I've only found work related files, nothing of interest. I'll keep plugging away to see what else surfaces, but don't hold your breath.'

'When's the autopsy been scheduled?' Fiona asked.

'Early Wednesday morning,' Nick told her, 'I was hoping either you or James would be able to assist me.'

'I'd love to mate but I'm giving evidence this week in Bristol relating to The Flannigan matter,' James informed him, 'I'm sure Fiona will be happy to do the honours.'

'You mean Benny Flannigan, aka "The Butcher of Barnstaple",' Fiona scoffed, 'I see that snivelling, self-important boor Ignatius Robb QC is acting for the Defence. I've heard from my confidential sources he's rubbing both hands together with anticipation waiting to cross-examine you again. Are you ready to spend another torrid, half day grilling in the box, dear brother?'

'You would have to bring that up,' James mused.

'When was it, last August…the Dickson trial if my memory serves me right?' continued Fiona, 'something about not performing blanks or controls on the plant evidence.'

'It wasn't my fault. It didn't help that the Deputy Crown prosecution team got my Gas Chromatograph readouts mixed up with the Government Lab HPLC results from another entirely different matter,' protested James, slightly embarrassed. 'Not this time however, sister dear. I'll be getting my own back tomorrow. No holes in this one. All the evidence, forensic and circumstantial points to Benny carving up the victim with a large "Bowie like" hunting knife and for him to walk away from this one will be a bloody miracle.

We've gone over the irrefutable chemical evidence a dozen times linking the leather scabbards in Benny Flannigan's flat with the Bowie knife used as the murder weapon. He used an unusual homemade concoction of bee's wax and sandalwood oil to condition the leather knife sheaths found in his bedroom. A combination not found in any known proprietary leather conditioner product.'

'So?' Fiona still wasn't convinced.

'Infra-Red spectra indicated strong similarities with the waxy material I extracted from the bowie knife handle to the material on the sheaths. The alcohol soluble fraction from both samples gave matching GC/Mass Spectra for the sesquiterpenes typical of sandalwood oil.

Bloody marvellous. Glad it's you, not me,' Katie chuckled. She always enjoyed hearing of her brother's success stories. He certainly knew his stuff when it came to Forensic Science. Not many cases got the better of James.

Fiona turned the conversation back to Liam Mercer, 'It must have been a calculated murder Nick, especially if your theory of Liam being drugged comes to fruition.'

Nick nodded his agreement, 'I'd almost bet my house on the fact Liam's killer did their homework. I don't believe for one moment they just happened to encounter each other on the cliff top resulting in a random fracas. Although there is the possibility Liam may have been injected with the unknown substance a few hours before arriving on the cliffs. We should know this once we conduct full toxicology.'

'Which may put Liam's wife in the picture, if the injection took place before Liam set off for his morning walk?' Katie calculated, 'It'll be interesting to get her version of events and find out how solid their relation was.'

'We'll know more after the autopsy,' Nick said casually, 'no use jumping to conclusions. It's the hard-core forensic evidence we're after, not assumptions.'

****

The following morning after a barely adequate breakfast Katie and James set off towards the Coast, hoping to catch the eccentric Lois St John. They encountered the usual bottlenecks driving through Totnes and again exiting the ancient market town of Kingsbridge, before getting stuck behind an old, rustic combine harvester up the steep incline of West Alvington Hill along the A381. Being the height of summer the narrow Devon lanes became blocked with tourist traffic, only offering a handful of passing bays. With the hedges full of wild plants and growth well over two metres, visibility was poor around sharp corners. Locals knew to use their horn alerting oncoming traffic of their presence, visitors did not, sometimes with disastrous consequences.

After a frustrating ninety minutes, James finally turned off the engine of Fiona's red TVR at the bottom of Coronation Road in Salcombe, a ten-minute walk from the art gallery in Union Street owned by Lois St John.

A light sou'easter moved fitfully in off the harbour providing scant relief on what could otherwise be described as a sweltering summer's day. Screeching gulls hovered over the waterfront scrounging for food as young children busied themselves with crabbing lines. More daring individuals ran and jumped off the side of the walkway, laughing and screaming as their warm bodies plunged into the giant ice bucket known as the English Channel.

The gallery belonging to Lois St John was in a winning position for tourists, no doubt making her a fortune during the warmer months, jammed in between an old worldly tearoom brimming with visitors tucking in to Devonshire cream teas and a small, sailing apparel retail outlet.

James and Katie entered the brightly lit gallery which heralded the grand title "Canvases of Colour" above the glass door.

'Anyone here?' James called out, glancing around the immaculate space, its walls crammed with paintings and drawings of local landscapes and maritime scenes, most bearing astronomical price tags.

'Won't be a moment I'm just mixing some paints,' a woman's voice answered from somewhere out the back, 'feel free to browse.'

James continued to study some of the paintings on the wall whilst Katie took a seat in an inviting sofa. Most of the paintings were very good, probably half justifying their ticket price; one or two were on the bizarre side and a couple offered little to the viewer. The majority could be described as intriguing; Lois certainly knew how to capture the quintessence of her subjects, using bright contrasting colours in nearly all the works.

James, staring with interest at a North Devon seascape, rendered expertly in impasto oil with a palette knife jumped as Lois suddenly materialised next to him. She'd drifted silently into the room, her boat shoes lifeless on the concrete floor.

'I can do that for fifteen hundred pounds if you take it today,' she offered, pushing her slim-line glasses firmly back onto the bridge of a nose turned up at the end and peering closely at the visitor. She was barely more than five feet tall, her long grey hair high on the top of her head in a very messy bun, 'You don't look like a local. Here on holiday?'

'Eh, not exactly,' James replied, 'I'm from Bovey Tracey, so I guess that's near enough.'

Lois merely grunted as if she didn't think living on the edge of Dartmoor classed James as a local in her neck of the woods.

'I'll leave you to keep browsing unless there's something I can assist you with. Are you together?' She'd caught sight of Katie half dozing on the red settee and shot her a scornful look. 'I'll have you know that Italian leather lounge is very expensive. If I see a mark or scratch after you've gone, I'll know where to direct the bill.'

'Yes, we're together and if your sofa is damaged in any way, I'll happily pay the costs,' James informed her, 'our visit pertains to one of your paintings, a beach scene.'

Lois' laughter rang out loudly, echoing throughout the gallery. 'My dear boy, I paint lots of beaches. You'll have to be more specific.'

'This one has about five people relaxing on a beach but in one corner there appears to be someone toppling from the cliff. It's quite a dramatic painting as I recall, just what I want for my bedroom wall.'

Lois offered a scathing look. 'I guess we can't all be accountable for taste on where we choose to hang paintings. The one you're describing is "Falling Memories". That particular work of art is not actually one of mine.'

'Really, I believe it had your signature on the bottom,' Katie remarked, rising from Lois' Italian modular and moving closer to James.

'That's as maybe but I can categorically state I did not paint that picture,' Lois informed them, sounding frustrated, 'Someone obviously thought it clever to add my name to the bottom making it look like my handy work. I know my own work young lady and that painting was not crafted by me.'

'If you didn't paint the picture, who did?' James asked, with interest.

'That young man I cannot answer,' Lois replied, 'I found it on my doorstep one morning with a little note "Please exhibit me". I did just that and all hell broke loose. You see I didn't notice a person in the right-hand corner plunging from the cliffs. More fool me. That painting caused me a lot of grief.'

'So, the style doesn't appear familiar in anyway? No particular artist you recognise?' James pressed.

'Not at all, I had so many people quiz me about the painting, but I can truthfully say I have no idea who the artist could have been. However, I do know what the painting relates to.'

Sounding convincing James had no reason to doubt Lois wasn't telling the truth.

James produced his business card briefing Lois St John on the real reason for their visit.

'You'd better come out the back to my studio.' she informed them, 'I could do with a break from the gallery. Just give me a moment to lock the front door and put up the *"Gone Fishing"* sign.'

James smiled. Lois was indeed a character.

The studio was intimate but well lit, surprisingly cheerful from the combination of skylights and white washed walls. Six easels supporting works in varying stages of completion lay scattered about, leading to speculation Lois worked on several paintings at once.

'Some of these take months to finish,' Lois explained to James, who was engrossed in a small, seductive pen and ink harbour scene. 'On average I paint for nine hours a day, sometimes more.'

'Do you ever tire of it?' James asked causally, almost tripping on a box of oil paints.

'Certainly not,' Lois replied indignantly, 'the day that happens I'll be six feet under. Now what's your poison?'

'Nothing for us thanks,' Katie piped up, as Lois pointed in the direction of a flat pack wine cabinet, housing several bottles of liquor.

'Not even a small tipple?' Lois pressed with gusto.

'No, but thanks all the same.'

'I'm sure you don't mind if I have a drop,' she said firmly, 'it's not something I do every day, but if we're going to talk about the Mercer boy I need something.'

Lois moved across to the cabinet and retrieved a half-empty bottle of bourbon covered in paint smears. She poured a generous amount of the heady, amber liquid before taking a seat by the window. James and Katie sat down opposite her to take in the water views and passers-by.

'Nice spot, but the rent is ridiculous,' Lois remarked, watching them take in the Salcombe waterfront. 'Damn rich entrepreneurs come to the South Hams and buy up all the properties before charging us locals a small fortune for trying to make an honest living. 1764 saw the first holiday home built here, that's when the troubles began. Back in the days of smugglers, houses were not built directly on the waterfront as it was deemed unsafe. It was much better for people to keep their distance from those with bad blood. Now the smugglers have gone, we're left with all and sundry constructing homes in the most desirable spots, forever spoiling views for others.'

James not one for small talk enquired once more about the painting, 'I was hoping you would be able to tell me about the painting and the death of young Daniel Mercer, but I don't suppose you know all that much if you didn't paint the picture.'

'That's where you're wrong,' Lois informed him, 'I was the one on the beach that day with the camera. I took the photograph with a telephoto lens, which led to the painting. As it happens Daniel's parents work for my estranged husband Judge Malcolm Frobisher, I can probably divulge a few interesting facts.'

'Mind if I record our conversation on my smart phone?' Katie enquired politely. She didn't feel she and Lois had got off to a great start and wanted to amend things by being extra courteous.

'Be my guest,' Lois replied, 'what I have to say is no great secret. No different to the statement I once gave the police.'

Katie placed the phone on the table next to her. Lois looked at Katie for her cue to begin talking and did so when she got the nod.

'I remember the event as if it was only yesterday,' Lois began, clutching her glass with two hands as if afraid it would leap into the air out of reach.

'Sonia, that's Daniel's mother, invited the "Artisans" to Daniel's tenth birthday party. The "Artisans" are tyro painters who get together in my gallery once a week, Thursday nights to be precise. The party was being held at the home of Lady Scott-Thomas, Daniel's godmother, but as the afternoon wore on it spilt over onto Mill Bay beach.'

'We've met Lady Scott-Thomas,' James broke in.

Lois pulled a face, not commenting.

'Do you know Sonia Mercer well?' Katie asked, 'I take it you do if you were invited to her son's birthday party.'

'I've met her on several occasions,' Lois replied, 'I would often attend work functions with Malcolm. One had to be polite to all his work associates and show interest in their lives, even if you found them excruciatingly boring.'

'I take it you also knew Liam Mercer?' James enquired.

'Yes, I knew them both.'

'Were you aware of Liam's recent death? It would appear he fell from the same cliffs as Daniel.'

Lois nodded briefly, a sad expression on her face, 'I read about it in the local gazette. I can't believe tragedy has struck that family twice; first little Daniel, then Liam. It's a cruel world, Mr Sinclair.'

'Do you know if Liam Mercer had any enemies?' James asked, keen to get solid background info on Liam.

'Like I said Mr Sinclair, I really didn't know him that well. We only met in connection to Malcolm's work.'

'Tell us more about your paintings,' Katie broke in, 'Would you describe your work as ah! say a little eccentric?'

'I like to describe them as unusual rather than eccentric, but not everyone can associate with my chaotic style,' Lois replied, knocking back her straight bourbon and noisily pouring another, not seeming to care if it was early in the day.

'Quite controversial would you say?' Katie ventured, studying Lois with interest to see if her facial expressions gave anything away.

'I paint what I see, not what people want and that often causes mayhem amongst the purer of us,' she explained.

'You mean those with lofty religious values,' Katie remarked.

Lois gave a shallow laugh. 'Not just religious people, my dear girl; my paintings can offend all walks of life. When the painting in question was shown at one of my exhibitions it became very controversial. Several people tried to have it banned, declaring it was in poor taste to depict a young child distant to his death. I swear, I had no idea what the painting meant. If I had, I'd never have exhibited it the way I did. I may be a bit different, but I'm not heartless.'

'What exhibition are you referring to?' Katie asked intrigued.

'We held a grand exhibition evening at the Salcombe Yacht Club back in September 2013. It's an annual event, where local artists get to showcase their latest works,' Lois explained, 'we got fifty high-powered guests to that one, along with the media and the general public of course. My publicist did a marvellous job promoting the evening, which we called "A Canvas of Life". On reflection that name itself wasn't the best considering "Falling Memories" was being exhibited.'

'Did the painting sell that evening?' James enquired, taking over the interviewing.

'Yes, as a matter of fact it did. If my memory serves me correctly it was reserved within the first twenty minutes, for well above the asking price of three thousand pounds.'

'Can you recall who bought the painting?'

'Not off hand. You'll need to speak with my publicist cum personal assistant, Gwyn Lacey, who keeps records of all sales. She'll be around on Thursday morning if you'd care to drop by again.'

James responded, making a mental note to do just that.

'That damn painting nearly cost me everything,' Lois went on to say, 'even after I got rid of it, I still received threats along with criminal activity.'

'What happened?' Katie asked.

Lois took a deep breath before letting out a hefty sigh, 'I had fireworks thrown through my letter box, the studio ransacked, the gallery façade spray painted. Whenever I ventured out at least one person would hurl abuse or objects at me. Things got rather heated for a while. I eventually retreated to my flat in South London, only returning several months later when things settled down.'

'Did the police ever charge anyone with the attacks on you or your property?' James enquired.

'They investigated everything, but it was hard to pinpoint the activities to any particular person. Often the attacks were random, probably a few activists thinking it clever to go around terrorising a local artist. There was an upside to all of this of course, the unwanted publicity boosted my career. The sales of my paintings tripled over night. Not that I didn't feel guilty, mind you. I never wanted to profit through other people's grief.'

Although said with a reasonable amount of conviction Katie didn't fully believe everything Lois was saying.

'So, you can categorically swear you have no idea who painted "Falling Memories"?' James pushed once more.

'No idea at all,' Lois replied calmly, 'that, young man remains a real mystery.'

'How did Liam and Sonia react to the painting?' Katie quizzed.

'Very nice about it, in fact. They understood I had nothing to do with the construction of the painting.'

James produced the photograph of "Falling Memories" from the inside pocket of his jacket. 'Can you tell me exactly who the five people are in this photo?'

Lois didn't even bother looking at the photo. 'That my dear boy is easy,' she replied smoothly. 'Dieanna Payne, a former member of my art class, her husband Barry is a current member and happens to be one of my protégés. Louise Warman who was Daniel's nanny, my husband Malcolm Frobisher, and Liam and Sonia Mercer.'

'Do you have addresses and contact numbers for all of them?' Katie enquired.

'I can look them up for you. Honestly, my dear girl, I hardly think the photograph has any real significance. It's just a harmless group enjoying Portlemouth beach. We've been acquaintances for a number of years.'

'I'm sure you're right;' James replied casually, 'however, we can't leave anything to chance when investigating a possible murder.'

With no more questions to hand James and Katie thanked Lois before exiting the gallery onto the busy, narrow thoroughfare. 'One thing now makes sense,' Katie said, as they meandered past the old boat sheds, 'I strongly believe the person who placed the print into the envelope wanted the police to know that although Lois took the photograph, the painting wasn't her handy work.'

'I'm not sure I follow,' James questioned, 'how do you draw that conclusion?'

'I get the impression they wanted us to look closely at Lois but also uncover another link.'

'You've still lost me,' James stared at his sister, concerned she had succumbed to mild sunstroke.

'I need to do more work on the profile of our killer, but I'm inclined to believe we could be dealing with a pathological murderer,' Katie dutifully explained, 'If I'm right with my assumptions, they will want us to uncover the truth as to why they committed this murder as much as the fact the crime was committed. They usually do this by guiding you to people affiliated with the deceased in a game of cat and mouse. To sum it up in one easy sentence, we might be bogged down in this matter for an eternity.'

****

Liam Mercer hurried towards Southernhay Gardens in Exeter annoyed his watch had ceased working. He was due at No. 3 Court twenty minutes ago, his colleagues would hardly be impressed. He envisaged the Chief Crown Prosecutor shaking his head, mumbling obscenities, *ready to issue a rebuke. Reaching the intersection, he glanced in both directions waiting impatiently for the lights to change. Anticipating the green, he launched off the pavement hearing the screech of tyres long before he spotted the black Mercedes saloon rocketing straight for him.*

Momentarily stunned Liam darted back on the pavement, the car clipping his left side as it sped away. It happened so quickly there was no chance to grab the number plate, barely a split second to recognise the model of car. Throbbing heat stabbed his upper thigh, he reeled in pain clutching drunkenly for a lamppost as he attempted to control his erratic breathing. His head felt light, his vision starting to fog.

'You all right mate?' a young lad questioned, having witnessed the incident. 'Don't know what you've done to piss someone off, but that Merc driver deliberately accelerated heading straight towards you. You were bloody lucky.'

Chapter Two

The two friends sat at the rear of the Old Mill Cafe deep in animated conversation. A week of record temperatures had been rudely and abruptly cut short by a strong cold front barrelling down from the Arctic and sweeping in from Russia. Holidaymakers had vacated early and the towns and villages along the Devon Coast were eerily devoid of activity. Dustings of snow were recorded in Northern Scotland.

'We've hit a snag,' Nick informed James, idly playing with the rustic sugar bowl. 'Detective Chief Inspector Mick Rose is on leave this week and his replacement DI Rod Wetherill won't let us near Liam Mercer's office. We have no chance of getting background information on his employment or searching for other clues, not yet anyway.'

'What's his problem denying us access?' James asked, raising the collar of his leather jacket to ward off the cold creeping in under the rear entrance. 'Surely, he knows Mercer's office should be classed as a potential crime scene.'

'He says it's his jurisdiction and we're to leave well alone,' Nick replied, adding sugar to his coffee before stirring vigorously, and tossing the spoon back on the table, 'something to do with letting his squad conduct the groundwork. I suspect he wants to earn some kudos and impress the Chief Super whilst he's filling in as DCI. Ambitious bastard I hear who doesn't like Moorlands either. Believes the Force can do without outsiders. So, I'd be careful.'

'Does he now?' James scoffed indignantly, 'we'll see about that.'

He picked up his mobile phone punching in the familiar numbers which usually got him through to DCI Rose at the Exeter CID. After a few rings a crisp voice echoed down the line.

'Inspector Wetherill, how can I help you?'

'Good afternoon, sir, this is Doctor James Sinclair from Moorland Forens –'

'I know who you are,' Wetherill snapped, before James could finish his sentence, 'what do you want?'

'I understand you informed my colleague Doctor Nicholas Shelby that Liam Mercer's office is off limits, why is that, sir?'

'I thought that to be obvious, Sinclair?' Wetherill answered, his voice taking on a disinterested tone, 'my squad have already conducted a full sweep of Mercer's office, found nothing, so no need for you lot to waste time nosing around.'

James fought back anger, 'With all due respect to you and your officers sir, Moorland Forensics has been assigned this case due to known complexities. Liam Mercer's office could hold vital clues that can't afford to be overlooked. It is crucial we do our own search of Mercer's office in line with the coroner's expectations.'

'If you're unhappy with my decision, Sinclair, I suggest you put your complaint in writing to the Commander. Now if that's all, I'll bid you good day.'

He rung off before James could utter another word.

'Charming chap,' James muttered under his breath, placing his mobile back on the table and taking a sip of his lukewarm latte. 'Well Nicholas my friend, it looks as if I'll need to contact Rudy Jenks to get past the Pitt Bull Terrier.'

Within half an hour of speaking with the Commander, James and Nick were smugly on their way to Liam Mercer's office situated in the city centre of Exeter. Commander Jenks had granted 100% unconditional access for Moorland Forensics to do their own sweep of Liam's office and had gone so far as to say he'd be dealing with DI Wetherill directly if his obstructionist attitude continued.

Driving through Exeter Nick turned into Magdalen Street towards Southernhay Gardens, steering his vehicle into the car park at the back of Exeter Crown Court near where Grays Law Firm had their three-floor office, parking adjacent to a near new Maserati Spider. James a keen classic car enthusiast hopped out to take a closer look at the gleaming white machine. An attractive young female with short curly blond hair leant casually against the driver's door. She looked up and smiled as James and Nick approached.

'Nice car,' James commented, not able to restrain himself as he ran his hand over the smooth body work of the Italian creation. 'Is it yours?'

'I wish,' the young woman laughed, flashing a row of even white teeth, 'it belongs to my boss Liam Mercer. I'm Tabitha Fletcher, Liam's personal assistant.'

From the way Tabitha spoke of Liam in the present tense it became apparent she had not been informed of his death. James braced himself to break the news. After introducing himself, he gently guided Tabitha to a secluded part of the car park to notify her of Liam's death.

Tabitha caught hold of his arm for support. 'No that's not possible, it can't be.'

'Liam's body was discovered at the bottom of East Portlemouth cliffs. We are treating his death as suspicious,' James went on.

Tabitha's eyes misted with tears. 'Good God, who could have done such a thing?'

'That's what we intend to find out,' James reassured her, 'when did you last see Liam? Think carefully, anything you remember could be helpful to enquiries.'

'Um! I can't remember,' Tabitha stuttered, the colour draining from her face. 'Jesus Christ, Friday night, I guess. This is all such a dreadful shock I can't think straight. I've only just returned from a conference in Brighton.'

'Take your time,' James instructed, helping her into the back seat of Nick's Government issue Renault.

Tabitha took a deep breath, puffing out her cheeks, 'I am almost certain I saw Liam Friday night, but it must have been quite late.'

'Would it help if I jogged your memory?' Nick interrupted, stepping forward, 'someone spotted you leaving Mercer's home just after 11pm, the evening prior to his death, which would have been the Friday.'

James tried to hide his surprise. Nick had deliberately kept this information from him, so he could spring it on Tabitha; a clever ploy. He often did in depth research and background checks on the deceased, he always said it helped him explore the body as a person not merely as a surgical instrument. James on the other hand mostly preferred to keep his work pegged purely at a scientific level, only investigating what he felt was necessary.

Tabitha looked at Nick, 'Yes, that's correct. There were papers Liam needed to sign. I'd been at the office working late when I realised I didn't have his signature.'

'And the signing couldn't wait until Monday morning when both of you would be back in the office?' Nick probed. 'Exactly what was so urgent Ms Fletcher that required Liam's signature after business hours?'

Tabitha remained calm, offering an explanation. 'I'd overlooked a key witness for a court hearing which was due to commence at 9:30 sharp on Monday morning. I needed those documents to subpoena someone to court. Liam works from home on Mondays and Tuesdays.'

'Was Liam's wife at home when you called round?' James asked.

'Apparently, Sonia was in bed,' Tabitha replied softly, 'of course, I couldn't be sure of that. I'm just going on what Liam told me.'

'Did you stay long?' This question was fired by Nick.

'About one hour. Liam opened a bottle of red and we sat talking about the pending court case.'

'Ms Fletcher, what exactly was your relationship with Liam Mercer?' Nick enquired.

From the stunned expression on Tabitha's face Nick's question caught her off guard. 'We were business associates,' she replied, fixing him with a steady glare.

'My colleague and I need to look around Liam's office,' James broke in, remembering the real reason for their visit, fearful a full-blown altercation might erupt between Tabitha and Nick. Nick often felt the strain from working long hours and found it hard keeping his short fuse temper in check, usually lashing out at any one in range.

'Yes of course, I'll show you the way,' Tabitha offered, seemingly glad to step out of the firing line.

Liam's office was on the third floor of the imposing brick building, blessed with an expansive view to the estuary mouth. Exeter was an impressive city on the River Ex. There had been a significant settlement on the site going back to before the Iron Age, most likely a repository from where tin and copper mined on Dartmoor was traded to merchants from Europe and the Mediterranean. The Romans built fortifications in the area and the Saxons gave it its name, their most important cultural and trading centre settlement in the Kingdom of Wessex.

Still cordoned off with police tape Nick lifted the yellow ribbon to allow them access through the main door.

'We'll probably be a couple of hours,' James advised Tabitha, placing a laptop and large briefcase on a black designer chair. 'I don't suppose there's chance of a coffee?' He used his winning smile, which melted the heart of every female.

Tabitha beamed, happy to make herself useful. She hurried off to the tiny kitchen positioned to one side of the entrance hall.

'Must be quite a shock for the poor girl,' James remarked, as he donned gloves and started rifling through papers scattered on a nearby filing cabinet.

Declining a reply Nick moved across to a bookshelf and began reading some of the spines. 'Your ubiquitous Law Reports,' he commented, 'not much of interest.'

Initial sifting through drawers and cupboards revealed little of import. Tabitha returned a few minutes later with the espressos, before muttering something about needing to take cheques to accounts on the first floor. She disappeared, leaving the guys to continue their search.

Nick walking past an ornate Victorian bookcase tripped over a worn tuft of carpet, nearly spearing head first into the side of a corner desk. 'Bloody hazard.' he winced, rubbing the side of his left ankle. He was about to dismiss the incident when something caught his eye. With James' help the two men dropped to their knees pulling at the tattered fibres of the offending carpet until they came apart to reveal loose wooden floorboards. After some fiddling and tugging, Nick wrenched one of the boards free, eventually wriggling onto his stomach to reach into the space below.

'There's something stashed here,' Nick advised James, 'think it's a parcel of some sort from the feel.'

'Well! Hurry it up,' James urged impatiently, fixing his eyes on the door, 'we don't want Tabitha walking in if we're about to uncover something of interest.'

'Okay, okay, for Christ's sake, I can't go any faster.'

Nick kept pulling at the small bundle, finally easing it up in both hands before throwing the package on to James. Both men sat back on the floor and stared wide-eyed as wads of mint fresh fifty-pound notes bound with large rubber bands tumbled onto the carpet.

'Wow what a find,' Nick whistled in amazement, 'this is a big horde of cash.'

As the initial shock dispersed, along with a fleeting temptation to pocket some for themselves, the money was frantically placed into a clear plastic bag inside the empty brief case to be reserved for laboratory examination. If the notes had never been in circulation before they could do specific checks to determine where they had come from.

'How's it going?' Tabitha enquired, from a position just outside the doorway, careful not to step inside the office which was clearly out of bounds to non-officialdom.

'Best if you don't stick around,' Nick advised, managing a weak smile, which didn't quite meet his grey eyes.

'Right, I'm off home. Here's my number should you need me for anything.'

Nick took the small "stick-it" note Tabitha held out to him. 'I'm sure there'll be more questions we'll need to ask at some stage. We'll be in touch.'

Tabitha tottered out of the room balancing on her heels, leaving James and Nick to continue searching the small office.

'This must be a photograph of Daniel,' Nick said, lifting a framed photograph of a young lad of about ten. His winning smile showed two missing front teeth. His hair was snow white, framing large opaque eyes. The photo was dropped into the brief case alongside the cash.

'Apart from the money there's nothing out of the ordinary here,' James stated, flexing his tired muscles. 'We'd better grab Liam's office-based computer on our way out for analysis. Obviously, the police forensic team didn't see it as a worthwhile exercise, they've left it sitting on his desk.'

Nick grunted, 'Too lazy you mean. Any hard work would bring them out in a cold sweat.'

James laughed as he placed the laptop into a bag and dropped it next to the brief case.

'Turning up all that money was a find,' James proclaimed, as they headed back down the stairs, 'by the way, how's your ankle?'

'Bloody sore.'

****

The Mercer's grade two listed, whitewashed stone cottage stood a quarter of a mile from the main road on the outskirts of West Alvington, a stones-throw from Kingsbridge. After ringing the door bell and waiting several minutes the door was opened by a tall, balding middle-aged man dressed in denim jeans and a white cotton T-shirt, a heavy three-day stubble adding to a dishevelled, sleep deprived look.

'I'm here to see Sonia Mercer,' James informed him, producing a business card, 'I'm the Forensic Scientist heading up the investigation into the death of her husband.'

'You'd better come in. I'm one of Sonia and Liam's business associates, Luke Green,' he stood aside for James to enter a spacious lobby, 'you'll need to go easy with Sonia, she's still suffering from shock.'

James followed Green into an immaculate living room cluttered with antiques, imparting an uneasy claustrophobia, a feeling reinforced by the low ceiling and period oak beams. James found it necessary to duck his head as he entered.

'I'll let Sonia know you're here,' Luke advised, turning towards the door. 'Please take a seat, Mr Sinclair.'

James did as instructed, opting for one of two large armchairs in the Liberty style surrounding an inglenook fireplace.

A red-eyed Sonia Mercer eventually emerged, gliding into the living room where she took up residence on a turquoise leather lounge.

'Have you any news?' Sonia enquired, reaching for a cigarette from a packet resting on the arm of the lounge.

James shook his head, 'It's too early to determine exactly how your husband died, Mrs Mercer. We need to conduct various forensic tests before we'll have those answers. There'll be a full investigation which will include an autopsy overseen by the local Coroner.'

'I didn't kill him, if that's what you're thinking,' Sonia blurted out.

'I'd just like to ask a few questions,' James continued, ignoring her blunt statement. As a commonplace defence mechanism, it was not unusual for someone to declare their innocence when being informally questioned.

Sonia's body took on a more relaxed demeanour as she leant back on the couch exhaling on her cigarette, 'There's not much I can tell you, Liam went for an early morning walk on the Portlemouth cliffs and never came back. He often walked in the mornings, especially on days when he wasn't in a rush to get to work.'

'On the day Liam died had you argued about anything before he left the house?' James enquired, jotting down notes in a dark blue leather-bound notebook.

Sonia shook her head.

'Do you know if he'd recently had a disagreement with anyone, a work colleague perhaps?'

'No.'

'I understand the location where your husband's body was found happens to be the very same which claimed the life of your son a little over five years ago. What can you tell me about the death of your son Mrs Mercer? Can you think of a possible link between the two deaths?'

Before Sonia could answer Luke Green interjected, his face a mottled purple as rage began to seep through his veins. 'Look here Sinclair, are these questions really necessary. We know Liam's dead. No amount of questioning is going to bring him back, or Daniel for that matter. Sonia should not be subjected to this sort of interrogation.'

'As with all suspicious deaths, we need to undertake a thorough investigation,' James replied evenly, 'I understand this isn't easy, but we need to establish a motive for Liam's death. Anything Sonia knows about the death of her son may help our current endeavours.'

Sonia gave Luke a brief smile, coupled with a look to indicate she had no objections with the way James was conducting his questioning. Luke clearly miffed, sunk further into his chair, watching James carefully, ready to pounce if he crossed the line.

'Daniel's death was a tragic accident,' Sonia began, her voice unsteady, 'as young lads do they look for all sorts of adventure and Daniel obviously went too close to the edge of the cliff.'

'Was there anything about your son's death which seemed odd or suspicious?'

'No. The only thing I recall is Daniel complaining of feeling dizzy around lunch time, his eyes were red and swollen.'

'Did you report this to the investigating officers?' James quizzed, intrigued by this information as his mind went into overdrive.

Sonia clearly thought otherwise, 'Yes, I reported it to several people, but not one of them seemed to think it relevant in anyway. Like I said Mr Sinclair, my son's death was a tragic accident.'

James made a note to check things out in more detail when he next caught up with Nick Shelby. He would be keen to trawl through the Coroner's report and take a close look at toxicology. Changing tack, he returned to discussing Liam Mercer, enquiring about his position as an assistant Crown Prosecutor.

Sonia looked decidedly relieved at no longer having to answer questions about her son. 'Liam had a challenging job Mr Sinclair. He was a workaholic and even though we were in the same building we could go literally days without seeing each other. You might be best to speak with the senior partner Judge Malcolm Frobisher if you want more information. I'm afraid nothing I can tell you will help your investigation, Liam and I always worked on separate matters. If he had enemies due to work related issues, I wouldn't have a clue, nor do I know why someone would want my husband dead.'

James rose slowly to his feet. 'Thank you, Sonia that's all for now. We'll keep you posted on the autopsy date and when you'll be able to make funeral arrangements.'

****

An aura of unproductive activity greeted James walking in through the glass-panelled doors of the small local office of the Newton Abbott Star, a young unkempt reporter sat slouched in a chair conducting a telephone interview, a second randomly reviewing photographs and a third typing tardily on a keyboard with obvious lack of enthusiasm.

James scouted the room for Tom Markham, eventually spotting him at the rear behind a desk, his feet resting on an empty chair, engrossed in the Sun form guide. Although the owner of the Star, by virtue of a lucky inheritance, Markham could often be found hanging out in the branches, preferring the chase for a story rather than running the paper properly from the central office in Newton Abbott. It also allowed him to disappear from meetings unannounced and indulge his weakness for the greyhounds. For this reason, he appointed himself Chief Reporter.

James quietly strolled across the room forcefully removing Markham's feet, placing them on the floor so he could sit down.

'Bloody idiot Sinclair, you'll give someone a heart attack creeping up on them like that,' Tom complained, 'what the hell are you doing here?'

'How well do you know the journalist who covered the Daniel Mercer hearing about five years ago?' James shot at him.

'Old Scooter? I know him fairly well. Why?' Markham replied, chewing on a pencil.

'I was hoping you might tell me where I can find him?'

Markham stifled a yawn, 'Let me think. Yes, he officially retired three years ago. I believe he's residing in Churchstow, down in the South Hams.'

'Would you be able to find his address?' James pressed.

'I can try. What's this all about anyway?'

'I'm interested in uncovering more details on the death of young Daniel Mercer,' James offered, not wanting to give too much away. Any slight sniff of a story and Markham was likely to turn it into front page news embellishing it with fabrication far removed from the truth.

'You're wasting your breath on that one, Sinclair. Scooter nearly died covering that story. Half the people that came forward were full of shit, the other half insane. It turned into media frenzy straight out of a TV soap.'

'Something you'd know all about,' James replied with a facetious smile, dodging Tom's swinging right hand, 'I take it Scooter has a proper name?'

'Yeah, Reg Applegate, got his nickname from scooting around on his ancient Heinkel moped covering stories. I'll find his address and drop it by in the morning in exchange for a few bottles of vintage red.'

'What else do you recall about Daniel Mercer's death? You must have proof read what went to print.'

'The allegations that surfaced made by Louise Warman of being raped by Liam Mercer two months earlier made better headlines than the actual death of the young boy,' Markham informed him, 'Warman was Daniel Mercer's nanny. Stunning young woman in her twenties, with a body most would envy.'

James looked surprised, 'Tell me more.'

'Not much to tell really. Liam Mercer was a well-known womaniser and when he didn't openly get what he wanted he apparently resorted to force. Of course, working for Judge Frobisher, Liam was bound to get away with any wrongdoing. Poor Louise didn't stand a chance.'

'Do you think Liam Mercer was capable of rape?' James enquired, knowing Tom had ways of obtaining inside information on matters that interested him.

Tom nodded, 'There was never any doubt in my mind but proving it would have been difficult if it had gone to Court. No one's going to believe a young woman over a well-respected lawyer, particularly when he's a high-profile counsel for the prosecution.'

'Especially a crooked one,' James mocked.

'Yep, especially a crooked one,' Tom echoed, 'now if that's all, piss off and leave me in peace.'

'Well, I hope this Applegate fella had better work ethics than you lot,' James taunted, waving his forefinger at the press team, 'look at them all, snails on Prozac.'

James smartly exited the building, ignoring the large protests which followed. He made no friends with the local journalists and planned to keep it that way.

****

Glancing nervously at the car clock, Fiona cursed loudly. She was already fifteen minutes late for Liam Mercer's autopsy. Katie's old Punto, requisitioned at the last minute, decided to stall twice through the main street of Exeter and the beeping of horns did nothing to foster a genial mood as Fiona finally wrestled the ageing euro box into the car park at the back of the Coroners Court.

Rushing through security doors, she practically vaulted up the four flights of stairs to where the autopsy was scheduled. Heading straight for the female changing rooms she quickly donned her protective gear to join Nick in the lab.

'Car trouble?' Nick sympathised, having seen her arrive in the notoriously unreliable Fiat.

Fiona chose to ignore this remark, wishing she hadn't locked her keys in the TVR. 'Gee, it's cold in here Nick. What have you got the thermostat on? It may be warming up outside but inside feels like Siberia. I don't know how long I'll last in these sub-zero conditions.'

'It suits me perfectly,' Nick replied, affording her a cheeky grin, 'besides, too much warmth and the smell in here would be horrendous. Double gown if you must.'

'I'm going to have to,' Fiona remarked, as she began to scrub up in preparation for the autopsy, 'I see you're eager to start.'

'Yep, thought we'd get cracking then we can head to the pub for a drink,' Nick announced, his laid-back Kiwi attitude coming to the forefront, 'I'll get you to write some notes if you don't mind.'

Fiona grabbed a clipboard and paper, 'I take it we're starting with an external examination first?'

Nick nodded, moving over to where the body of Liam Mercer lay on a trolley. He took a breath and began.

'Firstly, I agree with your initial findings at the beach. The broken neck was caused by impact with a rock and enough to cause immediate death. Well done on that one and picking up the possible strangulation attempt as well.

Looking closely at the throat you can see tiny, wound synthetic rope fibres embedded under a thin layer of epidermis. They're similar, if not identical to the polypropylene sheets used on headsails or the halyards to hoist a main sail. This has already been confirmed by high power and electron microscope imaging, proving it was clearly our instrument for strangulation.'

'Hardly a clue considering half the local population is involved in sailing or boating of some description,' Fiona replied sceptically, moving rapidly on the spot to keep warm.

'But nevertheless, a clue,' Nick reminded her firmly, 'what we do know is someone definitely tried to strangle Liam Mercer. Now what we need to determine is if he was still alive when he toppled from the cliff or was strangulation the actual course of death? We've already established the three-centimetre gash on his right cheek would have occurred during the fall.'

Fiona busied herself with detailed notes as Nick continued. 'It would appear Liam Mercer probably put up a bit of a fight, but for some reason he didn't have a lot of energy to really defend himself. I can't be sure until the blood tests come back from the lab, but it's highly probable he had some form of sedative or psychotropic in the blood stream. If you recall I initially discovered a small puncture wound at the base of his neck.

My theory is: after being injected with a possible tranquilizer someone lunged at our victim delivering a hefty push and hey presto over the edge he goes crashing onto the jagged rocks below – ouch. Although, I very much doubt he felt a thing. I imagine his heart would have stopped beating on the way down. I just need confirmation on measurements before drawing a firm conclusion.'

Nick paused for a few moments before reaching for a scalpel to begin the internal examination. Once he'd exposed the chest cavity removing the heart he continued, 'If you look closely at the heart you can see Liam experienced a massive cardio infarction caused by shock. I doubt he felt much after that as death would have occurred instantly. A heart attack was the actual cause of death; however, foul play could be a contributing factor.'

'That's a blessing,' Fiona muttered, 'crashing onto the beach wouldn't have been a memorable experience.'

'It would appear the subject had a light breakfast of cereal and coffee before he died. There are no other stomach contents.'

After a further two hours Nick removed his gloves scribbling a few notes of his own. He then continued to speak into the small tape recorder housed on a nearby bench.

'The initial result of the autopsy indicates Mr Liam Derek Mercer died under suspicious circumstances and not solely from natural causes. Although suffering a lethal heart attack, his death would not have occurred had he not fallen from a great height.' Nick switched off the tape recorder. 'We now have a full-blown murder investigation, Ms Sinclair.'

Fiona moved to one side of the lab and started to shed some of her protective clothing. 'I'll duck in the shower, change and be ready in fifteen minutes for that drink you were talking about earlier.'

'Right you are. I'll just pop Liam back in the fridge and hop in the other shower. Feel free to join me if you feel like sharing for extra warmth?'

'No, I'll be fine,' Fiona laughed, disappearing into the ladies' cloakroom. Nick had an irrepressible charm which at times proved tough to resist.

****

Entering the outskirts of Exeter city centre James secured a parking spot in one of the narrow side streets. It took him a further ten minutes to locate No. 2 Court where Judge Frobisher was residing and greater time to wait for him to break for lunch. James was unsure of the reception he would receive from Frobisher; so far, he'd refused to speak with any of the investigating forensic team.

Frobisher looked annoyed as James approached waving a business card under his nose, enquiring if he could spare a few minutes to discuss the death of Liam Mercer.

'I don't get long for lunch,' Judge Frobisher grumbled, throwing his arms up in despair. James swiftly reviewing his hefty size drew the conclusion he didn't appear undernourished from rushed lunches.

'We'd better go into my office,' Frobisher continued, leading the way down a set of steep steps to a rabbit warren of rooms, 'walls around here tend to have ears.'

James followed Frobisher into a cramped room with one tiny window overlooking the River Exe. From the distinct odour of rotting wood and mould it clearly didn't attract much sunshine. Not quite the furnishings he'd envisaged for such a high-profile Judge.

Frobisher tactfully eased himself into an old lounge chair causing the springs to creak and groan. 'Now how can I assist today?' He opened a small brown paper bag and retrieved a bought sandwich, taking a large bite. 'Salmon and cucumber from the canteen, surprisingly good.' he spluttered, with mouth full. 'I hope you don't mind me eating?'

'You go ahead,' James instructed, preferring to stand, 'I'd like to ask a few questions in relation to Liam Mercer, what can you tell me about him, was he a respected partner?'

'One of the best prosecuting lawyers I've ever worked with,' Frobisher replied heartily, 'Liam was a true professional and a damn good bloke.'

'Were you aware of any tricky cases he worked on which may have made him enemies?'

'Great Scott! Man, all cases create some form of friction,' Frobisher replied, removing a piece of salmon from his front teeth with a fingernail, 'every time someone gets sentenced an enemy is created. The legal profession doesn't make friends Sinclair, that's not our job.'

'Were you aware of any threats made against Liam?'

Frobisher shook his head before delving into the brown parcel for another sandwich, 'Liam never mentioned anything to me.'

'I'm beginning to learn there was a lot of controversy surrounding the death of his son back in 2013. The Mercer's nanny alleged Liam raped her, only months before Daniel died. What can you tell me about that?'

'I can't tell you anything,' Frobisher remarked, resting his chin in his hand. 'I only read that story in the local and national press. Liam never chose to discuss it with me. However, it's my belief the woman made the whole thing up to seek attention. Not uncommon you know.'

'Did the police formally charge him?'

'Can't remember, sorry Sinclair, I'm due back in court. That's all I've got time for,' Judge Frobisher eased up out of his seat brushing a few wayward crumbs off his fluorescent pink tie. Without even a proper goodbye he strolled out of the room indicating the meeting was over.

James quickly realised he'd been duped. Judge Frobisher had not really provided any new facts regarding Liam Mercer. He'd used years of experience as a lawyer and judge to avoid any direct questioning. The meeting had been a complete waste of time.

****

Liam sat behind his desk idly fiddling with the pink cord of a client brief and staring blankly into space, his mind unfocused on work vainly trying to ignore the persistent ringing of his mobile phone. Finally, he took the call...

'Liam it's me,' the voice at the other end spoke, 'have you remembered you and Sonia have tickets for tonight's Shakespeare

performance at the Theatre Royal in Plymouth? She'll be cross if you arrive late.'

'I'd completely let this evening slip my mind;' Liam replied truthfully, 'thanks for reminding me.'

SIX HOURS LATER

'How was the show, I thought I'd phone to enquire before you went to bed. Luckily, I rang earlier to remind you of the performance or you would have taken a serve from Sonia.'

Liam was not in the mood for personal conversation, 'If you must know I had a shit night. My fucking laptop was stolen from the boot of my car when we were in the theatre.'

'Oh, that's awful. I imagine a lot of confidential files were stored on the hard drive, which you wouldn't want falling into wrong hands.'

'Precisely, now if you've only called for a chat, don't bother. We can catch up another time.'

'Yes, but...'

Liam hung up, leaving the caller in mid-sentence.

'Well of all the insensitive things to do,' the caller muttered out loud, slamming down the phone.

Fury etched across their façade they stormed across the room and poured a drink to overflowing, before settling down onto the sofa, 'I was just about to tell Liam how I feel his pain, but maybe not. I think I'll rev up this nice little laptop and find out exactly what Liam's been up to. He really can't trust anyone.'

To the accompaniment of a chilling laugh Liam's flip computer hummed into life at the press of a button, revealing all his deep dark secrets. The caller hugged themselves with glee.

Chapter Three

'The toxicology results have come back positive to a moderate amount of Valium in Liam's blood stream,' Nick began assuredly, addressing his captive audience in the instrument room at Moorland Forensics. Leaning forward with elbows resting on the Infra-Red Spectrometer he continued with his brief on the autopsy, 'This is why he didn't put up much of a fight. I'm also pretty certain Liam dabbled in cocaine and possibly heroin from the sub microgram amounts detected in blood and soft tissue, also confirmed by GC/Mass Spec, but there's no indication he was a junkie. I'm still having difficulty determining the exact cause of death, so further tests are on the cards.

Also, the attempt at strangulation was just that. The trachea and windpipe were only slightly traumatised. No way near enough to prevent breathing; Fiona agrees with me.'

'So, what exactly took place on the cliff top prior to the fall?' Katie enquired, 'the struggle sounds minuscule so can you still determine if Liam was murdered?'

Nick shrugged his shoulders, 'We don't have conclusive evidence indicating if Liam accidentally fell from the cliff or if he was pushed. If he was pushed it wouldn't have been a hard shove, which could easily mimic a fall. I suggest we return to the crime scene and take another scout around. We need to look at things from all angles.'

'This won't be an easy case from the scientific perspective,' James acknowledged, frustration creeping into his voice. We've got to be pragmatic. I don't reckon revisiting the crime scene is going to do anything. We could be blundering around for ages down there following obscure leads and meaningless dead ends coupled with supposed "physical evidence". I suggest we work closely with the local police to discover who may have wanted to harm Liam Mercer. We can certainly prove someone drugged him, but it will take a lot of luck to determine if the fall from the cliff top was accidental or deliberate.'

Nick shuffled in his seat, 'Yep, you're right on that one, Jim. No court will convict anyone merely on speculation or circumstantial evidence. The Crown Prosecutor wouldn't even contemplate charges. However, we must be seen to be doing our job.'

****

Two weeks after the discovery of Liam Mercer's body the Moorland team, bending to Shelby's wishes, reluctantly took the hard decision to temporarily relocate to Salcombe for a few days making it easier to conduct further interviews and tests. Katie rang around to find suitable accommodation eventually securing a two-bedroom waterside town house only shouting distance from Lois St John's Art Gallery, which was more than adequate as a short-term base.

'I hope the weather is not going to turn for the worse now we've arrived,' Katie commented, glancing at a darkening sky as the last of their belongings was stowed away.

'For sure we'll cop a few summer storms with all this tropical moisture in the air,' James replied casually, 'let's hope the forecast for tomorrow is more favourable. We'll be conducting the four-mile coastal walk starting and ending at East Portlemouth. Nick will be joining us to assist with measurements. We need to get some idea what happened to Liam Mercer just before he fell to his death.'

Exactly on eight o'clock the following morning the Forensic Team stood shivering on the top of Portlemouth cliffs. Light showers ghosted in from the Channel enveloping the town of Salcombe in a shimmering grey mist. In days gone by it would have been perfect conditions for opportunists who worked the rugged coastlines guiding ships on to tortuous rocks.

'Bloody miserable, can't even see the harbour entrance,' Nick remarked, trying to psych himself up by opening his forensic case to retrieve a tape measure, 'I suppose we might as well get on with it.'

Katie pulled her light-weight jacket tightly to her chest to counteract the cold. The sou'westerly howled incessantly, threading a path directly off the Atlantic.

'This must be where Liam Mercer fell to his death and down there a few degrees off 90 would be the spot he landed,' Nick commented, standing as close to the edge as he dared.

Katie, not one for heights, found herself turning away seeing Shelby in almost the exact spot where Liam Mercer last stood. It gave her goose bumps and filled her with apprehension thinking about it. Whilst Nick and James began measuring areas and distances from the cliff, recording details into a flip tablet, Katie sat down on a wooden seat. On any other day the bench would command spectacular views all the way to Salcombe, stretching towards Kingsbridge on one side and South Sands the other.

'What little physical evidence we did find up here has been bagged and sent off for analysis,' Nick mumbled, wiping a few drops of rain from a chilled face.

'You know it strikes me as funny why Liam ventured so close to the cliff edge, away from the guided path,' Katie volunteered at last. 'Even if the perpetrator didn't mean to push him over the edge, they could still be done for manslaughter.'

'Not necessarily,' Nick advised, 'without eyewitnesses they could easily claim Liam lost balance and fell without so much as a finger being laid upon him, and no one could prove otherwise. Death by misadventure.'

Katie bit down hard on her lower lip. How she hated all this conjecture. None of it made any sense. At this moment in time it was clearly apparent Liam Mercer's assassin could get away scot-free.

With the cliff top investigation concluded the small group began the walk along the coastal path to Garra Rock.

'Watch where you step,' James instructed the others, 'a few heavy showers could see this path slippery and dangerous, possibly lethal.'

The last of the fronts was gradually driving the clouds inland and away from the coast. Far to the east the sun's feeble rays broke through the low scudding squalls. A warm afternoon beckoned.

Along the steep coastal path, a variety of sea birds nested seeking shelter from the inclement weather, their feathers tossed about by the relentless gales.

'Ah, now this is nice,' Nick remarked, stepping onto Sandy Beach at Mill Bay. 'According to the map, we continue following the coastal path along the edge of Sycamore Wood.'

The walk proved invigorating, a pleasant change from the mundane everyday grind compiling lab reports and sifting through forensic data. Once or twice the small party stopped to admire the panoramic view taking in Salcombe and Malborough, before deciding to make tracks for home.

'Not much more we can do here today,' Nick told the others, as they boarded the Portlemouth Ferry, 'I suggest we start chatting with a few locals, find out if they know anything about our victim. Tomorrow I plan to look into the death of young Daniel. I need to establish if there are any links between his death and his father's. I'll be heading back to Exeter but will call if I have any new leads.'

****

James picked up the phone on the second ring. 'Sinclair.'

'It's Nick, guess who conducted the autopsy on young Daniel Mercer? None other than Margo Betteridge, thought you might like to know.'

'Well, I can't see Margo leaving anything unaccounted for, she's the archetypical perfectionist.'

'Precisely,' Nick agreed, 'Margo would have conducted every test imaginable looking for Daniel's cause of death.'

'I take it she's still head scientist at The Royal Devon and Exeter Hospital?'

'Yep, they'll either drag Margo out of there kicking and screaming, or she'll be wheeled out on a gurney,' Nick laughed.

'I'll drop over and see Margo first thing after lunch, Margo's sure to give me the full story as to what the conclusions were.'

'Just one word of advice,' Nick added, 'Tread carefully on this one mate, there are a few things which aren't adding up. I can't quite put my finger on it, but I have a gut instinct this case could get messy if we dig too deeply.'

James acknowledged the warning as he switched off his laptop in readiness for the drive into Exeter. He had cleared his backlog of paperwork so the afternoon was free for a long overdue reunion with Dr Margo Betteridge.

Within the hour James swung his beaten Land Rover into the gravelled hospital car park in Exeter. Encountering the usual busy Thursday out patient's day it took nearly ten frustrating minutes to secure a parking bay, followed by another five to pay for a ticket and display it on his windscreen. A further ten minutes passed to reach the west wing where the labs were based. If not for his keenness to reacquaint with Margo Betteridge he'd have given up long before.

Once inside the building, the distinctly sweet but repugnant odour of disinfectant reached his nostrils.

The science department labs had recently been renovated with a new floor added. James unfamiliar with the revised layout followed makeshift, printed signs along narrow corridors and up two flights of stairs until he finally made it to Margo's hideout.

After a recent review of internal procedures, the laboratories were now ensconced behind locked doors. Explaining the reason for his visit and flashing identification to an over officious security desk clerk he was buzzed into a small waiting room.

'I'm looking for Doctor Betteridge?' James announced.

'The Operations Lab,' the overweight guard grunted, 'down the corridor to the end, second door on your right.'

Following the simple instructions, he located Margo hunched over a wooden bench surrounded by stacks of petri dishes, her face only inches from an old computer monitor.

'Margo, how lovely to see you,' James planted a kiss on her right cheek.

'Well, if it isn't young James Sinclair,' she smiled warmly, getting to her feet to give him a firm hug, 'you've done all right for yourself, my lad. Saw your recent papers in the journals and the book of course, I'm extremely impressed with the way your forensic career is progressing. I must have taught you well.'

'Extremely well,' James replied honestly, being very fond of Margo and genuinely pleased to see her.

'What brings you to my humble lab?' Margo asked, turning her attention back to the computer screen. 'With this new security system in place I don't get many visitors. The days can drag.'

James laughed, 'Right there, it's not an easy place to access, sign of the times I guess, I was hoping I could tear you away to chat about a certain matter you worked on in 2013, the death of a young lad in East Portlemouth, Daniel Mercer.'

Margo's soft, ageless features mirrored a look of surprise as she moved across to a nearby sink washing her hands before scrubbing them with liquid soap.

'Sorry, there's some nasty flora on that agar, methicillin resistant Shigella. Anyway, I can't for the life of me imagine why that case would interest you,' she remarked, grasping paper towelling and drying her hands vigorously.

'The boy's father has just been found under similar circumstances,' James explained, 'I was hoping you could fill me in on any details that stood out surrounding Daniel's death, spot any similarities, peculiarities, that sort of thing.'

'I see. Give me a few minutes; we can head across the road to the local coffee shop. Better environment to chat.'

James waited patiently for Margo to shut down her computer, give a young lab assistant a few instructions before heading out through a side door leading the way to a quiet café in Dryden Road.

'You're taking me back a few years dragging up that case,' Margo informed James, taking a quick look around to ensure their conversation wasn't in ear reach of other coffee imbibers, 'I'll have to see what I can remember. What exactly would you like to know?'

James summarised in a few brief sentences the state of play and the accumulated facts leading to their current impasse in relation to the death of Liam Mercer.

'It all sounds suspicious to me,' Margo told him bluntly. 'Especially as you say they both died on their birthdays and the same location.'

James waited patiently for Margo to reflect on a case buried in the darkest recesses of her mind. She would have conducted numerous autopsies since Daniel's death, so it would take a while to dredge up past events.

'I can't be sure our findings were accurate,' Margo began, a little hesitantly, 'it was an odd death to work on.'

'In what way?' James pressed. It was not like Margo to have doubts.

'Well for a start, it was not easy trying to determine if young Daniel fell to his death or was pushed,' Margo explained, 'as you'll be aware James, an added complication to this type of death is a push can actually be intentional or accidental creating extreme confusion for an enquiry. I recall the position of the small body lying on the rocks gave no real clue. My personal thoughts were if Daniel had been pushed it was not with any great force, more like a nudge. However, like I said we then needed to determine if someone tried to murder Daniel or if it was a tragic accident.'

'Who assisted with the autopsy?' James asked, raising his hand to attract the attention of a passing waitress.

'Patrick Clarke,' Margo replied, 'Patrick is very through, we went over that little body meticulously but always came to the same conclusion: "Accidental death caused by misadventure". I remember the parents accepting the verdict, but Daniel's godfather kept agitating for a second investigation.'

'Who's his godfather? Someone we know?' James asked, scanning the menu.

'A wealthy entrepreneur, I forget his name, but I can dig through files and email the information through to you. It may take some time; a lot of the paperwork has gone into storage boxes in Bristol.'

'That would be useful, thank you. Anything you can lay your hands on would be appreciated. Now, about bruising on the body? Were there any signs of abuse?'

Margo shook her head. 'We found no old bruises or unusual marks to indicate Daniel was an ill-treated child. There were a few mandatory broken bones caused by his body crashing onto the rocks, apart from that no other physical damage.'

'Tell me Margo, how well do you know Judge Frobisher?'

Margo surprised by the question pulled a face, 'I choose not to know him if I can help it James,' she replied, palpable loathing in her voice, 'our paths occasionally cross when I'm called as an expert witness, either in Court or at chamber briefings. Ghastly man, if you want my honest opinion.'

'I had the pleasure of meeting him the other day,' James replied, 'he didn't leave a lasting impression on me.'

'Frobisher doesn't like it when things don't go his way,' Margo muttered, thoughtfully perusing dessert on the specials board.

'Does he show integrity?' James probed.

'He's not got an honest bone in his fat stumpy body,' Margo exploded, 'one word of warning James, if you're thinking of getting one over on him don't, he has connections with hard-core criminals inside and outside the prison system. Stay clear of him.'

'Come on, surely your beliefs are speculation. Such a high-profile person can't be that bad,' James laughed.

'Think what you will,' Margo answered stiffly, 'I can categorically state, Judge Frobisher is the epitome of wicked.'

'Can you recall how long the investigation into Daniel's death went for?' James continued, wishing to keep the topic of Daniel on track.

'It was done and dusted inside three weeks. We honestly couldn't find any concrete evidence to suggest foul play.'

'If you recall anything will you give me a call?' James pleaded, hoping something would trigger Margo's memory if she thought long and hard about the case.

'Most certainly,' Margo smiled, 'James, you must come over for dinner one evening and bring your gorgeous sisters along. Myles would be delighted to see you all. He's near completion of his eighth sci-fi novel and would love to brag about it to anyone willing to listen.'

James nodded, 'I'll call you in a couple of weeks and we'll arrange something. Now let's eat, I'm starving.'

Margo's description of Mal Frobisher bothered James as he drove back home along the A38, being so deep in thought he missed the turn off onto the A303. It was out of character for Margo to intensely dislike a person. She obviously had good reason to detest the Judge. Maybe she was privy to more than she was letting on. Margo was a shrewd individual, not always wanting to part with all the facts, often keeping cards close to her chest, as a form of defence.

****

'DI Wetherill is petitioning the Chief Coroner to sign off on Liam's death as an unfortunate accident, one caused by misadventure,' James informed Fiona, as he gave her the updated brief late on Thursday afternoon.

'How the hell can he push for a ruling of accidental death? That's a load of bullshit, and he knows it, all our start-up evidence indicates credible foul play,' Fiona had difficulty containing her rising anger. Working excessive hours to get to the bottom of Liam Mercer's death she was not about to sit back and let crucial evidence be swept under the carpet. 'Wetherill's a bent copper. He's hiding something, you can be damn sure of that.'

'I tend to agree, but what?' James quizzed, 'if he's putting the case to bed we've not a hope in Hades of getting to the truth behind Liam's death. All our efforts would have been in vain.'

'If you think I'm giving up on this case brother you're very much mistaken,' Fiona replied stubbornly, 'you either need to buy us more time or pretend we have some firm evidence of unequivocal foul play. The other option is to ignore his finding and carry on this investigation regardless until we come up with something.'

'Without the Commander's permission to continue Fi we'd be skating on thin ice,' James cautioned his sister, 'we step circumspectly, or we could land in serious strife.'

'That's as maybe, but Liam Mercer was murdered, I know he was,' Fiona insisted, 'somewhere out there his killer is roaming free, quite possibly capable of killing again and I for one am not about to let that happen. You know what else I think, Wetherill knows a lot more about Liam's death than he's letting on.'

'Perhaps he does, but you'll have a hard job proving it.'

'I figure if we can conduct all the necessary tests here in our own lab no one's going to be any the wiser. What I need from you is the following and as quickly as you can. Are you up for it?'

James shot his sister a warm smile, reaching for his tablet. 'Fire away. I've never seen you this passionate about a case before, Fiona.'

****

Matt sank into a chair to brief the Forensic Team on what he'd located in the depths of Liam Mercer's computer. He was fatigued, his mood noticeably subdued.

'The drive was a real cow to decipher. I have my suspicions Liam only recently purchased a new computer and installed the latest protection and anti-theft software,' he began, recalling the late nights during the week spent poring over data, 'lots of files were corrupted and a virus had played merry hell with the deletions. Anyway, to cut to the chase the most notable case Liam Mercer worked on was *The Langham Trial.*'

He paused for a few moments repositioning, so his legs outstretched before him, 'Michael Langham was a well-known art critic for the Art Monthly, prosecuted by Mercer in 2011 over an assault charge. He was sentenced to a five-year unsuspended jail sentence. Unfortunately, I've not been able to uncover finer details.'

Matt flicked through his wad of notes before continuing, 'In October 2012, Langham committed suicide. At a press conference Liam Mercer made a comment to say, "One less bad penny in life's corrupt wishing well." As you can imagine it was not the best statement to make. Langham's widow threatened to sue and swore she'd get even with Mercer.'

'There you go, motive to kill,' Katie said, her psychological mind coming to the forefront. 'Where can we find Langham's widow to ask questions?'

'All the very best with that one,' Matt replied, 'I've conducted extensive research, but she's nowhere to be found. Claire Langham has vanished into thin air.'

'If Claire Langham did kill Liam Mercer why wait several years to seek revenge?' Fiona interrupted.

'Perhaps she needed to plan things to the last detail,' Katie explained. 'Let's face it, unless you kill in a moment of frenzy, a planned murder would require meticulous preparation and a build-up of fortitude.'

Fiona shuddered. 'That's an awful lot of hate to construct.'

'What else do you know about the Langhams? Were there children?' James directed his question back to Matt.

'One daughter now in her early twenties,' Matt added, consulting his notes again.

'I suggest we try to get an interview with the Super at Exeter CID and see what information he's prepared to part with,' Fiona remarked, 'he might be willing to divulge some hard facts on Claire Langham and any police protection she was offered. If the senior constabulary is uncooperative try DCI Rose, he's often happy to provide inside information.'

'You do realise if Langham's widow is our killer, she could have more murders planned,' Katie informed the small group, 'if she's seeking revenge for her husband's death there could be several people responsible, her profile may fit that of a serial killer.'

James slowly blew out his cheeks, 'Great, the more we dig the bigger the hole.'

Katie slapped her brother firmly on the back, 'Where's your sense of adventure? This sort of intrigue is perfect for my ever-churning psychological mind. Got anything else Mr Tyler, before we call it a day?'

'Only that Mercer and Frobisher are proprietors of "The Palette" wine bar bistro in Salcombe, very prestigious by all accounts. It would be worth checking the place out. Neither particularly strikes me as model citizens, could be the ideal cover for illegal activities.'

'Or just a nice place to unwind after a busy day and enjoy a bottle of vino,' Nick grinned, rising to his feet, 'I love the way you always default to the dark side of life Matthew, mate. For once you may have read things all wrong.'

'We'll see,' Matt chided, 'I'll wager you one hundred notes I'm right on this one.'

Nick reached over to shake his hand, 'May the best man win ol' buddy, may the best man win!'

'What was the final tally on the cash bundle in Liam's office?' James asked, not bothered about a friendly banter between the two men.

'It's been counted a dozen times and the amount is sixty thousand pounds exactly,' Nick replied.

'Wow, as much as that?' James whistled, 'was there anything on Liam's computer which might indicate the origin of the cash?'

Matt shook his head, 'No, perhaps the proceeds of some elaborate extortion operation. Maybe he was blackmailing someone, but who and why I have no idea.'

****

Alone in the main foyer of the Court House, Liam searched his jacket pockets for the digital front door key; standard procedure for those staying back after 9pm required personal devices to exit the building.

'Damn,' Liam fumed, checking his jacket once more, only to find them empty, his mobile also missing. Cursing the recent security overhaul, he tried the large metal door with gusto, anger rising when it wouldn't budge. Eventually, he sank down on the cold tiled floor watching as the overhead lights flickered for a split second before going out, plunging him into total darkness.

'Is anyone here?' Liam called out tentatively. When no reply came, he felt somewhat relieved.

Returning to his office was not an option, once inside the foyer the only exit was by the main door, now securely locked.

The temperature in the Court House was dropping dramatically; a blast of cold air surging through the ducting system.

Dressed only in lightweight clothing appropriate for the season, Liam felt the chill penetrate the back of his neck. The clock on the wall struck eleven, then twelve. Time ticked by slowly, he huddled in a corner to keep warm. Where were the bloody cleaners?

Shortly before 2am as he drifted in and out of slumber, Liam was alerted to the reception phone ringing insistently. Strange, when he'd tried making a call earlier the line was dead. Fumbling in the near darkness, he finally lifted the receiver.

'I wondered how long it would take you to pick up the phone,' a muffled voice whispered from the other end. 'I wanted you to see what it's like to be alone Liam, to be afraid of the unknown. You go around wrecking lives and for once you needed to know what it feels like to be powerless. Remember, I am watching you, Liam Derek Mercer.'

Chapter Four

The distinct, intoxicating smell of varnish, creosote and wood shavings seared James' nostrils when he sauntered through the entrance of the old converted boat shed. A young Asian lad entrenched at the counter of 'Driscoll's Fish and Tackle' looked up smiling as James approached.

Lady Scott Thomas' husband had been a priority on James' "must do list" for the last two weeks.

'I'm looking for Leicester Scott-Thomas,' James said, reciprocating the smile, 'I understand he's around here somewhere?'

The lad pointed to a side door, 'You'll find the old boy out yonder in Tindall's Boatyard.'

Gingerly descending a small flight of ancient, rotting wooden steps and drinking in a mix of petrol and turps fumes, James found himself in an enclosed yard and slipway, fronting onto the harbour, where men dressed in overalls were busy working on boats of varying size and configuration. Heads glanced up as James walked past.

Leicester Scott-Thomas was readily recognisable from a photo James noticed displayed on a side table at his home. He looked older in the flesh, his hair was thinning, now completely white, not the flecked sandy colour portrayed in the photo.

'I'm betting it's too rough to go out today?' James commented, joining Scott-Thomas who was repairing a ripped headsail on a sewing machine.

'Yep, Huey's howling in today. Force 7 from the South,' Leicester acknowledged, without looking up. 'Would be madness heading out to sea in these conditions. When the wind dies, we'll be back to mud flats. That's the drawback with estuary tides. Interested in buying a boat, lad?'

'Wish I could,' James replied, balancing precariously against the transom of a small, wooden, clinker planked Cornish Lugger, 'I'm James Sinclair, with the forensic team investigating the death of Liam Mercer, the unfortunate who fell from Portlemouth cliffs. Your wife was the person who stumbled across the body.'

'Nasty business that,' Leicester replied, finally glancing up from the workbench, 'Rosemary is still in a state of shock.'

'Can you recall where you were the morning Mr Mercer died?' James asked.

'Here working on this little beauty,' Leicester replied, nodding in the direction of a vintage Eight Metre Class racing yacht up on the hard in a corner of the shed. 'Feast your eyes on those gorgeous lines Sinclair. This gorgeous machine won the Gold Cup for Italy in 1951.'

'You've got me there. My knowledge of big boats is limited, only a dinghy sailor I'm afraid. But it sure looks the business,' James remarked.

'Proper job, sails like a witch. Unbeatable to windward,' Leicester added quickly. 'I've had plenty of tempting offers, especially from the Italians. They want to repatriate her to the Costa Smeralda, but she's not for sale. Boats have always been my passion. I grew up around the bay in Hope Cove. As a boy I was always sailing or fishing when tides permitted.'

'Can anyone vouch for you the morning Liam Mercer died?'

Leicester gave a sheepish grin, 'Yes, but Rosemary believes I was tuning a new mainsail off the Coast and I'd like it to stay that way. She doesn't mind me being at sea, but for some reason she hates me spending time in the boatyard. She's afraid I'll end up in the pub.'

Leicester stood up and stretched his thin, wiry limbs before continuing with his explanation, 'For years I was a heavy drinker.'

'That's why you lied about your whereabouts the morning of Liam's death,' James surmised.

Leicester kicked aside a large piece of plank with his right foot. 'I like to use the expression "fabrication of truth". Anyway, if you're wondering if I saw anything in relation to the young man's death the answer is an emphatic "no". I was up at four-thirty, grabbed a cappuccino at Bert Farr's place, before starting work in the yard around a quarter past six. Three others can verify this as they were helping varnish the deck bright work.'

'I'll get you to jot their names onto a piece of paper before I leave,' James instructed.

'What's your local history like?' Leicester enquired of James, clearly not having the faintest desire to discuss Liam Mercer's death any further.

'Only average,' James replied, slightly embarrassed, 'why?'

'This coastline is steeped in maritime history, old and recent,' Leicester proudly informed him, 'I'll wager you didn't know there were a number of shipwrecks around these parts. The earliest was a Bronze Age ship loaded with weapons and precious metal objects, probably a Phoenician oared cargo vessel. There's a documented wreck of a 17th century vessel which sank off Salcombe carrying the largest collection of Islamic coins ever found in England.'

'Remarkable.'

'On the subject of boats, I've another one even more stunning than this one,' Leicester teased, having captured James' interest, 'come take a look. I bought her from an old salt in Dartmouth. She's halfway through major restoration.'

James followed Leicester along the yard to where another wooden boat stood majestically on high beams, surrounded by scaffolding and plank walkways.

'She'll be worth a few quid when seaworthy again,' Leicester chortled, 'she's a double ended ocean cruiser, cedar on white oak.'

'Certainly, a fine-looking boat,' James commented, admiring the 35-footer's classic deep keeled form whilst running his hand seductively across the smooth wood.

Where do people get the funds to bring something like this back to life? He conjectured inwardly, serious envy beginning to surface.

Leicester mopped his deeply furrowed brow with a cloth, squinting at the bright sunlight. 'Fancy a beer, Sinclair? I was just about to head to the Portlemouth Arms, if you'd care to join me?'

James looked a little hesitate. As if reading his mind Leicester clapped him firmly on the back. 'Don't worry, mine will be a straight orange juice,' he informed him, 'I will never go back to that old demon.'

James' features instantly relaxed. 'In that case why not,'

Once they were seated in the low beamed pub Leicester struck up conversation again, 'Fire away if you have more questions to ask, Lad. I may not be able to help, but I appreciate you've a job to do. I feel more relaxed speaking in here. Me old yachtie mates can be a bit paranoid around police or other officials.'

James leaning forward over the bar took a sip of beer before asking, 'Did you know Liam Mercer, the man who died?'

'I knew of him,' Leicester replied, toying with his glass. 'For years I worked alongside Malcolm Frobisher as a Supreme Court Judge. I occasionally came across Mercer.'

'What impression did you form?'

'I don't think I gave him much thought. He knew his legal stuff all right, but apart from that I can't really comment.'

'Are you still working as a Judge?'

'Good God no, I gave that up a few years ago on doctor's orders when I copped a major health scare.'

'What was your relationship with Frobisher like?'

'Frobisher and I never saw eye to eye. He appears pleasant enough, but there's a much darker side to his nature. We tended to disagree on many occasions.'

Leicester took a long deep breath exhaling slowly. 'In recent years there were a few strange things going on at his chambers,' he enlightened James, 'I have my suspicions Frobisher and Mercer were involved in stolen art works or antiques around the South Hams, but no one's ever proved anything. I believe Michael Langham got close, look what happened to him.'

'Know much about that case?' James probed.

'Only from reading the papers and catching the local gossip,' Leicester replied, 'I can't quite fathom why that poor man got such a licking. From what I heard the evidence against him was a bit scant. Knowing Frobisher as I do, I'm inclined to believe it was a set up. Frobisher and Mercer wanted Langham out of the way and this was the best way to do it. I'd steer clear of Frobisher if I was you Sinclair, he's a ruthless bastard and that's on a good day.'

'I'll keep that in mind. Can I buy you another orange juice?'

Leicester shook his head, 'I'm heading over to Newton Abbot for the three thirty guineas. Got my money on a nifty little thoroughbred called "Piping Hot", horse racing is my other passion. I've got four horses all stabled at a livery near Loddiswell. I probably break even from all the bets I put on, another pleasure I keep from Rosemary,' Leicester chuckled as he held out his hand to James, 'thanks for the company, it's been an interesting afternoon.'

****

Matt strolled into the lab, launching his powerful frame onto the bench, which groaned under the weight. James, both eyes firmly fixed to a Leitz hi-power stereo microscope examining textile samples, grunted a muffled greeting.

'Anything interesting,' Matt gibed, trying to be facetious, 'don't you ever take a break?'

'It looks as if I'm about to,' James replied, pushing the microscope to one side, 'what can I do you for?'

61

'I just happened to bump into Assistant Superintendent Clive Brinks from the Exeter CID last night in the pub. Clive and I go back a long way from my Yard days, anyway, I took the liberty of questioning him about the Langham case.'

'And?'

'Get this. Not for one moment does Brinks believe Michael Langham capable of harming another human being, he says there was concrete evidence to prove Michael Langham was involved in large-scale corruption. The courts could easily have found him guilty based on the weight of facts brought to light, but for some reason they chose not to, instead sending him down on assault charges. DI Wetherill was the lead copper heading up the case who claimed to have misplaced statements and key evidence.'

'Sounds fishy to me,' James said, rubbing his stubble, 'what about Langhams' widow and daughter, do you have any details on either of them?'

'So far, I've only been able to gather snippets of info,' Matt replied, frustration evident. 'Shortly after Michael Langham went to prison for the assault charges Claire Langham and her now twenty-two-year-old daughter Michelle, were permanently assigned a protection care officer for fear of repercussions. Both would almost certainly have changed their names.'

'Do you have any clues as to where they might be now? Can we be sure they are even in the country?'

'Nope, the police protection program is binding. Only a few people would have that knowledge, DI Wetherill being one of them, as he was the lead officer in charge of the case, but he's not about to tell us in a hurry.'

'I wouldn't trust that slimy weasel to keep a secret,' James sneered, 'he's as bent as a boomerang.'

'Very funny,' Matt chided, 'but on a serious note I agree. Brinks couldn't tell me much more.'

James pondered for a few moments, before making his next statement, 'If Claire and her daughter were involved in Liam's murder; we'll flush them out eventually. Like the old saying goes: you can run…'

'Yes, but you need to be careful James,' Matt warned, 'if you try to find Claire Langham and her daughter you could be putting them both in harm's way. It's quite probable they're innocent with no link to Liam Mercer's death. I'd make it a priority to speak to them before you go delving into the past.'

'Point taken,' James said, emptying a can of energy drink, 'I'll see what I can discover and then decide how far I go.'

****

James entered Lois' premises on Union Street, finding no one in attendance in the gallery, he stuck his head around the doorway of the studio.

'Gwyn Lacey?' he enquired, addressing an attractive, platinum blonde, middle-aged woman washing up paint pallets at a rustic sink, her features fine with a hint of fragility, like French porcelain.

'Yes, you must be the scientific expert, James St Clair. Lois said you might be dropping by.'

'Sinclair.' James corrected.

Gwyn dried her hands with a nearby towel, offering the right one for James to shake. 'I was about to head to Waves Café for a bite to eat. Business is a bit slow. Care to join me James?'

Her suggestion was accepted.

With the gallery door securely locked Gwyn led James through narrow side streets to a secluded eatery a stone's throw from the waterfront.

'So, tell me, how long have you worked for Lois St John?' James asked, sinking into a high-backed chair desperate to unwind after a hectic week.

Gwyn wrinkled her forehead. 'Almost three years. I organise the art exhibitions and help out in the shop.'

'Can I assume you also have a talent for painting?'

Gwyn smiled weakly, warming to her guest, 'I dabble a bit, but not up to the standard of Lois. She really is a marvel, earning quite a name for herself in art circles. That's woman's going places.'

'What can you tell me about the infamous painting "Falling Memories"? Do you happen to know who bought it?'

Gwyn shook her head, 'The night the painting sold was one of our busiest. I didn't take down any particulars.'

'Is it unusual not to jot down details?' James pressed, pouring a glass of water from a courtesy jug.

'Unfortunately, it's quite common, James. You see, we get distracted at these exhibition nights, entertaining guests is the main priority. It's vital to ensure members of the media entourage get looked after as well as customers. If we treat journalists well, they tend to write favourable reviews, these shows can make or break local artists. You've got to suck up to the gay gallery mafia as well or you'll never sell a painting. They run the art scene in this country. I could probably go back through the receipts book. Someone might have entered it into the computer customer list.'

'Do you remember if it was a man or woman who bought the painting?'

Gwyn laughed, 'That much I can recall, it was a gentleman of average height, I'm guessing to be in his late fifties early sixties, good looking for his age, somewhat distinguished, with a public-school accent, certainly not what I'd call a proper Devonian.'

'Had you seen him before?'

Gwyn shook her head, 'No, I don't remember seeing him before.'

'Did he say why he wanted the painting?'

'No. Something about liking the vibrant colours, with the boat in the foreground appealing somewhat. I don't think he knew any of the people depicted in the work. We didn't engage in conversation. Sorry, I'm not much help, am I?' Gwyn stammered, flustered at the loss of memory.

'You're doing fine. Now tell me, what's Lois like as a boss?' James enquired, hoping to put Gwyn at ease.

'How confidential is our discussion today?'

'It's one hundred percent confidential,' James assured her, 'I don't expect you to totally dish the dirt on Lois, unless there's something you think I should know to aid our ongoing investigation.'

'I'll tell you what I can, and you shall be the one to judge if it's useful or not.'

James signalled to the passing waitress ordering a large cappuccino and a slice of warm banana bread. The invigorating sea air gnawed at his insides and he'd heard the food at the café was of exceptional standard.

'Would you say Lois is erratic?' James ventured, 'I've often heard artists can be very temperamental with extremely short fuses.'

'Oh, Lois is okay as far as talented people go, I suppose,' Gwyn replied hesitantly, dabbing her lips with a serviette, 'I've only seen her flare up twice and on both occasions, it was justified, the first was directed at a young art student who poked an easel right through one of Lois' prize winning water colours; that girl was extremely clumsy, the other when a critic referred to her in a national newspaper as *having the artistic talent of a blind, three-legged mule.*'

'How well do you know Lois' husband Malcolm Frobisher?' James asked, leaning back in his chair, listening with interest as Gwyn parted with her knowledge.

'Ah, the supreme court judge,' Gwyn giggled roguishly, 'I've probably met him twice.'

'Would you describe him as a pleasant chap?'

'I hardly know him James. However, I don't think I'd want to get on the wrong side of Malcolm Frobisher. I feel uneasy when he's around but can't quite put my finger on why.'

'So, there's nothing else you can really tell me which could help my current investigation?' James concluded, draining his coffee.

'Not really.'

James pushed aside the cup and plate, rising to his feet. 'I appreciate you taking time to speak with me today Gwyn. Lois is lucky having such a level-headed assistant.'

'The pleasure's mine, Mr St Clair.'

****

'Now what brings you to see me in quick succession?' Margo enquired of her visitor, entrenched in the hospital library, thumbing through a stack of medical journals. 'I'm certain this isn't merely a social call, Jim.'

'You've got the uncanny knack of being able to read my mind,' James laughed, planting a kiss on her rosy cheeks and pulling up a chair, 'tell me Margo, when you were working on the Daniel Mercer matter did you encounter any problems or even interference?'

'Why do you ask?' Margo fired back, 'I thought we'd discussed this matter only a few days ago.'

James took a deep breath. 'If you must know I've been speaking with one of the duty Sergeants at Exeter HQ, who vaguely recalls the investigation of Daniel's death turning into a bit of a farce. He mentioned something about the forensics being riddled with problems.'

'What do you mean by problems? No investigation is ever straightforward. I think at our last meeting I mentioned it was a strange case.'

'Well, was there anything that struck you as unusual? Anything you felt was out of place?'

Margo fell silent, lost deep in thought. It was a few minutes before she spoke again.

'My memory's not what it was James. I've worked on so many cases since the Mercer one. Let me see what I can remember.'

James allowed Margo thinking space. With any luck her brain neurons would get the jolt they needed.

'Stressful, that's it, with a string of bizarre hiccups along the way,' Margo piped up at last, recognition spreading across a visage miraculously unsullied by years of horrendous working hours and the impossible demands of a part time Government pathologist.

'What do you mean by hiccups?'

'Well dramas might be a better word to use,' Margo replied candidly, pushing aside the medical journals and leaning heavily on the table in front of her. 'We had a break-in one night and some DNA samples were stolen. We decided it was kids messing around. Then the T-shirt Daniel was wearing at the time of his death became coffee stained,' Margo paused as the details flooded back, 'the forensic tests were plagued with issues of some sort or another, right from the start.'

'Did you redo the DNA tests?' James asked.

'Of course,' Margo scolded, sounding a little indignant, 'but with evidence now contaminated we weren't sure our findings were meaningful. Yes, I'm sure of it now, the Daniel Mercer case was not just odd it was manic.'

James looked keenly at Margo, waiting for her to continue.

'The second lot of tests conducted indicated Sonia Mercer was not Daniel Mercer's biological mother,' Margo said, lowering her voice a notch, noticing reproachful glances from the hospital librarian.

'Did these findings eventually reach the public?' James asked.

'Not by the usual channels,' Margo snorted, 'someone spilt their guts to the press.'

'Any idea as to who the source was?'

Margo shook her head, 'I can categorically state it was not my lab technicians, although some cretin was hell bent on divulging the confidential test results. That investigation plagued me for an eternity. The moment the findings hit the papers my phone didn't stop ringing. The hearing was put on hold to do some serious explaining to Regional Home Office, the boys in blue were all over the lab. Liam Mercer's legal team got in contact threatening to censor the Crown and we were forced into damage control. Not something I'd ever want to go through again. Maybe that's why I had difficulty remembering a case I'd much rather forget.'

'Has it ever occurred to you that perhaps the results didn't get leaked?' James suggested.

Margo looked at James blankly, 'I'm not sure I follow?'

'Well, suppose someone already knew Sonia was not Daniel's mother. What if that person also knew your lab would conduct full DNA tests which would uncover this bombshell? This being the case there's every possibility they disclosed the information to the press, using your team as scapegoats.'

'I guess anything's possible,' Margo muttered, 'why would anyone do that? It's absurd.'

'Who knows?' James replied earnestly, 'with your permission Margo I'd like to reopen the forensics on Daniel Mercer. Would you allow me full access to all your previous data and files?'

'Why of course, but on one condition,' Margo conceded.

'Yes?'

'You keep this to yourself, just your immediate team. I do not want to run the risk of any outsider getting wind of this.'

'You have my word. Thanks Margo, you're a gem.'

'I don't need flattery,' Margo repudiated, 'we'd better return to the lab. Denise over there wants to close for lunch. If we upset the old battle axe, I'll never hear the end of it.'

Back in the confines of the lab Margo leaned against a swivel chair, removing her left shoe giving her aching foot a gentle massage.

'You'll find all the files in the second drawer of that filing cabinet over there,' she instructed, indicating an old metal three draw cabinet resting against the back wall of her office, 'when you're done please return each file just as you found it, and lock up afterwards.'

'Yes, me lady,' James smiled, dodging Margo's right arm, which teasingly came close to giving him a cuff across the back of the head, 'oh, and Jim, if you do discover anything of interest, I'd like to be the first to know.'

'Sure, before you go Margo, one last question. Did you notice anything unusual about Daniel's eyes whilst conducting the autopsy? Would you say he could have been suffering from a severe allergy of some description?'

'Strange question,' Margo said, a little perplexed, 'It's so long-ago. I can't recall much of the finer details. If we did find anything it'll all be documented. Clarke is not one to overlook things, very thorough is our Patrick. If that's all, I'll leave you to it, I'm lecturing to a group of German medical students this afternoon in Bristol, I daren't be late.'

With Margo heading out the door James, set to work going through the almost illegible, hand written notes penned by Patrick Clarke.

'Typical bloody medico,' he mumbled, needing to re-read the scrawl several times in case he missed any vital evidence.

After an hour of fruitlessly scouring the reports James stumbled upon something of interest. Clarke had documented a paragraph of intrigue. According to his conclusions, Daniel was suffering from an allergic reaction at the time of his death. Clarke going on to declare he believed the reaction to have been caused by seafood, perhaps oysters. James sat down reading aloud Clarke's report:

In my capacity as the Coroner appointed pathologist, I believe Daniel Liam Mercer, aged ten years, had a severe reaction to shellfish ingestion, possible tainted. This condition may have been caused by pathogenic bacteria toxins, parasites or an allergic reaction to the shellfish protein, but it is difficult to determine which. I am also inclined to believe the deceased suffered a severe anaphylactic shock and this in part caused his death. I noted the following: excessive swelling around his trachea, hives on his torso, legs and arms. Although not witness to Daniel Liam Mercer prior to his death I am confident he would have experienced bouts of vomiting, a drop in blood pressure and breathing difficulty. Medical reports also indicate Daniel Liam Mercer was a chronic Asthmatic needing Ventolin and additional medication for this condition.

James was dumbfounded. He had not come across the information in any previous reports he'd read at the Exeter Coroner's office.

Placing the document back in the filing cabinet, safely locked away, he puzzled over his findings. Could it be possible Clarke's statement had simply been overlooked in the final report, or had someone deliberately kept it under wraps?

****

Liam reached to touch his aching head, the stomach cramps worsening as a wave of nausea unfolded. He'd felt fine when he'd gone to bed last night, now he thought he was dying, barely able to raise his head off the pillow. He tried to think what he could have eaten to churn his stomach so violently. There was a chicken and salad roll eaten at lunchtime, it must have been that. The canteen prided itself on fresh quality food, but on this occasion, they must have received a bad batch of meat.

Liam glanced at his iPhone, persistently buzzing on the bedside table. He chose to ignore it, not in the mood to speak to anyone. Drifting in and out of a fitful doze, he slept most of the afternoon. When he finally awoke, he gulped a small glass of water before gingerly leaning across the side of the bed to turn on the phone, which registered a staggering fifty-five messages.

Jolting to the present Liam realised all fifty-five messages were identical, from an unknown caller. "So sorry you've been taken ill," the messages read, "Let's hope you don't die, die, die, die, die..."

Chapter Five

Within two weeks of the meeting with Margo, James and Nick successfully petitioned the Crown to officially re-open the case on Daniel Mercer, allowing access to copies of the documents at the Home Office in Exeter. Due to strict security guidelines James was not permitted to remove any of the files, all information had to be kept on site.

For several days he sat behind an old oak desk scrutinising all the case notes, police reports and forensic results. Again, he failed to come across any report indicating Daniel had suffered a severe reaction at the time of death.

Once James had compiled all detailed notes relating to Daniel's death, he convinced Nick to have the police draw up and distribute posters urging people to come forward if they had been on Mill Bay Beach the day Daniel Mercer died. The intentions were to flush out anyone who witnessed Daniel acting strangely or appearing distressed moments before he fell. Bright, eye-catching bills were displayed within a ten-mile radius of the coastal village of Portlemouth: in local stores, on church notice boards, in schools and village halls. Notices were also placed in the local newspapers and village life magazines. Finally, a make-shift police operations unit was set up in the local Portlemouth hall at the centre of the village, in the hope some soul would come forth with vital information.

Initially, Sonia Mercer had been vehemently opposed to the idea of her son's death being dredged up again, but over time she succumbed to the hubris, throwing her hands up in dismay.

'Do what you must,' she conceded at the media conference, 'you'll be lucky to unearth new evidence. My son's death is cloaked in mystery and so far, no one's been able to prove anything to the contrary.'

At cessation of proceedings, and with James trapped giving a television interview, Fiona approached Sonia seizing the opportunity to delve into Daniel's medical history. Sonia was alone, standing outside the Portlemouth Hall, smoking.

'Sonia, do you mind me asking if Daniel had any allergies?'

'Daniel was a chronic asthmatic,' Sonia replied. He was on regular Ventolin and Atropine, as a toddler. He also had a nut and shellfish allergy. Dr McGregor said his allergies were likely to get worse as he got older, which is not always the case. Apparently, it's more common for teenagers and adults to have these types of allergies than very young children.

'How did Daniel manage his allergies?'

'Due to the severity of his condition we always made sure Daniel carried his medication with him, which included an Epipen. We wouldn't let Daniel out of the house without it.'

'Was Daniel comfortable using the Epipen if needed?' Fiona enquired.

Sonia nodded, 'Oh yes, he's used it on several occasions. Daniel was quite mature for his age. He understood his ailments and how to deal with them.'

Fiona made a note of this in her small note pad before asking her next set of questions.

'The day Daniel died were you aware if he had been exposed to nuts or shellfish?'

Sonia looked confused, 'It's possible, there was a variety of food for his birthday party, spread out on fold up tables on the beach. Why are you asking me this? I don't see how any of it is relevant.'

'It's all routine questioning,' Fiona replied sympathetically, 'are you also aware if Daniel had his Epipen with him the day he died?'

'I don't know, I assume he did, although…'

'Although what?' Fiona urged.

'I don't recall it being amongst his belongings when the police returned his duffle bag. Daniel always kept it in a small pouch attached to his bag.'

Fiona tried to cover her shock, 'Thanks for your time, Sonia. I'll be in touch if I have subsequent news for you.'

****

'You did well to discover details on Daniel's allergies from Clarke's medical notes,' Nick commented to James, as they sat in the demountable waiting patiently for volunteers to come forward. 'Although I still have concerns over Fiona's comments relating to the Epipen. I've checked the contents listed in Daniel's bag at time of death and no Epipen is noted. With or without the pen the leading question is, whether anyone played a part in Daniel's death or if his medical condition was the pre-disposing factor. The other possibility that arises would be if Daniel's fall from the cliff was the consequence of losing control of his senses, misjudging the distance from the edge of the cliff.'

'It's all too ambiguous for my liking,' James sighed, 'the other thing to take into consideration is; if someone knew of Daniel Mercer's allergies, they could easily have exposed him to the shellfish before ensuring he goes onto the cliff top. The chances of him falling would have been extremely high, something the person was bound to have known. That same person could also have taken the Epipen from his bag.'

'In other words, it would have been easy for someone to murder Daniel Mercer and get away with it? Making it look like a tragic accident,' Nick surmised.

'Precisely, therefore we need to see if anyone can remember anything of significance on the day Daniel died.'

DCI Rose and the press team soon dispersed leaving James and Nick consuming the purgative commonly known as "police instant coffee".

Stifling a yawn James prodded Nick awake from a micro nap when a young man appeared in the doorway, kitted out in tight jeans and a stained England Rugby shirt. His earnest green eyes searching the room eventually settled on the two seated at the desk. Still unsure the man ventured slowly across the wooden floor, pain etched on tanned, chiselled features.

James pulled up a chair for the young man to sit down and after brief introductions Richard De Crespigny recounted what he remembered about the day Daniel Mercer fell to his death.

'Watching him fall was like a slow-motion football replay,' Richard explained, 'back then I was only fifteen, not much older than Mercer. My friends and I weren't part of the official birthday party, but we were offered food and refreshments, it became quite a social event. I remember looking up at the cliffs when I heard the boy scream, wondering if my brain was playing tricks.'

'Was this the first time you'd been to this particular beach?' James asked, jotting down notes.

'No. I spend a lot of time around Portlemouth and Salcombe. My parents own the local sailing school, that's where I sustained my injury. Got my leg caught in an outboard motor, had a few operations, but it's never going to get better. Something I learn to live with.'

'Did you notice anything unusual on that particular day, anyone acting suspiciously or looking out of place?'

Richard took a moment to answer, 'I remember a plump lady taking photographs. She was just clicking away with her camera, but no one seemed to mind. I think someone mentioned she was an artist, a local woman, but I can't remember her name.'

'Did you see Daniel playing on the beach prior to his death?' Nick enquired, rubbing tired eyes.

'Sorry I can't be certain of that one,' Richard replied, 'time distorts the memory. There were a lot of children playing on the beach that day. I assume he was there amongst the throng but can't single him out.'

'Is there anything that happened which triggers a particular memory to Daniel's death? Did you hear comments which made you suspicious or hear of anyone making threats?' this question was asked by James.

'Not really,' Richard paused, easing his left leg into a different position. 'However, one thing did strike me as strange, there was a woman who became extremely manic after the event. I'd say she was in her mid-thirties, very attractive, nice figure.'

'Manic in what way?' James asked.

'She started screaming before collapsing on to the sand; a scream so loud I had to block my ears. I'm guessing she was a relative of sorts as she turned deathly white before wailing like a banshee. It took a local doctor over twenty minutes to calm her with sedatives before the paramedics arrived.'

Nick fiddled with his tie not trying to hide a bored expression. 'Anyone watching such a catastrophe is bound to be upset,' he snapped, still cranky from being woken from his afternoon siesta. 'Is there anything else you can tell us, Mr De Crespigny?'

Richard shook his head, 'Not really. I hope I've been of some assistance.'

James jumped in before Nick could let fly a cutting remark, 'Thanks for your time Richard we'll be in touch if we require anything else.'

'Well that was a waste of time,' Nick turned to James, as De Crespigny limped away, 'Let's hope we get something useful out of this exercise, so far we've learnt buggar all.'

'Patience is a virtue. Christ, how much sleep did you get last night?' James cajoled, helping himself to a glass of water from the cooler. 'Any information we obtain today will be useful to Katie in building a history of events. These things can't be rushed. We need to piece everything together in the hope eventually a proper picture emerges. Hey up, what's she doing here?'

Nick turned his head towards the door, where Lady Scott-Thomas stood speaking with a junior police constable. She was dressed in a bright-pink outfit with matching hat and high heels, clearly not wanting to appear inconspicuous.

'Yoo-hoo,' she called out loudly, 'you've set yourselves up nicely, haven't you? Quite the little detectives, all you need now is a buddy Miss Marble.'

'Marple,' Nick corrected her.

'Yes, that's what I said, Marble.'

James wasn't quite sure if she was being naïve or taking the mickey but wasn't about to waste time finding out. 'I take it you have something important you'd like to relay going back to the death of young Daniel?' he quizzed.

'Yes indeed. I'd not really thought much about it until recently. When I heard you'd set up camp in this makeshift facility I felt it my duty to part with any knowledge that might be of assistance.'

'What exactly do you remember about that day?' James asked, trying his best to appear enthused.

'A lot of shouting, that's what I remember,' Lady Scott-Thomas began, easing into a chair, carefully placing her bag on her lap, 'it was meant to be a day of celebration, but as far as I recall it wasn't exactly that. Daniel was such a lively child, always getting into mischief. I remember hearing raised voices not long before he died.'

'Did you see Daniel venture onto the cliff path?' James prompted, 'was he alone, or did he have someone with him?'

'I don't know, it's so long ago,' Rosemary Scott-Thomas replied, looking flustered, 'perhaps my coming here was not such a good idea if I am having trouble remembering tiny details like that.'

'Take your time, if you need a glass of water or a coffee you only need to ask.'

'You're too kind,' Lady Scott-Thomas beamed, 'Please call me Rosemary. Perhaps your assistant here would be kind enough to fetch me a drop of Sherry. I know they keep a spare bottle over in the hall kitchenette for emergencies, second cupboard on the left, third shelf.'

James tried not to laugh as Nick stood up to meet the demands. As soon as he was out of earshot Rosemary leaned forward to whisper in James' ear. 'I believe I saw something I should be telling you but can't quite be certain as time does have a habit of playing tricks with the memory. What I do know is Daniel was arguing with his father before heading in the direction of the coastal path. Something was not right, and the next moment Daniel was over the edge and well…'

'So, you don't believe Daniel's death was an accident?' Nick interrupted, returning to the interview facility with a small glass of Sherry.

'Well if you put it like that, then probably yes Mr Shelby. The argument was very heated, and I am quite certain I heard someone threaten young Daniel.'

'How certain are you it was Liam Mercer?' Nick probed.

'I can't really be sure. It would be wrong of me to speculate; however, it could have been Liam Mercer.'

'We don't work on conjecture,' Nick answered flippantly. He hated working off assumptions, he needed clarification and evidence.

'How confidential is our discussion today?' Lady Scott-Thomas enquired, as she turned to face James, 'I need to know I will be safe if I give you information.'

'Very confidential,' James reassured her.

Lady Scott-Thomas heaved a sigh of relief, glancing slowly around the room to make sure no one else was in earshot. 'In that case James, I retract my first statement. I am one hundred percent certain one of two men I saw following Daniel along the footpath was his father.'

'You said there were two men?' James quizzed, 'do you know who the other man was?'

'Yes, the Honourable Malcolm Frobisher.'

'What do you make of that?' Nick asked, after Lady Scott-Thomas had swept out of the hall. 'Is she right and if so, did Liam and Frobisher kill Daniel?'

'Who knows, we'll have to notify Mick Rose; it's his area of responsibility. They'll want to have a lot more than that to even dare pull the Judge in for questioning. Let's be pragmatic about this, I don't reckon they have the political clout or fortitude to do it. And even in the highly unlikely event that Rose gets to put the third degree on Malcolm Frobisher no way he'll confess to killing a ten-year-old child.'

****

A few nights later, James took a call from Nick Shelby. 'It's taken a while for me to put everything together on Daniel Mercer but now I have the formal report and summary, I think you'll find the conclusions rather fascinating. I'll swing by early tomorrow on my way up north and give you a detailed update.'

In the morning, just before nine, the small team hovered around the bench in the Moorland lab, expectantly waiting for Nick to deliver his findings into the death of Daniel Mercer.

'From all the evidence James and Fiona have brought to light we suspect his death was no accident,' Nick announced. 'From the eye witness accounts, in conjunction with the autopsy results, it appears Daniel Mercer was given eye drops which caused extensive blurred vision. On top of that he consumed small quantities of shellfish to which he may have experienced a severe allergic reaction. Once up on the cliffs Daniel would have no sense of direction due to his blurred sight and suffering anaphylaxis, this in turn means he did not know he was venturing close to the edge of the drop. I strongly believe the killer knew this result was highly probable; they wanted to make Daniel's death appear to be a tragic accident.'

A lump formed in Katie's throat. It appeared to be a cold calculated murder, almost flying under the radar, a murder which would prove difficult to solve.

'Now the tricky part is establishing who could have done this and what their motive would have been,' James spoke up, 'DCI Rose and his people are going to work closely with us to establish a list of those who knew the Mercer family well, someone who might have played a part in Daniel's murder. Unfortunately, at this stage there are no clear scientific avenues left which will assist us moving forward. We know what caused Daniel to fall, what we don't know is who was behind it.'

Nick glanced at his watch. 'Sorry, but I've a staff interview in Bideford. Let's call it a day and meet at my office tomorrow morning at eleven to review more evidence. I've asked Rose to join us as his assistance will be pivotal.'

****

Rod Wetherill looked up impatiently as James bound unceremoniously into his office. 'What do you want?' he fired crossly, 'I have enough on my plate without forensics turning up unannounced.'

'I'm just trying to establish why the final report pertaining to the death of Daniel Mercer was lacking in some of the finer detail?'

James said coolly, leaning over the desk so his blue eyes made direct contact with Wetherill's, 'I've gone over the reports and there's very little in the way of documented facts to back up the conclusions arrived at. From my knowledge and analysis, it would appear the police taskforce at the time didn't bother getting eyewitness accounts, which in my opinion left the case wide open.'

'If you're accusing me of not doing my job properly Sinclair, don't,' Wetherill snapped.

'No one's accusing anyone of anything Detective Inspector, I'm merely trying to establish some facts,' James remarked smoothly.

'Sounds to me like you're meddling in something you know very little about,' Wetherill replied curtly, 'my officers followed all the right channels. We went over the evidence with a fine-tooth comb but never discovered anything other than Daniel Mercer died of natural causes, a tragic fall from a cliff that's all it was, nothing more, nothing less.'

'Well forensics states otherwise,' James remarked stubbornly, 'That's me doing my job properly.'

'Then forensics is wrong,' DI Wetherill retaliated, starting to rise from his chair, 'I'd stop meddling in matters that don't concern you Sinclair. Now if that's all you've come about, I suggest you leave, some of us have important work to do.'

Before James could comment further the Superintendent entered the room having overheard part of the conversation. 'James, I have to agree with the DI,' he weighed in, 'no evidence ever pointed to Daniel being murdered. Best leave this one alone.'

'Sorry I can't do that,' James answered crisply, 'my job, gentlemen, is to uncover scientific evidence and that's exactly what I plan to do, with or without your full co-operation.'

James stormed out of the office annoyed that forensics and police investigators were not on the same side.

Returning to the office, James turned on the espresso machine and dropped in a strong black capsule. An instant stimulant was required, knowing it was only a matter of time before Chief Superintendent Ashcroft was on the blower to complain about his recent confrontation with the DI. As he sat behind his desk absentmindedly shuffling papers the shrill of the phone rang in his ear.

'Sinclair, you can't barge in to CID upsetting Wetherill,' the Super barked. 'What on earth is that about?'

James was working overtime to keep his temper in check. Not a good idea to lose it with the big boss. 'I'm uncertain why he would be so upset,' James replied smoothly. 'I was only doing my job, questioning the integrity of the final police report, which doesn't seem to match scientific evidence.'

'The case on Daniel Mercer is closed, has been for quite some time. I fully support DI Wetherill with his police findings.'

'Sorry sir, but I don't,' James replied firmly, 'I can't understand why the Detective Inspector reacted that way, unless he's got something to hide of course.'

James caught a muffled groan on the other end of the phone. 'You'll have to be careful how you proceed with this investigation, Sinclair. DI Wetherill is within his power to make life very uncomfortable for you. You may even find he refuses the Moorland team future access to files containing classified information.'

'That sounds like a threat to me,' James retorted, realising he was beaten.

'No one's threatening you James. I'm just telling you to go lightly,' Bob Ashcroft replied in a softer tone, 'I know you're a damn good forensic scientist but watch your step. There are a lot of senior people who will stop you in your tracks if you tread on their rather large toes. Do you understand?'

'Yes, sir.'

****

Katie waited in the reception foyer of the Lemon Tree Hostel, a private facility owned by a local wealthy vicar and his wife who dabbled in property development. The stark, minimalist, two-storey complex, sat in sumptuous grounds in Holden Forest overlooking the nearby sprawl of Exeter. It catered exclusively for those with a terminal illness providing luxurious comfort to the very end. At five hundred pounds a night it was a privilege not within the reach of the average punter.

'How may I help you?' the young nurse on reception finally enquired, projecting an abnormally white smile, 'are you here on a visit or do you wish to make an enquiry about booking someone in?'

'I'm looking for Louise Warman,' Katie replied casually.

'Second room, on the right,' the young nurse instructed, barely looking up from the desk, 'I can only allow you twenty minutes. Louise is very weak and gets exhausted easily. We don't expect her to last the month.'

Entering room 5, Katie encountered Louise propped up in bed reading a magazine. She looked thin and frail, far beyond her twenty-seven years.

'I was expecting you,' Louise commented, placing the magazine on the bedside table. 'The moment I read about Liam's death I knew I'd be inundated with visits. I assume you're a police woman wanting to ask me further questions about the rape allegations?'

For a moment Katie was lost for words. Breathing was obviously difficult for Louise, the volume in her voice barely more than a whisper.

'You want to ask me about Liam Mercer? Am I right?' Louise wheezed, turning up her oxygen supply.

'Yes, but I understand this must be very awkward for you,' Katie mumbled, a little hesitantly, 'I'm a forensic psychologist, not a police woman. My name's Katie Sinclair, I'm with a company called Moorland Forensics. I don't want to cause too much distress, but hope you'll be able to talk to me about Liam Mercer.'

'Having terminal cancer is difficult Ms Sinclair, reminiscing about being raped is easy in compassion,' Louise sighed.

'Were you angry when Liam got off with what he did to you?' Katie asked, taking up a position on the side of Louise's bed, following her instructions.

'Angry no, disappointed yes. I did nothing to encourage what happened to me.'

'You were close to Daniel, weren't you and very good at your job.'

Louise managed a faint smile which lit up her sparkling blue eyes. 'Daniel was a beautiful child, it broke my heart to resign as his nanny, but I was left with no choice after what happened. I could hardly live in the same house with a man who brutally attacked me.'

'I understand as a result of the hearing Mercer was never charged, why was that?'

'My lawyer informed me the prime forensic evidence got destroyed, whatever that means,' Louise wheezed, 'without concrete evidence to go on, it merely became my word against his, an open and shut case.'

'Louise, do you believe Daniel's death to have been an accident?' Katie knew this was a leading question and one Louise may not be prepared or able to answer.

Louise reached for a glass of water, this itself proving to be a very slow, drawn out process. Katie offered to help but Louise raised her hand in protest. The remaining piece of independence left in her body was not going to be taken away by anyone. Once she had drunk Louise answered the question.

'Yes, I do believe Daniel was murdered. Now I have a question for you, Ms Sinclair. Do you still picture in your mind what happened to you? You were young and naïve like I was, it couldn't have been easy.'

Kate was incredulous. She wanted to reply, but no words came. Was it that obvious to a stranger she herself had been through a similar torture?

'It's okay to let go,' Louise replied softly, 'you need to let go, otherwise it will haunt you for the rest of your life.'

'Have you forgiven Liam Mercer for what he did to you?' Katie asked, desperate to change the subject.

Louise smiled weakly. Turning to Katie she caught hold of her hand squeezing it tight. 'I had to forgive, without absolution there is no resolution.'

****

Brandy balloon in hand Lois lazed on the leather settee, lost in a snifter of cognac as James strolled in to the studio just after three the following afternoon. She gazed up smiling.

'Jim Sinclair, how lovely to see you, be careful of the paint tins scattered about and don't step on the canvas. I'm experimenting with a "Jackson Pollock style" of painting. You literally throw a lot of paint onto a blank canvas and create a masterpiece. I'm having a go with thin acrylics, not ducos and aluminium paint. Well that's the theory,' she laughed, waving across to her creation occupying a significant portion of the studio floor.

James returned the smile, 'Perhaps one day you'll teach me how to draw, Lois? No "Blue Poles" or anything. Just simple stuff, Art was intimidating for me at school.'

'That's why you found solace and gratification in the scientific disciplines. I'm sure you can be taught how to paint Jim; of course, having the inborn talent helps enormously. In a nutshell, learning how to draw is the key. You must be taught how to "see". It comes from looking inside the subject and capturing its essence, not just representing it. Then you need to place the subject in its environment. All the great painters had it, from Titian and Rembrandt through to Matisse and Picasso. Great art creates a kaleidoscope of emotions and feelings in the viewer.'

'I can sort of get what you're saying,' James replied, wondering if he was in for a long winded, but enthralling lecture. Lois was eccentric, but she certainly knew how to spin a good yarn.

'What I call the "Great Tradition of Western Art", it's always been there,' Lois continued, only too happy to have a captive audience, 'you can sense its presence even in the early Cro-Magnon cave paintings of Europe. A Cezanne still life, as an example succeeds beautifully because it generates feelings of comfort and insecurity both at the same time. Now with what do I owe the pleasure?'

'More questions I'm afraid, this time they relate to your husband Judge Frobisher,' James forced, reluctant to switch from Lois' fascinating insight.

'Malcolm if you don't mind James,' Lois corrected him, 'I certainly don't hold him in such high esteem as others. He's just plain Mal to me. Now what is it you want to know?'

'We believe Judge Frobisher, sorry Malcolm, may have tried to protect Liam Mercer over an alleged rape charge, although he flatly denies it. Was this ever discussed with you?'

Lois gave a look of reproach, 'I can assure you Malcolm is a very gracious man, not in the habit of covering things up. Really James, you need to do your homework better. In case you hadn't realised the woman in question was young Daniel's nanny, when you get consenting adults living under the same roof things are bound to happen, consensual sex being one of them.'

'Not according to the police report.

'Yes, well they don't always get it right,' Lois objected, 'things get distorted, especially when that so and so Tom Markham plays around with his alarmist press releases, printing unmitigated garbage. He's a frightful specimen of a human being.'

James concealed a wry grin. He understood where Lois was coming from as well realising the clever plight to steer the topic of conversation along a different avenue. 'Did Malcolm discuss in any detail the alleged rape of Louise Warman?' he asked, 'after all, he was probably Liam's closest confidant. I am sure the subject must have been raised on occasions?'

Lois gripped her glass firmly, a custom James had witnessed on more than one occasion. 'Not with me it didn't James, Malcolm tries to keep clear of forming opinions or discussing another person's issues. He's not one to delve into idle gossip. Whatever people think about Malcolm, he has high morals.'

James doubted this very much but didn't want to burst Lois' bubble if she really believed her estranged husband was a paragon of virtue. So far, from what James had learned of Malcolm Frobisher, he was totally immoral.

'Can you tell me anything about Louise Warman?' James asked. 'Did you know her well?'

'I met her at social gatherings and of course when she did a few odd jobs at the Warehouse.' Lois replied, draining her brandy.

James looked perplexed as Lois went on to explain. 'When Louise accused Liam of rape her role as Daniel's nanny instantly ceased. Liam being the kind man he was felt sorry for the poor wretch, providing her with a filing job at a warehouse in Devonport. Law firms are big businesses James, too much paperwork to be stored in small offices. Malcolm and Liam decided to invest in a secure toll filing, computerised record system business where documents could be stowed for easy access. Louise was employed on a full-time basis to keep those files in order. She was lucky if you ask me. I'd have thrown the book at her for wasting everyone's time including police scientifics. Utter lies are all that came out of that woman's mouth.'

James refrained from comment, 'Does Malcolm still operate this Warehouse you mention?'

'I very much doubt it, but that's something you'll have to ask him,' Lois replied, 'Malcolm goes through fads, once he tires of something he moves on to a new venture.'

James preferred the term 'scheme' not 'venture' but didn't want to rock the boat. He thanked Lois for her time, making a mental note to check out this Warehouse at some point to see what really went on there. He didn't for one moment believe in any documents filing business. Malcolm might be able to fool Lois, but not everyone could be taken in that easily.

****

The small brown envelope lay on the inside doormat, covered by junk mail. Sonia almost overlooked it when picking up the brochures. The plain, nondescript letter bore Liam's name in bold letters. It lacked postage stamps, clearly hand delivered, probably overnight.

Liam away till the weekend on business, Sonia took it upon herself to tear open the envelope and peek at the contents inside. After years of mostly turbulent marriage, Sonia no longer desired the need for secrets. It had been a long time since she'd trusted her husband, reading his mail wouldn't shock. That was the common-sense logic she usually employed.

The poem, typed on expensive watermark paper was brief and to the point, not flattering:

Roses are Red, Liam is Blue, oh shit! You've stopped breathing, what happened to you?

Sonia was not particularly surprised, certainly not unsettled. Any number of people could have penned this note; Liam was not Mr Popular, especially in his line of work.

She carefully folded the note before placing it back in the envelope and burying it at the very back of a chest of drawers. She wasn't going to bother Liam with such rubbish. Lately, he'd not been looking well, and she didn't want to add to his stress. His sleep was often fitful, interrupted by the same unconscious outbursts. He mumbled the same sentence every night: "Claire Langham is after my blood. She's going to kill me."

Chapter Six

Margo Betteridge had resided in the small hamlet village of Loddiswell for most of her professional life. Situated a few kilometres from Kingsbridge, just off the B3196, her quirky, converted barn lay nestled in a small lush valley, hidden from view behind a clump of Sycamore trees.

Arriving unannounced in the middle of a monsoonal, summer downpour, Fiona carefully drove her TVR across a narrow arched stone bridge and on to a red gravel driveway parking in between two large conifers, then making a calculated dash to the front door.

'Fiona Sinclair. You're a sight for sore eyes,' Margo shouted above the din, as she dragged Fiona inside and out of the torrent, 'get that wet jacket off before you get hyperthermia.'

Fiona obliged, peeling off her rain-soaked jacket and hanging it over a nearby radiator.

'I'll whip up hot chocolate,' Margo said, 'there's a log fire burning in the living room. Get in there and get comfortable. I'm afraid you won't get to see Myles on this occasion; he's in Auckland at a writer's workshop. All right for some.'

Fiona dutifully followed Margo's instructions, strolling into a large open living space, more inviting and much warmer than the hallway. The original barn features: high oak beams and sand stone walls sat well within the colour scheme of warm oranges and creams. Pride of place was a character wood burner giving comfort as the rain pelted against the tiny windowpanes.

Fiona made herself at home, settling onto the expansive sofa where she listened to the developing storm and the distant roll of thunder. Margo joined her a few minutes later, bearing drinks and a tray of fresh scones and jam.

'Although it's lovely to see you Fiona I take it this is not a social call?' Margo smiled, ensconcing herself on the lounge opposite her visitor. 'What line of enquiry are you currently working on?'

'You're quite the detective,' Fiona laughed, reaching for a plate. 'I hope you don't mind me dropping by without calling, but I'm anxious to know if you worked on the forensic evidence collated in relation to the rape of Louise Warman? She was the young woman who accused Liam Mercer of rape.'

'I do vaguely remember the case,' Margo replied hesitantly, passing Fiona the hot chocolate, which was gratefully accepted. 'Trevor Williams was the lead medico assigned to that one. I assisted. Due to Liam Mercer's senior legal position, Williams was the only person allowed full authority. My biochemists performed the lab tests under my direction.'

'From the tests conducted could you confirm Louise had been raped?' Fiona probed.

'Not entirely, but as I recall there were traces of semen and lots of acid phosphatase, indicating she had sexual intercourse within hours of the alleged assault. Honestly Fiona, you and James know how to switch my memory into gear. James has been quizzing me about Daniel Mercer and now you want to know about Louise Warman.'

'There's no rest for the wicked,' Fiona teased, 'with the evidence that came to light, could it have been consensual intercourse?'

'It's possible, but there were signs of physical violence, coupled with severe bruising, so I don't think it was that straight forward,' Margo replied, 'I also remember Louise sustained quite a deep cut above her left eye requiring several stitches. The crazy thing is, as we were finalising the paperwork a fire broke out in the lab destroying all forensic samples, so any evidence of sexual intercourse was immediately erased.'

'Did you not find this to be a tad suspicious?' Fiona enquired, opting for another cream tea.

'I guess I did, but there wasn't a lot we could do about it,' Margo replied stoically, 'without concrete evidence the case was automatically closed. It was also during a time when our lab was overloaded with work and terrible as it may sound, we were pleased to see the matter finalised, so we could move onto another.'

'Did the fire get investigated?'

'Yep, and although everyone suspected the fire in the solvent store was deliberate, we had no real proof. A lot of things didn't add up back then, but we were damned to know what to do about it.'

'What else can you tell me about Louise Warman? Have you spoken with her since the investigation took place?'

Margo's face changed, sadness in her eyes, 'Last I heard, Louise was being treated for cancer without much success. You can try talking with her GP: Elsbeth McGregor, although, she may not be willing to part with anything useful. You know what medicos can be like with confidentiality.'

'Don't I ever,' Fiona empathised, 'any assistance regarding Louise's medical records would be greatly appreciated, Margo. From the scientific angle I'm keen to find out more about past events relating to Louise. It may help with the current police enquiries.'

'Leave it with me and I'll make that call in the morning,' Margo replied, 'I can't see a problem. McGregor and I crewed together at Cowes Classic Week a couple of years ago. Now if there's no more I can assist with, let's stop talking shop. I want to hear everything your family has been up to. I've a leg of Dartmoor lamb we can roast and a great Bordeaux I'm dying to crack, complimented by an array of vegetables fit for a king. It's so lovely to see you Fiona, it's been far too long between visits.'

****

'Have I caught you at a bad time?' James enquired, amusingly watching Lady Scott-Thomas struggle with a folding sun lounge, which refused to bend at the hinges.

Cursing she capitulated throwing the recalcitrant chair into neighbouring rose bushes. 'Not, at all, come this way. We can sit in the summerhouse. The seats there are at least of the comfortable variety and won't cause scorn. I'll have Nancy bring homemade lemonade. God knows I could do with a bit of zing after the day I've endured. Now, what can I do for you? I doubt you're here to discuss the weather, although today happens to be a fine one, Devon at its best.'

'I caught up with Leicester last week,' James informed, settling himself into an inviting French cane armchair, 'your husband's a wealth of knowledge on yachts.'

She looked keenly at James. 'I'm pleased the dear has a rewarding hobby. Shortly after retiring Leicester suffered a nervous breakdown, drifting into chronic depression.'

'I imagine that was difficult for you both?'

'It was. He sought professional help, and thankfully he's now doing well. Dr Finch really is a marvel. If ever you need a psychiatrist, he's your man.'

'I'll keep it in mind, tell me Rosemary, what triggered the breakdown?'

'Pressures at work, Leicester had many disagreements with Malcolm Frobisher, which in the end started to take its toll.'

'Do you remember if they rowed about anything in particular?'

'Oh well, they were constantly at each other's throats,' Lady Scott-Thomas offered quietly, 'Frobisher is a man of forthright opinion, who takes affront at anyone else with a differing view.'

'So, he doesn't rank high on your list of favourites?' James surmised.

'Not at all, I can't fathom how Lois St John can even bear to have contact with that man. I'd have divorced him years ago, but she's bizarre in many ways. She still turns to him for financial advice where quite frankly *I* wouldn't bother. Lois is a bright woman, she needs to start making an independent life for herself.'

James pondered his next question, guessing the reaction it would cause.

'Rosemary, how well do you know your husband?' James leaned back, eyes fixed keenly on the older woman's face.

Lady Scott-Thomas managed a shallow laugh. 'What sort of question is that my boy? Perhaps you need to rethink your topic of conversation. I'm inclined to believe the sun has got the better of you.'

'It's a reasonable question, considering I'm in the throes of a possible murder enquiry,' James commented.

'Now, wait just a minute,' Lady Scott-Thomas bit back, 'if you're suggesting for one moment my Leicester had anything to do with the death of Liam Mercer, you're very much mistaken. You need to be careful what you're implying. I have friends in high places and don't take too kindly to idle accusations or impertinence.'

'I'm not meaning to be out of order, simply doing my job,' James replied smoothly.

'I happen to know Leicester extremely well, we've been married for over thirty-five years,' Lady Scott-Thomas fired back, 'Leicester's no killer.'

'I can understand your immediate annoyance,' James said, ensuring his voice took on a softer approach. 'However, with all lines of enquiry we need to tackle things head on, so we can eventually rule them out.'

'Yes, I see, but you're going down the wrong path if you believe Leicester could murder someone in cold blood. Leicester is not always a man of many words, but he has a good heart.'

'I really wanted to establish what his rapport was with Malcolm and Liam, if he bore a grudge.'

Lady Scott-Thomas laughed. 'Of course, he harboured some resentment, especially towards Frobisher, but Leicester doesn't have time to dwell on the past. As long as he has his boats, he's a happy man. Now how about that glass of lemonade? I'm sure you won't refuse. You must work terribly hard James, spend a bit of time with me and I will expand your knowledge on the history of this part of the world.'

Exhausted from the intensity of the last few days James decided to take Rosemary up on her offer. He welcomed a rest from the lab and all the never-ending trials and tribulations that went with it.

****

'Hello Jimmy, how lovely to see you,' Jo threw her plump arms around his neck, planting a kiss on both cheeks. As usual her make-up was over the top, bright red lipstick matching her flowing skirt, which in turn complimented her shoulder bag and shoes. Her distinctive High Veldt Afrikaners accent, betraying an unbroken line back to the Boers rose sharp and lucid above the hubbub of the court precincts. 'You're looking devilishly handsome as ever. Do you have time for a drink, eh my friend?'

'Sorry, not today,' James replied, trying to edge away from the courtroom secretary, cursing his rotten luck running into the biggest flirt and most notorious gossip in the Courts. 'I'm surprised to see you here, Jo. I thought you'd returned to the Republic on long service.'

'Not for another few months,' Jo volunteered, 'I'll be heading back to Johannesburg late October.'

'I'd better dash,' James lied. 'I'm on my way for a meeting with the Crown Prosecutor and mustn't keep them waiting.'

'I caught up with Katie a few weeks back,' Jo piped up, competing to keep up with James' long stride as he tried vainly to escape. 'Isn't it wonderful news she's considering a job with the Supreme Court? We could do with a new Forensic Psychologist joining the team, especially someone of her calibre. I bet you'll miss her though, she's been a real asset to your organisation.'

James wondered if he'd heard correctly, stopping to stare at Jo, his mouth agape, 'Pardon, I'm not sure I follow. I'm not aware of any moves Katie wants to make.'

Jo looked mortified as she stood staring back at James, 'Wow, I'm sorry. Perhaps I got my wires crossed. Nice to see you James, better let you get to your appointment.'

James was left stunned, his mind in overdrive as Jo hurried down the courthouse steps, disappearing out of sight around the corner.

****

It was almost four by the time James walked into the Moorland office. A light rain and low swirling mist drifting down from the escarpment did nothing to enhance a fractious mood, compounded by a fouled spark plug on the A38.

Katie never once mentioning her intentions on a career move had him bursting with combative irritation.

Throwing his summer-weight jacket over a stool, James didn't even consider a 'hello' as he slid into the seat behind his desk, unconsciously picking up a wad of computerised gas chromatograph read outs. Fiona and Katie both engrossed in work, failed to acknowledge his arrival.

Silence reigned in the office, broken only when Fiona announced she was heading into Newton Abbot to catch up with a friend and would see them both tomorrow. No sooner had she departed James turned on Katie, his blue eyes slits of dark emotion.

'I bumped into Jo Van Der Westhuizen today when I was entering Exeter Crown Court. She informs me you've applied for a position as a Forensic Psychologist to practice within the Supreme Court. Had you not thought to tell me?'

Katie looked up from her computer, facing the angry eyes head on. 'I've merely expressed an interest in learning more about the vacancy,' she replied, trying to keep her voice steady as it became etched with resentment, 'an old University colleague emailed me with the job description suggesting I consider applying.'

'I thought we were a team,' James fired back, 'our decision to set up Moorland Forensics with our Grandfather's money was a passion for all of us. To throw it away on a whim would be madness. You'd destroy us all.'

'Don't be so melodramatic,' Katie replied, fiddling with the scientific calculator on her desk, 'surely, you don't expect us to remain joined at the hip forever. What if owning a family business isn't enough for me? What if I need more of a challenge?'

'You make it sound drab,' James fumed, 'aren't we good enough for the mighty Katie?'

'Now you're being ridiculous,' Katie fought back, 'you know what James, I really wasn't too keen to move on, but after your little outburst I think I will apply for the job.'

James stood up facing his sister, 'If you do decide to leave you will damage Moorland Forensics. Is that what you want?'

'No of course not, but perhaps for once I want true recognition for the work I do. I'm sick of being an afterthought in all our investigations, someone who's called upon only because you and Fiona have nothing better to do and decide to try involving a forensic psychologist. I know I'm good at my job and have a lot to offer, yet for some reason you seem to forget that and quite frankly, I've had enough.'

Topping off her outburst the youngest sibling marched out of the room slamming the door with such force her brothers' framed qualification jumped off the wall and smashed on the floor.

****

James sighing heavily, tore open the envelope he'd received in the mail a few days earlier, not bothering to check who it was from. Fiona had questioned him about the letter, but James had kept it unopened on his desk, ignoring her curiosity. Finally shaking out the contents he was surprised to discover a photograph of a baby, probably no older than three months. He turned the photo, finding a hand-written note on the back:

Jason Robert Sinclair, aged 13 weeks. The son you've always wanted.

James kept staring at the young infant, short curly locks of dark-brown hair with matching chocolate eyes.

He hadn't believed Lauren when she told him she was pregnant. Their relationship had been a six-month fling when Lauren's husband was stationed in Afghanistan. James never wanted ties, now he'd got more than he bargained for. He stuffed the letter back in the envelope before shoving it to the rear of the desk drawer. The picture he placed in his wallet.

****

For most of the week the atmosphere in the Moorland office remained glacial. James and Katie barely spoke to each other and when they did it was work related, short cryptic sentences. Katie spent half the day at the cafe across the road, occasionally texting or emailing if she needed a response to something.

Fiona, caught in the middle, tried keeping the peace without taking sides. Both her siblings could be stubborn, and she wasn't about to place bets as to who would back down first. She hoped eventually they'd make peace before their petty squabble had lasting effects on business. A few times she had to remind them of looming deadlines, both seemed so preoccupied.

Towards the end of the week James spent most of the day shut away in the lab, surfacing a couple of times to venture up town for a beer and sandwich, before returning to work on some tissue sample digestions and extractions. Shortly, before four-thirty on Friday afternoon he turned up in the office to make an announcement.

'Cancel anything you had planned for tonight ladies. We are going to the opening of a new art gallery in Dartmouth, "Visions in Blue". I've been on the phone to Lois St John who's keen for us to attend. Seems she sent an invitation in the mail, but it must have gone astray.'

Katie grimaced, 'Why do we need to attend some dreary function organised by Lois St John? I can think of plenty of other activities for a Friday night, other than standing around staring at boring works of art. No thanks, you both go. I'll stay home and wash my hair.'

'Sorry, but you don't have any say in the matter,' her brother replied briskly, 'I need a psychologist present to analyse all the guests, one of them might happen to have strong links to Liam Mercer's murder. Have you forgotten the tiny detail of a controversial painting exhibited by Lois being left at the murder scene? Someone painted the damn thing and tonight might tell us who.'

'I think you're being farfetched thinking the opening of a new gallery will lead you to new evidence;' Katie replied tactlessly, 'besides, my knowledge of arty types leads to the conclusion they are all a bit weird, ever ready to push their extreme Structural Post-Marxist views; so it'll be a waste of time for me to form any real opinions on who might have murdered who and with what. You could host a murder mystery night and get more clues.'

'Thanks for those invaluable words of wisdom,' James fired back crossly, 'right now, you're still part of the Moorland team and

I need you to spend time creating profiles. If you don't like it you can say your goodbyes now, and don't bother ever coming back.'

Katie was stunned. Part of her reaction was meant in jest, but James obviously didn't see that. Heading upstairs to find something suitable to wear she hoped by the time she re-emerged her brother would be in a better mood. They couldn't go on arguing this way, she needed to organise a suitable time to sit down and talk to him in a logical fashion. If she were to move on to a new position, it really needed his blessing.

Within an hour the siblings were heading for Dartmouth in the Land Rover, James opting for the scenic coastal route via Torcross and along Slapton Sands. The evening was balmy with scores of people making the most of the late summer weather on the beachfront, even as it neared seven o'clock. Katie secretly wished James would turn off the arrow straight bitumen, so she could join the tourists for a quick dip in the beckoning ocean. However, she remained silent as he made a sharp left turn, pushing the old "Landie" up the steep climb towards Blackpool Sands, resigned to the fact any comment, positive or otherwise, would not be welcomed by her brother whose face still projected a look of contempt. He'd been moody for most of the day, his temperament becoming worse after recently opening a small blue envelope he'd kept sitting on his desk for almost a week, the contents of which he was not willing to share. Fiona had done her best to try and prize the information from him, without success. He just shrugged, claiming it was nothing of real consequence.

'Most likely a threatening note from a husband who's discovered his wife is one of James' trophies,' Fiona joked to her sister, knowing their brother was renowned for bedding married women. 'He needs to break that habit before he lands himself in serious trouble.'

Katie concurred, nodding and whispering back, 'Yes, but you and I both know he won't give up the good times that easily. He loves the fact he can live the life of a satyr with no strings attached. Although one day he'll make a great husband, so long as he can ditch his errant ways.'

At the top of the coastal road a sweeping seascape vista unfolded. A guided missile frigate, its stark outline defined by the sun's last westerly rays could be clearly seen a few miles off Start Point, slowly navigating its way up Channel to the Devonport Dockyards.

Passing through the small village of Strete, James indicated to turn right off the main road, deciding to take the back way into Dartmouth via the castle. He sounded the horn a few times, a common practice for locals necessitated by the high hedges and narrow roads. Many an impatient holidaymaker had their sojourn tragically cut short by a head-on collision, not realising how deadly Devon's lanes could be.

'Impressive,' James commented as Dartmouth Castle soon hove into sight, the tension in his face suddenly lifting, 'I didn't know it was over 600 years old, built by…'

'No need for the history lesson,' Fiona interrupted jovially, 'we had a class tour at school. I remember the guide waffling on as if it was last week. John Hawley 1388. Gun tower added early Tudor Period. Saw action in the Civil War and in use up till start WW2.'

Silence returned for the remainder of the drive into Dartmouth, James realising his sisters were not up for one of his long-winded dissertations on local history.

Dartmouth came into sight as James headed towards the main hub of the town. Passing the new gallery 'Visions in Blue' a noise erupted as guests, media, artists and gallery staff overflowed onto the pavement, wine and beer glasses in hand. No doubt Lois would be pleased by the turn out.

After driving around for almost fifteen minutes James darted into a spot opposite the boat float, a short stroll along the road from the gallery. He'd almost feared the need to drive back out of town or secure a spot in one of the side streets near the Naval College. That would have resulted in an incumbent twenty-minute walk.

'It's a shame the Harbour Bookshop closed,' Katie commented as they walked along Fairfax Street, 'I used to love browsing the shelves for a good thriller. It became quite iconic having once been owned by the late Christopher Robin and his lovely wife. I believe they opened it in 1951 to escape city life.'

On arrival at the gallery, James squeezed past the throng carelessly blocking the entrance way, before making it through to a large reception area. He was greeted by Lois standing at a small table covered with name tags. She was the epitome of elegance in a flattering, turquoise trouser suit, set off by an outrageous art deco emerald and diamond necklace.

'James dear boy, how lovely to see you and your beautiful siblings,' Lois beamed, planting a kiss on his lips, 'Gwyn is around somewhere, she was thrilled you could make it tonight. Head through to the back room where the refreshments are, I expect you're all in need of a drink after your drive.'

'I see you're a firm friend of the lovely artist,' Fiona teased as they made their way towards the rear of the building.

'It's all part of the job, dear Fi,' James teased, 'watch and learn, dear girl, watch and learn. All good forensics make friends with possible perpetrators, they say *keep your friends close and your enemies even closer*.'

'Since when have you considered Lois to be an enemy or even murderer for that matter?' Fiona enquired, giving her brother a firm dig in the ribs. 'Ah look, there's Lois' husband. He doesn't appear happy to be here.'

The three turned and made their way over to where Malcolm Frobisher was encamped leaning over a make shift bar on an outside terrace. 'Propping up bars is obviously what he does best,' Katie mocked, lowering her voice a notch.

James sidled up to the Judge, 'Evening Frobisher, I see Lois has pulled together quite a gathering? Your wife is certainly a remarkable woman.'

'Indeed, she is, although I'm not sure how wonderful it is to have so many "would-be's" from the art crowd all gathered in one spot,' Malcolm wheezed, puffing on an acrid Cuban cigar. 'Most are hangers-on with something up their arse and a penchant for guzzling free booze. Not a pretty sight as the hours tick by, old boy.'

'Not really your thing?' Katie enquired, helping herself to a glass of champagne from a passing waiter.

'I attend these functions under great duress,' Malcolm informed Katie, as he signalled the barman for a double whisky, 'Occasionally Lois drags me along where I dutifully smile and nod in all the right places. Thankfully, I'm partially deaf in one ear, so most of the time I don't hear what people are saying, that can be a real godsend. How about another beer James, you don't appear to be drinking much?'

'I really ought to go steady on the alcohol consumption,' James replied, waving his car keys.

'Nonsense, a few won't hurt. The trouble with you scientific types is you don't know when to relax. Tell me, how's your investigation going into Liam's murder. Have you caught the bastard yet?'

Fiona and Katie wandered off to look at some paintings, whilst James stayed to keep Frobisher company.

'Every day we're one step closer to catching them,' James solemnly replied, accepting a beer from the youth behind the bar.

Frobisher downed his drink and ordered another, 'What rot, come on let's be honest, you haven't got a bloody clue, have you?'

James turned the beer glass uneasily around in his hands, hoping the topic of conversation would switch away from Liam's murder. Frobisher was the last person he wanted to discuss things with.

'I knew Liam's shady past would catch up with him eventually,' Frobisher continued, 'The problem is, he bragged about it, the worst he could have done.'

'Bragged about what?' James pressed, realising Frobisher was more than a bit under the weather and likely to let something slip if he was kept talking.

'The one thing men brag about of course, sex. They can't help talking about who they did it with, when and how many times. When Liam told me, I literally fell off my seat. She was the last person I thought he'd sleep with, well I suppose that's because I knew who she really was,'

Frobisher tapped the side of his nose with his finger, 'Mum is the word,' he belched loudly, followed by a sassy laugh.

James had difficulty following this cryptic conversation, 'Are you talking about an affair between Liam and a mysterious woman, the woman who happened to be the mother of Daniel Mercer?'

'Of course, I'm talking about Daniel's mother,' Frobisher acknowledged, 'Liam had no idea what impact it would have later, how could he have known? All I can say is, it's an interesting family tree. Branches are sticking out all over the place. What should be an elegant Japanese Maple now resembles a Sitka Pine.'

Frobisher threw back his head and laughed, before wheezing heavily, 'Oh, dear James, some people do get themselves into a mess, don't they? You know I envy your line of work, at least your patients never complain, you don't have to deal with overzealous women.'

Malcolm chuckled, signalling for another drink, 'Back soon,' he declared, easing strategically off the bar stool to stand on wobbly feet, 'I'm off to the little boy's room, hang around.'

'I sincerely hope Malcolm's not been bothering you, James?' Lois enquired, rushing up to James as Malcolm rumbled towards the restrooms. 'He tends to become loud and obnoxious when drinking. Not a good look.'

'On the contrary Lois, he's been providing me with some insight into Liam Mercer's past, which could help my investigation.'

'Really, what's he been saying?'

'Just enlightening me on Liam's previous relationships,' James replied truthfully, 'all a bit jumbled but given time I'm sure I'll work it out.'

Lois laughed nervously, 'The man is full of malt whisky, James, I wouldn't attach too much credence to anything he's been saying.'

Malcolm swayed back to his bar stool, groping Lois on the bottom before sitting down. James found it all rather amusing, but Lois didn't. Her right arm came up to issue Malcolm with a resounding slap on his forearm. 'If you're going to start playing up, you can leave,' she ordered sternly.

Malcolm grinned, 'Yes, your honour, whatever you say your honour, my little, arty-farty dear.'

James, deciding it was time to do a bit of circulating offered his apology then moved across the room to introduce his sisters to Gwyn Lacey. They found Gwyn bustling about like a mother hen, showing guests selected paintings and drawings expertly spaced and grouped on the whitewashed walls. Fiona couldn't help noticing the hefty price tag which went with most of the works. A few were good and perhaps worth what Lois was asking, but the majority seemed expensive and quite ordinary.

'I'm delighted you could make it tonight,' Gwyn smiled, her grey eyes flashing beneath the mandatory rows of quartz down lighting. A red sequined cocktail dress enhanced her slim, shapely figure and for the first time James realised how attractive she was, for a slightly older woman. 'We've done well to attract this many hi-profiles,' Gwyn gushed, 'I understand local author Beverley Murtle is around somewhere. Rapper "Wrapper Paper" has also honoured us with his presence.'

James was amused, 'Well, hopefully they'll help boost tonight's event. I understand half of tonight's takings will be donated to local charities?'

'Having celebrities here will certainly bolster our sales,' Gwyn beamed, 'by far our biggest draw card is Lady Scott-Thomas. She's quite a celebrity in her own right. Whenever Rosemary turns up at a function it's bound to be a huge success. The local media buzz around her like bees to a honey pot. She's always popping up in the tabloids, either through her charity work or who she's seen out and about with. Last week's Daily Mail had an article about her dining with the Danish Royals on their yacht.'

'I never would have guessed,' James responded, struggling to be heard above the gallery noise, 'I don't know that much about her really, apart from a few meetings in relation with a current case we're working on.'

'Well, you can't just call yourself a Lady,' Gwyn explained, swept up in the euphoria of the evening and knocking back a glass of champagne in one go, 'you have to earn the title.'

'I suppose you do,' James replied, 'so, tell me Gwyn, how does Rosemary manage to claim such an accolade?'

Happy to have a moment to share her knowledge, Gwyn revealed facts on Lady Scott-Thomas and her aristocracy, 'Her great grandfather was the fifth Earl of something or other, who owned a good chunk of Devon at one point in time. One of his daughters married into European aristocracy. The Habsburgs, would you believe.

Everyone knows it's de rigueur for Rosemary to head up to London once or twice a month to mingle with the rich and famous, including the polo crowd. Her personal wealth is estimated at around eighty million pounds.'

James grasped a nearby pillar for support. 'Wow, I had no idea. Although, her Portlemouth house is reasonably impressive with its views over the Salcombe estuary, it doesn't blatantly advertise her true worth.'

Gwyn laughed, 'You need to study Rosemary in more detail James. You'll find many top-notch properties listed under her name. I know for a fact she owns a large country estate in Gloucestershire, not far from where a member of the present royal family resides. Over twenty bedrooms so I'm told, each decorated in its own individual style.

Lady Scott-Thomas has been born and bred with money, although it's her father's business interests and investments that earn the big bucks. He's done alright for himself, probably double her net worth. Once a month he still chairs the company board meeting, assisting with takeover bids and such using his astute business brain.'

'What sort of business are we talking about?' James enquired, watching Katie stifling a yawn, not at all interested in hearing about the magnitude of wealth associated with Rosemary Scott-Thomas.

'Rosemary's father is majority shareholder in one of the largest maritime construction conglomerates in Europe,' Gwyn explained. 'Based out of Southampton for the most part, but there's also a major operations centre on the Clyde and an impressive regional office in Exeter. Essentially, naval vessels and oil field infrastructure, I understand. Milton's in his eighties now, but he's still a shrewd businessman. Oh yes, the Scott-Thomas family are up there with the best of them.'

Gwyn eventually disappeared to greet some more guests, leaving James working the room chatting with several beautiful women, single or otherwise. He was never put off by a woman with a partner, he saw it as a challenge to conquer. Women of all ages were drawn to him and at least one woman there tonight would find herself seduced by his irresistible charm.

After a while, with a few phone numbers punched into his mobile, James re-joined his siblings who had congregated near the bar to take in Lady Scott-Thomas mingling with guests. James was amazed at her popularity, bizarrely akin to a member of the royal family out on a walkabout, presented with flowers and gifts, which were dutifully passed to an assistant.

'Lady Scott-Thomas how lovely to see you, is Leicester not with you?' James pushed forward as she came near.

Rosemary reached out, catching hold of his hand. 'Good gracious no, he won't be seen dead in the same room as the honourable Malcolm Frobisher. As soon as Leicester learnt Mal would be here tonight, he was adamant he would not be attending.'

'Shame, I could have done with a chance to talk yachts. Perhaps I could get him to take me for a sail one day.'

'I'm sure he'd be delighted. I'm afraid I've never been one to potter about on small boats, too bumpy for my liking, I loathe spilling even a drop of champagne.'

'Yes, lumpy seas are a menace,' James agreed, 'Seasickness is the…'

'Oh, if you'll please excuse me there's Lieutenant Commander Beau Robins from the Royal Navy with his wife Jacqueline,' Rosemary cut him short in a rude fashion, 'it would be wrong of me not to go and say hello.'

'Been dumped I see,' Gwyn joked, seeing him staring at the back of Lady Scott-Thomas as she waltzed across the room, practically flinging herself on the unsuspecting Commander.

'Looks that way,' James replied, ruefully, 'can I get you another drink?'

'That would be nice, a chardonnay if you don't mind.'

James left Gwyn in a quiet corner of the room whilst he chased down the drinks. Upon his return he witnessed Gwyn standing next to Malcolm Frobisher, his face a look of thunder.

James edged slowly forwards, deliberately shielding behind guests as he tried to eavesdrop on the conversation. Frobisher had a fat blotched hand firmly around Gwyn's left wrist like a vice, preventing her from going anywhere.

'You need to learn to keep your mouth shut sweetheart,' Frobisher hissed, 'there are a lot of people who would love to know all about your past Gwyn. I take it that's the name we're using tonight?'

Frobisher threw back his head and laughed, 'You're an intriguing woman Gwyn, and what's more, when I beckon, you're always going to put out.'

'You fucking bastard,' Gwyn foamed, through clenched teeth, 'one day you'll be sorry for what you've done. I'll make you pay.'

'Oh, I doubt that very much,' Frobisher smirked, 'me, I have nothing to fear, but you my dear, that's another story. Shall we say eleven o'clock tonight at the corner of Fore Street? I for one will be looking forward to our little rendezvous. Please don't keep me waiting, you know how cross it makes me.'

Gwyn wrenched herself free from Frobisher's grip, 'One day you'll rot in hell for all your sins. Someone will put an end to your sordid, pathetic life.'

Gwyn, not noticing where she was going, collided with James as she hurried away from Frobisher. 'Hey slow down, you okay?' James enquired, seeing the panic and fear in her eyes.

Gwyn took a deep breath. 'Yeah, I'm just exhausted from a very long day. If you'll excuse me James, I think I'll call it a night, perhaps we can have that drink another time. I feel a migraine coming on.'

'Yes of course, I understand.'

'What was all that about?' Katie enquired, having observed with interest the drama between Gwyn and Frobisher.

'I'm not really sure; however, when I first met Gwyn Lacey and questioned her about her rapport with Malcolm Frobisher, she led me to understand they hardly knew each other, now I believe differently. Something's going on between those two, and I'm not merely speculating sexually. Gwyn lied to me, and I'd like to know why.'

'She's a strange one,' Katie remarked, cheeks reddening slightly from one too many champagnes, 'it is if she's trying to be as something or someone she's not.'

'Interesting observation,' James replied, always keen to listen to Katie providing one of her psychological spiels.

'It's in the voice and mannerism. Noticeably her body language when she was next to Frobisher. The sophisticated, urbane professional Gwyn Lacey evaporates, leaving a colder, more calculating individual.'

'Yes, I see what you mean,' James said, declining another alcoholic beverage from an attractive waitress, 'maybe it was merely a flight persona, not uncommon when someone feels threatened.'

'I don't agree,' Katie replied steadfastly, 'I'm pretty sure Gwyn Lacey harbours a few skeletons in the cupboard, and it appears to me, Frobisher is threatening to let them out.'

Before James could comment further, a noticeable hush descended in the gallery signalling the start of the charity auction. 'I think this is our cue to disappear,' James whispered to his sisters, gently guiding them to the nearest exit. 'Let's slip off before we're noticed.'

'Smart move,' a young woman commented, following them towards the door, 'what idiot is going to spend big money on paintings you can't guarantee are originals? This place is loaded with forgeries, but either people are too dumb to notice, or they don't bloody care. No wonder legitimate local artists are finding it hard to make a living.'

James stopped in his tracks, about to ask a few questions of his own when the woman hurried off, heading down the road and disappearing into a poorly lit car park.

'What was that all about?' he turned to his sisters.

'Most probably a bitter woman who has spent too long on the turps,' Fiona giggled, 'talking of which, James pass over your car keys. I'm probably the only sober one amongst us, best if I were to drive.'

James only too glad to take a back seat, did as instructed. 'I'm drober as a fudge,' he teased.

'Well, tonight our Judge wasn't sober;' Katie remarked, 'in fact, he was pissed as a newt.'

****

'For God's sake why didn't you stop me?' Katie protested, groaning in pain. 'I only meant to have a couple of drinks last night.' Her head was about to explode into a thousand pieces, she'd already thrown up twice.

'Take some aspirin and drink plenty of water,' Fiona advised, 'why don't you pop upstairs and crash on the bed for a while, I can answer the phone.'

100

'Sadly, that's not an option,' Katie mumbled, 'Louise Warman's GP Elspeth McGregor is contacting me at eleven. This may be the only chance I get to talk with her.'

'You'll have to soldier on then,' Fiona mused, 'I don't have much sympathy for self-inflicted pain.'

At eleven sharp Katie received the phone call she'd been waiting for. Fiona sat listening to a few one-sided comments mixed with exclamations, anxious for the conversation to end so she could be provided with an update.

'Now this is interesting,' Katie informed Fiona, finally finishing the phone call from Elspeth McGregor at her Kingsbridge surgery. 'According to Dr McGregor, Louise Warman registered well above safe levels of radiation in her blood and tissue samples. Although it was only an opinion and what she gleaned from reading and talking with associates, Dr McGregor believes having this much potentially carcinogenic radioactivity in a person's system was probably not accidental, what's your thinking, Sis?'

'She's right,' Fiona replied, recalling her University tutorials. 'No one goes around deliberately exposing themselves to possible sources of radioactivity or ingesting contaminated food and water. There would need to be low to moderate exposure over a reasonable time span or heavy flux exposure over a short time period.

Chernobyl is a good example. Workers at the nuclear plant, near the damaged core, received massive doses of radiation and died quickly soon after. As did some unprotected workers involved in rescue and plugging activities of the core in the coming days and weeks. People away from the site who received low to moderate doses didn't show symptoms of radiation sickness or cancer for months or years later. If Louise Warman got the cancer from radiation, it's my guess she was exposed to low levels over a moderate time span say 1 to 2 years. It's highly unlikely she got or was given a massive dose from a high intensity source. Do you have any idea exactly how Louise Warman could have absorbed such dangerous levels?'

'One theory McGregor has is Louise might have been exposed to a toxic environment whilst working at an isolated warehouse in Devonport, as you would know it's not uncommon for old building sites to leak radiation. Guess who owns the Warehouse in question? Our dear friend Judge Frobisher. If Dr McGregor's assumptions are correct, Frobisher could have deliberately allowed Louise Warman to spend hours each day working in a toxic environment, knowing she would eventually die.'

'Come on, Sis, you're in fantasyland with that one,' Fiona chuckled, 'no one is going to allow anyone to suffer in such a way. Besides, it would be quicker and easier to dispose of someone by any number of the usual more direct means.'

'Just think about it; slow maybe, but almost impossible to diagnose and very little evidence left to pin on someone. We all know what a bastard Frobisher can be.'

'Yes, but surely Frobisher wouldn't stoop that low, allowing someone to die a slow and painful death. Everything we have gleaned about him in the last few weeks is basically hearsay and he's a judge for Christ's sake.'

'He wouldn't care,' Katie rebuffed, 'the man gives me the creeps and I am pretty sure his psyche profile fits. Malcolm Frobisher would stop at nothing to get what he wanted. Elspeth suggests we follow up with a certain Professor Abe Torrington at The Physics School in Cardiff. He's a world-renowned authority on radionuclides in the environment. I think it'd be a good idea for James to get in touch, he probably knows the guy anyway. This is more in line with his expertise than ours.'

'Do I hear my name being used in vain?' James asked, strolling into the office after an arduous session spent at the Home Office, 'Are you going to tell me what you're talking about?'

Katie quickly brought her brother up to speed.

'Ah, now it's interesting you should raise that subject,' James commented, as he dropped into the chair behind his desk, 'on my way to Exeter this morning I received a call from Mick Rose, who informed me Louise Warman passed away in the early hours of this morning. Rose has been pressing Louise's father to give permission for a full autopsy to be conducted, including histology. If he consents, I'll collect some of Louise's clothing, so we can begin the examination, which might give us some indication to what she's been exposed to and when.'

The office went quiet for several, palpably difficult moments, before Katie let out a long drawn out sigh.

'You know that warehouse of Frobisher's has been on my mind ever since Lois mentioned it,' continued James, 'I'm free tomorrow and I've got the address somewhere, guess a nice drive down to Devonport is in order.'

****

102

'You okay, Mercer?'

'I need my med, medication,' Liam stammered, 'over there, in my kit bag.'

The bag was brought over and tipped upside down, the contents cascading noisily onto the tiled floor. A frantic search began for a puffer and small bottle of pills.

'They're not here,' Liam wheezed, 'I need those damn, fucking pills for Christ's sake.'

A small audience had gathered in the courthouse foyer, watching the commotion unfold. No one seemed to know what to do.

Liam's eyes glazed, his breathing shallow. He was now on his knees turning blue, gasping desperately for air which refused to re-inflate his lungs. He was 100% certain the pills and puffer had been placed in his bag when he'd left home early that morning.

'Out of the bloody way,' Tabitha Fletcher ordered, roughly shouldering people aside to get to her boss, 'oh, my God Liam, what the hell happened? I found your medication sitting on your desk, it's not like you to leave it behind.'

Liam forced a feeble smile, allowing Tabitha to administer the medication through a puffer and spacer to maximize the effect. Almost immediately, Liam's condition began to improve.

'Let's get you out of here,' Tabitha instructed, helping him onto his feet.

'Thank you,' Liam mumbled, letting Tabitha guide him down the courtroom steps and out into the hazy sunshine. 'You saved my life.'

'Perhaps that's an exaggeration; however, you can buy me a drink later.'

Unexpectedly, Liam desperately caught hold of Tabitha's left arm. 'No, I'm serious Tabs, they're out to get me.'

Tabitha laughed nervously, 'Who's out to get you?'

Liam turned his ashen grey face towards her. 'The Langhams. They're finally closing in on me. The way things are going I'll be lucky to make it past forty.'

Chapter Seven

'I've been spinning my wheels for half an hour,' Frobisher fumed when Gwyn finally turned up on his doorstep, 'don't mess with me Gwyn or you'll be sorry.'

She pushed past him, striding into the living room where she fixed a large brandy. 'Go fuck yourself. I'm only here to tell you, you can stick your paintings up your arse, I've had enough.'

Frobisher's eyes widened into saucers. 'I'd take that back if I were you, I've been keeping your pathetic secret for a very long time, but I'm happy to blow your cover if you start being obtrusive.'

'To be honest I don't care,' Gwyn answered back, 'Go find someone else to do your dirty work. I'm done with you and your sexual perversions.'

Drink still in hand, Gwyn marched towards the front door. As her hand reached the door handle Frobisher caught her from behind twisting her left arm across her back until she screamed in agony.

'You're not going anywhere,' Frobisher fired angrily, 'we had a deal, remember?'

Gwyn broke free, openly laughing in his face, 'The deal's off.'

'I'll say it again, don't mess with me Gwyn,' Frobisher warned, 'It would be so easy for me to get Moorland Forensics to run tests on the picture frames and guess whose DNA they would find? Walking out on me now, Gwyn my love, is not an option.'

Frobisher turned to head along the hallway; Gwyn in one rapid motion downed the last of the brandy and threw the glass towards Frobisher, narrowly missing his head.

'I'd get that nasty temper of yours checked out,' Frobisher advised, venom in his words. 'Good night Gwyn, it is always a pleasure doing business with you, or perhaps I should say, it's a business doing pleasure with you.'

Gwyn spat on the ground, 'I'd watch my back if I were you Malcolm, you never know when someone might come knocking.'

****

James was away early the next morning, driving directly to the old industrial estate on the outskirts of Plymouth, the site of Frobisher's warehouse. He returned early evening, in time to catch the girls locking up the office.

'Come on, I'll shout dinner at The Golden Hind,' he declared with bravado, 'You won't believe what I've discovered.'

Not wanting to pass up the chance of a free meal, Fiona and Katie followed James out into the main street where they made for the pub bistro. Settled into one of the restaurants booths with drinks ordered, James related the day's events.

'Looks like you were onto something after all Katie,' James stated, 'I went to the address I got from Lois. Appears she was right. The warehouse is on the run-down estate tucked behind an old navy boat yard; secured by bolts and padlocks it appears to have been disused for some time. I couldn't get inside, and there was no security around, the whole industrial site is deserted.'

'And?' urged Katie

'Walking back to my car I discovered an old codger hanging around outside the gate giving the Land Rover the once over; Ivor something or other, name's in my notebook.'

'No one ever gives your old bomb "the once over",' smiled Katie.

'Don't know if he used to own a "Landie" or what but I couldn't shut him up. Said he's part-time caretaker for the site. I'd estimate he'd be at least eighty.

Told me he worked in a Uranium smelter on the site as a teenager in the late forties and remembers being told by a long-time employee that 500 tonnes of Uranium ore from Russia and Finland were processed at the plant in the First World War to recover Radium and Uranium, essentially for medical cancer treatment use and minor military needs. He says the site was so badly contaminated with radioactive heavy metals that the Government had no option but to shut it down, they bulldozed the whole kit and caboodle into the ground around 1952.'

'Keep going,' prompted Fiona, opening a bottle of Merlot and filling three glasses.

'Here's the best part, there are no official records on why the site was razed,' James said, lowering his voice instinctively, 'it's even difficult to find anything confirming the plant even existed. Ivor claims the Ministry of Defence hushed everything up coercing the Council into falsifying their records.'

James paused, downed half a glass of red and looked excitedly at Fiona and Katie. 'It gets worse. There was a Tin smelter on the same site in the years 1880–1915. Levels of Thorium, a characteristic radioactive contaminant of tin slag, way above WHO safety levels, were detected in the ground fill when industrial warehouses and storage facilities were built on the site in the early 80's.'

'Thorium, that's a real nasty bastard,' interjected Fiona.

'Ivor swears by this information,' continued her brother, 'claims he saw the classified document, which they covered up as well. The upshot is, it was all swept under the carpet because construction on the site was well under way and corruption at Council and contractor level was rife. The Government hid everything.'

'Wow. It's my belief Frobisher and possibly Mercer knew about the dangers at the estate because of their high-level positions and contacts,' blurted Katie, 'Frobisher is shrewd, he's not going to lease something without doing his homework first.'

'Yep, but I have some good news,' James told her, 'you'll be pleased with this, I've been on the phone with Mick Rose and we've arranged to meet with Torrington next Wednesday. He's happy to fly down by himself. Autopsy and histology results will take the usual few weeks. Therefore, in the meantime the plan is to do a low-profile scout around the warehouse in Devonport, coordinated by Mick, who is desperate for answers. It's vital everyone stays quiet on this. If news of our discovery leaks, the perpetrators may attempt a cover up – that being the case we won't stand a hope in hell of getting to the truth. Louise Warman would have died a painful death, her assassin left to walk free.'

****

The two men, take away cappuccinos in hand, waited expectantly outside the arrivals hall at Exeter Airport, keenly studying passengers disembarking the mid-morning Dash 8 flight from Cardiff.

'That's him,' James murmured, pointing to a tall, lean distinguished type in jeans and T-shirt exiting the moving footway.

'I know you, James Sinclair, right? The Headley Conspiracy six years ago?' Clear recognition lit up Torrington's features.

In his early sixties and proudly "old school", Torrington was a legend in the field of radiochemistry. Well over six feet and still bearing a head full of greying-blonde hair he looked ten years younger. His face and arms nevertheless bore the tell-tale, red burn marks and scars, the legacy of forty years occupational exposure to radioactive materials.

Pleasantries exchanged Mick ushered them towards his unmarked Jaguar parked defiantly in the taxi rank, an enraged cabbie disappearing when Rose waved his badge.

Sitting in the back as Rose floored the Jag up the A38 toward Plymouth, James and Abe Torrington reminisced about their only forensic collaboration.

'I was lucky to jump the queue at Hinkley Point. Normally minimum access lead time is six months,' confided Torrington.

Not luck, recalled James, who at the time secretly called in a favour from his ex-Professor and part time Chief Advisory Scientist at the Office of Nuclear Regulation, George Gooding.

James' mind drifted back to the biggest MDMA illicit drug manufacturing conspiracy in British legal history. The usual spectrographic and chromatographic analytical techniques on the physical evidence and precursor chemical materials had failed to conclusively link the five separate illicit labs to each other, and to the primary source of pseudoephedrine supply in France. The Crown desperately needed the chemical 'fingerprint' match to reinforce the hearsay and circumstantial evidence.

James was working for the Crown on contract at the time, and as a last resort he brought in Abe to try NAA, scientific parlance for Neutron Activation Analysis.

By bombarding a sample with a high-energy neutron flux, elements present in the material would be irradiated giving off a characteristic radiation pattern for each element. NAA instrumentation could then analyse the resultant radiation spectra and give both qualitative and quantitative determinations of the elements present, down to sub microgram levels; essentially resulting in a highly specific, very sensitive chemical 'fingerprint'. Inconveniently, the ideal source of neutrons for this technique was the high-energy radiation flux present inside the core of a nuclear reactor...

'I took the evidence samples down to Somerset myself and personally loaded them into the pile,' Torrington recalled. 'Then I had to hang around several days for the high energy radiation of the materials to subside before scanning. The matches were almost perfect... very satisfying in light of the poor matches we got using ICP/AES and Mass Spec.'

'I've arranged everything for today's visit,' broke in Rose, eavesdropping from the driver's seat. 'There are a couple of techs coming along, requisitioned from Plymouth for back up. But I want this to be as low key and unobtrusive as possible.'

Torrington nodded his agreement. 'I believe it's only low to moderate level contamination we're looking for, right, so no need for heavy suits and breathing apparatus.'

'You shouldn't be exposed to anything for long,' James advised. 'The counters and sampling equipment I brought will do the trick.'

Parking some distance away, with a clear view to the main gate of the deserted yard, the three were soon joined by two technical officers and a Detective Senior Constable exiting an undercover surveillance van, positioned behind a derelict shipping container.

'I'll go in by myself with only one of you for support,' Torrington instructed, nodding to a technical officer checking his hip mounted radio. 'I'm used to conducting this stuff single handed.'

He turned on a high sensitivity radiation counter, stuffing a small lead lined case with plastic sample bottles.

Rose waved to the technical officer who immediately advanced through the unlocked gates with Torrington in tow. Reaching Frobisher's storage facility, he pulled out a pair of bolt cutters and snipped effortlessly through the side door padlocks. The pair then vanished inside, watched anxiously fifty metres away by the others from within the van.

'The trouble is, even if Frobisher knew the site was contaminated, he's hardly going to admit it.' Rose exclaimed, stepping outside the van to light up a cigarette. 'It'll be difficult nailing anything to him.'

'Perhaps you're right,' James admitted. 'We still need to gather all the evidence, then try and build a case. Matt Tyler is researching the deeds to this place trying to trace who the land belongs to. It'll be a drawn-out process linking anything to Frobisher, but it can be done. There's every chance he may have slipped up somewhere along the line. They often do.'

Twenty minutes passed before the voice of the technical officer crackled through the van. 'We're coming out, all good.'

Moments later Torrington emerged from the side door giving the thumbs up, quickly followed in short order by the support, looking furtively over his shoulder. The two walked slowly away trying not to raise suspicion.

At the van both men removed large disposable gloves and plastic shoe covers, dropping them into a contamination bag handed out by James.

'Well, that's a hell of a surprise.' Torrington informed the crew, taking time to catch his breath and running fingers through unruly hair.

'The place is mostly rows and rows of filing cabinets, with shredding machines and large waste paper receptacles. There's a small kitchen, office and bathroom out back. The concrete floor has broken up badly in places, revealing the compacted landfill underneath. Damp has also seeped half way up the interior walls. I got digital counter readings off scale around the base of the walls. Small pools of brackish water under some cabinets sent the counter crazy. The back-office floor is just loose boards over compressed dirt. And guess what is more scary, high-value digital readouts.'

Mick Rose and James exchanged smiles.

'What's your evaluation?' butted in Rose, anxious for confirmation.

'I reckon the place has been 'hot' since day one,' Torrington replied. 'Your info that the site used to be a uranium processing plant is a distinct possibility. Also, that theory from James about slag from a tin smelter in the landfill is probably accurate. I'll bet my house the samples are high in Uranium, Radium and the usual radionuclide suspects. High Tin and Thorium will confirm the slag theory.'

'Job well done, we better get out of here. Everybody has to shower and change.' ordered Rose, slapping Abe heartily on the back.

At a Bovey Tracey pub that evening James and Abe filled Nick Shelby in on the day's sensational events over a beer and steak.

'What do you think, Abe? Radiation poisoning then?' queried Nick.

'Two weeks and I'll have full quals and quants on the heavy elements and isotopes. But it's looking good,' Torrington replied.

'By the way, that reminds me,' weighed in James, 'tomorrow I need to pick up Louise Warman's clothes and check out her shoes. If we recover any suspect material, I'll get police forensics to shoot them over to you Abe. I'd love to get an NAA or ICP/MS match on the elemental breakdown.'

'Yeah, it's a bit too early to tell,' Torrington cautioned, 'but if Louise was working there, exposed to those radiation levels over any reasonable length of time, then I have to say she had no chance.'

'Her medical reports indicate she was a healthy young woman prior to taking on the Warehouse job,' added Nick, his brow deeply furrowed. 'Then in a relatively short space of time the poor girl is dead from massive cancer attack on her liver and respiratory system. I can't see any of this as being coincidental. Now we're loaded with the onerous task of finding the person responsible.'

'Certainly, an agonising way to die,' James murmured softly, looking guiltily at his t-bone.

'What would you do Torrington if you found your daughter had been subjected to such a horrible death?' Nick questioned, cutting into his own steak with great gusto.

'Kill the bastard,' Torrington replied bluntly, 'I'd choose something as equally painful to ensure they suffered.'

'Yes, I thought as much,' Nick said, raising a laden fork to his mouth, 'would you do the same, James?'

'Without a doubt, and when you put it like that, I think we may have found Liam Mercer's killer,' James had determination in his voice, 'if my assumption is right, we need to get to Geoff Warman before he decides to kill again.'

****

'Did you know your daughter was exposed to high levels of radiation, Mr Warman?' DCI Rose enquired, looking across at the ashen faced man. He looked older than his fifty-three years. News of his daughter's death had taken its toll.

Geoff Warman shook his head, 'No, not at first, but as Louise got sicker, it became evident something was amiss. When Louise wasn't getting better and her persistent cough worsened, I made her visit a GP in Kingsbridge. Dr McGregor specialises in respiratory diseases, so was able to shed some light on Louise's worsening condition.'

'It must have come as a dreadful shock when Dr McGregor gave her diagnosis,' Rose continued, 'I guess you were hoping for a miracle cure?'

'Of course, I bloody was,' Geoff retorted, 'I used to be a heavy smoker who worked in the Cornish mines. It didn't take long to conclude my daughter was dying. It upset me to watch her suffer, and there was not a bloody thing I could do to help.'

'What was your reaction when you discovered the truth behind her illness?' Rose quizzed, 'were you incensed when Dr McGregor showed you the full medical report?'

Tears misted in Geoff's hazel eyes, 'I will never understand why anyone wanted to harm my little girl. Lou was all I had left after my wife died in a horse-riding accident five years ago.'

James and Mick waited patiently for Geoff Warman to compose himself, when he did the anger started to surface. 'Frobisher and Mercer can both rot in hell for what they've done. My daughter suffered at the hands of those ghouls. I'm glad Liam Mercer's dead. I hope he suffered right to the end to match what Lou went through.'

'Did you kill Liam Mercer?' James asked softly, 'Did you decide to seek revenge for what he did to your daughter?'

Geoff let out a throaty laugh, 'A cripple like me, you think I did away with Liam Mercer? Believe you me, my mind may have wanted to kill both those bastards repeatedly, but my body has always let me down.'

Geoff Warman pushed off the thick crochet blanket covering his wiry knees, 'These legs haven't been able to bear weight for over seventeen years, Mr Sinclair. I got trapped down a St Austell mine when I was in my mid-thirties. I've been unable to walk ever since.'

A silence descended in the room as Geoff Warman buried his head in his hands, sobbing uncontrollably. James motioned to Rose, it was time to leave. The evidence was conclusive, even if Geoff Warman had wanted to, there was no way he could have killed Liam Mercer. The unlucky man had undergone enough interrogation, it was time he was left alone to grieve the loss of his daughter. For a brief second James felt the depth of the man's pain as he followed Rose out through the door, closing it quietly behind them. No man should ever outlive his child.

****

With Geoff Warman officially off the suspect list, James concentrated on other possible perpetrators. One person of interest was Barry Payne, whose wife Dieanna had been portrayed in the infamous painting "Falling Memories". James knew very little about the couple but intended to find out more by paying Barry a visit. He'd learned Dieanna was institutionalised in a psychiatric hospital on the outskirts of Ivybridge but wasn't privy to the reason why.

James drove into the village of Lower Batson, just as the dying sun gave way to a clear, moonlit evening. Barry Payne's property, a late Georgian, grey stone house sat on the edge of the village, surrounded by a white picket fence enclosing the ubiquitous rose garden. After a brief introduction, and the reason for his visit, James was shown into an elaborately furnished, rectangular drawing room framing a panoramic vista across the light dappled water.

'Nice place you've got here,' James commented, taking advantage of a red leather sofa.

'Yes, I've spent the last few years renovating every nook and cranny,' Barry explained, sitting in an adjacent chair. 'When my wife Dieanna was admitted into Tor Haven Psychiatric Home I needed a project to keep me occupied. Watching Dieanna slowly deteriorate was horrific, not dissimilar to watching a beautiful flower wither.'

'What exactly happened to Dieanna? I take it she'd been ill for some time?'

Barry shook his head, 'Before witnessing the death of young Daniel Mercer Dieanna was as normal as you and me, Mr Sinclair. In fact, she was an exceptional individual: very intelligent and remarkably sharp with numbers. Then things changed dramatically, she was mentally torn apart. Every waking hour after, the accident replayed over and over in Dieanna's mind, until finally she just cracked under the strain.'

'Did Dieanna receive any professional counselling immediately following Daniel's death?' James asked, au fait with the basics of clinical psychology from working alongside his sister, 'I find it hard to believe Dieanna was made to go through all this alone.'

'Oh, the Health Service authorities were extremely good,' Barry explained, 'But unfortunately, things were never the same afterwards. I've read a mountain of books and articles on trauma, breakdowns and stress, the brain itself is a very complex machine. No support she received was enough to help her move forward. Gradually regressing, until one morning when we were shopping in Torquay, she attempted to run in front of a bus. Thankfully she was saved by a quick thinking passer-by dragging her to safety. Professor Carl Clifford said her breakdown was the worst he'd seen. The men in white coats literally came and dragged Dieanna away. She became unsafe to herself and others. Adam Finch her psychiatrist was probably the most supportive. To this day he still visits Dieanna in Tor Haven. Finch did everything possible to help Dieanna recover, but it wasn't quite enough.'

'I can only begin to imagine how awful that must have been for you,' James commented, wishing he had brought Katie along to break the awkward silence, as he steered the conversation towards a fresh path. 'Tell me about your hobby as an artist? How long have you belonged to Lois St John's little art group?'

'About seven years all up, we're a select little bunch. I feel privileged to belong. Dieanna loved our weekly painting sessions. Got to say, she was a better painter than I.'

'What do you paint?'

'Oh, this and that,' Barry replied, non-committal, shifting position on the lounge.

'I don't see any of your creative efforts donning the walls of this beautiful house,' James remarked, noticing an absence.

Barry gave a hearty laugh, 'I find it vulgar when people brag about their talents, or lack of them in my case.'

'I think you underestimate your artistic talents,' James chuckled, 'Lois swears blind you happen to be one of her best pupils.'

'Lois and I go back a long way,' Barry replied, softly. 'I think she feels somewhat responsible for what happened to Dieanna, especially as she took the photo, which culminated in that dreadful painting.'

'Do you feel she's partly to blame?' James pressed, 'After all, you could hardly forget the death of Daniel Mercer when the painting was displayed in such a public way. I understand it made headlines in all the local and national papers.'

Barry shook his head, 'No, I don't blame Lois.'

****

Although Adam Finch was a dedicated professional, Katie hoped to gain comprehensive knowledge relating to Dieanna Payne by paying him a surprise visit. Their paths had crossed several times throughout their practiced careers, Finch on more than one occasion asking her out on a formal date. Each time she had politely refused.

Ducking upstairs Katie showered and changed before applying more than the usual make-up; her outfit a tight fitting mini-skirt, lacey red top relatively low cut, and three-inch stiletto heels. Her platinum blonde hair hung loosely around her shoulders with a slight twist. All up an extremely sexy package, which was the look required. Doctor Adam Finch was a womanizer who never could resist a pretty female, no matter what the circumstance. Arriving at the surgery resembling a sex goddess would drive him wild.

The car park was overflowing when she drove the nondescript Punto in through the open boom gate at the Ivybridge Psychiatric

Clinic. Vehicles parked haphazardly right up to the front entrance, indicated all four Centre doctors were seeing back-to-back patients. Katie didn't envy their line of work. She'd never been drawn to spending endless hours listening to other people's problems. Forensic Psychology had a greater appeal, enabling her to chat with everyday people who by dint of bad luck or otherwise found themselves caught up in unfortunate activities. A bonus being all the psychopaths Katie got to meet along the way – never a dull moment!

Parking hard up against the stone brick wall Katie collected her bag off the front seat and smoothed down her skirt.

She walked through the main entrance into a spacious waiting area, not your typical drab, sterile environment associated with most clinical settings. By contrast the décor was colourful, bright and exuded an upbeat ambience; thankfully cooled by the air con straining at full capacity.

'I was hoping I could see Doctor Finch,' Katie remarked, slinking up to the reception desk and bending seductively over the return.

The young male nurse not bothering to look up, remained steadfast focused on a computer screen full of scheduled appointments. After a few moments, he glanced at Katie shaking his head.

'Sorry, Doctor Finch is fully booked today. Could I organise something for next week? I can fit you in on Thursday at ten thirty.'

'It is rather important,' Katie pressed, forcing a smile, 'couldn't you possibly squeeze me in somewhere?'

'I'm sorry, but he's even working through lunch today and at five he goes to visit his hospital patients.'

Katie called on her best acting skills, placing her hand on her head and groaning. 'I'd like to see the Doctor,' she insisted, 'if I have another attack, who knows what I might do.'

'Wait here,' the nurse instructed quickly, jumping to his feet, mild panic showing, 'may I have your name please?'

'Katie Sinclair. I'm sure when you tell Doctor Finch my name, he'll see me.'

With reservation he moved to an adjoining door, knocked briefly and entered. After a few minutes he came out flustered.

'You're not a patient, are you?' he fired at Katie, with accusing eyes. 'There are rules to be followed if wanting a professional appointment.'

'I don't recall actually mentioning I *was* a patient,' Katie replied, trying not to laugh, 'I take it Doctor Finch has agreed to see me. Shall I go in?'

He nodded, heading back behind the reception desk, his face crimson.

'That was a rotten trick to play Katie,' Doctor Finch scolded, as she entered the sanctuary of his sparsely furnished treatment room, 'Brian's a damn good nurse.'

'I'm sure he is, maybe a little too politically correct,' Katie laughed, 'however, it was the only way I could get to see the "oh so very busy" Doctor.'

Adam Finch smiled, stepping forward to deliver a kiss on her left cheek, 'If you're here to interrogate me about any of my patients, the answer is a firm no.'

Katie ignored his remark, instead taking a seat in a black leather swivel chair, deliberately showing a bit of leg.

'Just a few little bitty questions?' she pleaded, with mock dramatics, 'nothing too taxing, I promise.'

'Katie, you know I can't answer your questions. I have to adhere to patient confidentiality.'

'Aren't you just a little curious which patient I'm enquiring about?' she teased, deliberately crossing her legs in a seductive fashion.

Adam sat down behind his desk letting out a groan, 'Go on, you might as well tell me, I get the feeling you're going to anyway.'

'Actually, it's your lucky day, I'm here to ask you about two patients. The first one is Leicester Scott-Thomas. From one professional to another, what can you tell me about him?'

'Katie please don't do this to me,' Adam scorned, 'I can't answer any of your questions, and that's final.'

'Okay, let's try this another way,' Katie persisted, 'I'll guess the answers and you can tell me if I'm right or not. Surely that's allowed?'

'Ah technically no, but if I don't agree to something I know you'll go on pestering me, and I'll never get through my backlog of patients .'

'Precisely, now according to Lady Scott-Thomas her husband was being treated for depression over a three-year period. Would you have prescribed the usual anti-depressants, such as SSRIs?'

'Yes Paroxetine, but not high dosages. Leicester was fed up and run down more than depressed. He just needed a little pick me up.'

'Did he ever show signs of anger? I mean real aggression?'

'Not that I ever witnessed, he always came across humble, even a little embarrassed he was being treated for depression, his appointments were scheduled after hours when there were few people around.'

'Nothing out of the ordinary for him then,' Katie remarked, scribbling away in her notebook.

'No not really, who's your next victim?'

'Dieanna Payne.'

Adam's expression changed slightly. 'Dieanna is complex,' he confided, 'I've treated Dieanna for a number of years. She's not straightforward. There are times when she seems extremely manic, other occasions I'd swear she's as normal as you and me.'

'What exactly is her condition?'

'Primarily post-traumatic stress syndrome. I'm sure you're fully aware, she witnessed the death of young Daniel Mercer, which initially created a catatonic state. She's burdened with anxiety, coupled with persistent nightmares.'

'Anything else in those *confidential files* of yours? Would you say Dieanna is capable of inflicting harm to others?'

'Ah come on Katie, what sort of question is that?' Adam asked, with a touch of frustration.

'One I'd like answered, if you don't mind,' Katie replied smoothly, offering a charming smile sufficient to increase any male's endorphin levels, 'This is important, Adam. I'm profiling one, possibly two homicides here and I'd like some insight.'

'Okay, if you want my honest opinion, yes she could be capable, but to what extent I'm unsure. The medication she's now on has stabilised the condition considerably, but psychotic episodes still occur when she hears voices.'

'And what exactly do the voices tell her?'

'I don't know,' Adam replied, 'Dieanna doesn't share those thoughts with anyone. Professor Fleming at Cardiff University has conducted a case study on her which makes for fascinating reading, I suggest you look him up, or borrow a copy from the Uni library.'

Katie ignored this proposal. 'I understand Dieanna has been admitted to Tor Haven for long term care. Do you get to visit her regularly?'

'Not as often as I probably should. I try to get out to the sanatorium at least once a month, but I'll always attend more frequently if staff have major concerns. I have an excellent rapport with the nurses, they call me if Dieanna's condition deteriorates in anyway.'

'Nice place is it, this Tor Haven, is it a suitable environment do you think?'

'Most definitely, Dieanna can't live safely in the community.'

'How much has she told you about the death of Daniel Mercer? Did she reveal any useful information?'

'It was months before Dieanna would talk to anyone about anything, and even then, it didn't make much sense. Her words were muddled, she kept babbling sentences repeatedly. The woman was badly traumatised.'

'So how come no one else on the beach ended up like that?' Katie puzzled, 'don't you find it weird?'

Adam glanced at his watch, shaking his head. 'I'm surprised you're asking me this question Katie, after all you're a very experienced psychologist, you of all people know how trauma affects the population in myriad ways.'

'Yes I agree, but it's somewhat bizarre Dieanna completely fell to pieces. I'm inclined to think there was something overlooked during her initial treatment. What sort of background checks did you run on Dieanna Payne, did she have a traumatic home life as a child? Perhaps her personality isn't entirely what you imagine it to be? There has to be some underlying factor no one's brought to light.'

'Now you're asking irrelevant questions,' Adam remarked, buzzing through his next patient, 'if we're done Katie, I really must press on.'

Katie winked at Adam, 'Call me next week and you can take me out to dinner.'

****

Liam half dozing in an armchair stirred when the phone rang.

'Liam, it's Tabitha, sorry to call so late on a Sunday evening, do you have the witness phone numbers for the Dobb's case tomorrow?'

The hands of Liam's Swiss chronograph watch glowed eerily in the semi-darkness showing ten-thirty. Although, he admired Tabitha's work ethic he wished she'd occasionally respect his private life. This was the seventh call he'd received from her since lunchtime.

'You'll have to hang on,' he instructed testily, 'I've left the numbers on the front seat of my car. I'll go get them.'

Grabbing his iPhone, Liam lurched out the front door along the side path to the tarmac driveway where he left the Maserati Spyder.

Unlocking the doors with the remote he reached over for the wad of papers, using the interior reading light to locate the sheet with the relevant information. Securing the car again by the press of a button, he started back towards the house. 'Got a piece of paper and pen?' he enquired of Tabitha on speaker phone.

'Yep, fire away.'

Liam busy reciting the numbers, distracted and unsighted on the sparsely lit pathway, marched hard into a large metal object, the sharp edge spearing his right knee. He let out a yelp of pain, rolling onto the ground, feeling warm liquid gushing from an open wound. The phone jolting from his grasp crashed onto the path, followed by the piece of paper.

'Liam, are you okay, what happened?' Tabitha's voice could be heard shouting into the phone, 'Liam speak to me, I need to know you're okay.'

But Liam was unable to respond. He lay motionless on the ground, his world slipping into darkness. The shock of the incident rendered him unconscious.

Chapter Eight

'For fuck's sake, how the hell did that happen?' James bounced his cell phone down on the desk with such force, he was lucky it didn't break. 'The bloody idiot, he should be more careful. Getting out of this one won't be easy.'

'How did what happen?' Katie asked, watching James bury his head in his hands. The office railway clock chimed six, after a long day her brother was buckling under pressure from endless stints in the laboratory, coupled with many disturbed and sleepless nights.

'Nick Shelby's only gone and let a street value of fifty thousand pounds worth of cocaine slip through his fingers.'

'Surely there has to be some mistake?' Katie quizzed anxiously, digesting this information, knowing all too well the massive impact it could have for so many people. 'Nick wouldn't be so stupid.'

'Oh, wouldn't he?' James muttered flippantly. 'Remember that Combined Task Force cocaine bust at the Yeovil terrace last month. About a kilo?

What was it? Operation Mango… Tango?'

'Indigo,' mumbled Katie.

'That's it. Indigo. I passed it on to Nick to do a comprehensive HPLC/Mass Spec analysis in Bristol, so we could trace its origin and somehow his Office got broken into and hey presto, all the cocaine has vanished. Try explaining that one to the authorities. I'll be in for a right royal bollocking.'

'Well, Nick will need to do the explaining, not you,' Katie advised, 'it really can't be helped.'

'That's where you're wrong,' James replied, trying to keep his voice steady, 'I didn't have the authority to pass the whole seizure on to Nick. He took it to help me out because I'm swamped with other work. I can land myself in very hot water for this, and the consequences could be dire.'

'Nick's high enough up the pecking order, he can think of something,' soothed Katie.

'It's my bloody fault, I should have taken the obligatory representative samples and immediately returned the bags to police forensics. Worse still, I forgot to sign it out on the computer inventory. You know as well as me, we never keep large quantities of illicit drugs here.'

'Seems a bit coincidental the break in occurred with so much "coke" on the premises,' Katie remarked, 'maybe it was an inside job.'

James shot his sister a questioning look, 'I'm not sure I like where this is going, Katie.'

'Yeah, well, I've always had my suspicions Nick is a cocaine addict. What if all of this was carefully orchestrated? That's a lot of stimulant to tie someone over. He wouldn't need to source it from anywhere else.'

James ruefully picked up his phone examining it for damage, 'Nick may dabble occasionally in a few substances, but he's no addict, and I do not believe for one moment he would deliberately cause me grief. When I confronted him, he was most apologetic, promising to do all possible to fix it.'

'Whatever,' Katie replied dismissively, shutting down the CCTV monitors and checking the alarm system. 'I'm not convinced Nick is entirely innocent James, but if you want to believe in him, so be it. Good night.'

As James sat pondering his next move, he wondered if Katie was right. Nick did show all the classic signs of being a heavy cocaine abuser.

****

The following Friday after work, Katie agreed to meet Adam Finch for dinner in Tavistock. He'd been in touch stating he had unearthed more information, which could be of interest to Moorland's present investigation.

Checking the vanity mirror and fumbling with her makeup purse Katie felt a tingle of excitement, tempered by niggling doubt. What if Adam thought their evening would turn into a proper date? Much as Katie liked Adam as a person and admired him as a psychiatrist, she wasn't ready for a relationship. Besides, he wasn't really her type, a bit two-dimensional, academic.

Before her mind could divert to another topic it brought her back to her Honours Year at University; the night her innocence was brutally stolen, resulting in a latent mistrust of all men. She found it

120

hard to imagine she would ever find the right man and live happily ever after.

Katie drove along the A30 at high speed, a tactic she often reverted to when dark thoughts encroached, turning off at the A386 exit and cutting across the high moor without a slackening of pace.

"The Flavour of India" a South Indian restaurant in Tavistock was one of her favourites. The food wasn't cheap, boasted a first-class fusion menu and the usual classics, top of the range wine list and an award-winning chef.

Securing a parking spot in one of the town car parks Katie made her entrance into the restaurant foyer, garnering looks of admiration from other diners.

'Wow look at you,' Adam whistled, as Katie joined him at a table overlooking the main street, 'you look hot.'

Katie blushed at the compliment, quick to deflect the subject. 'I'm keen to hear what you've got in connection to the death of Liam Mercer?' she remarked, allowing a waiter to take her jacket and position her chair, 'your phone call sounded very mysterious.'

Gee, you cut right to the chase. First, we order,' Adam instructed, passing her a menu, 'I'm starving.'

After ordering a banquet for two, Adam launched into what Katie was longing to hear. She sat back, eyes fixed keenly on his warm features.

'After your visit the other day, it got me thinking about Dieanna Payne,' Adam began, savouring the bouquet of a robust red. 'Although quite a nice facility, on reflection I can't understand why Dieanna was admitted into Tor Haven. Normally Post Traumatic Stress Disorder is treated with medications and regular clinic visits, not involving men in white coats.'

'So, you weren't the one to place her into Tor Haven?' Katie enquired, munching ravenously on an onion bhaji.

'Good God, no, I was dead set against it, but Carl Clifford the Head Psychiatrist at Trentmoor Psychiatric Services had the final say. He advised Dieanna was a danger to the community, and my opinion didn't count for much.'

'And you didn't believe she was a clear threat to others?'

'Perhaps now, after years locked in an institution, but not then.'

'This is heavy stuff, Adam. Why would Clifford make the wrong judgment?'

'It happens I guess, but this is where things start to get interesting. Part of Clifford's recommendation came about following submission letters from Lois St John and other local dignitaries. Lois believed Dieanna was manic. She certainly didn't want her to remain in her little art group, therefore she organised a petition to have Dieanna sectioned.'

'Why not just tell Dieanna she was no longer welcome at the Artisan's workshops?' Katie queried, puzzled why Lois should attempt something so dramatic as having a person sectioned under the Mental Health Act of 1983. 'It seems to me this action was way over the top, even by an eccentric artist such as Lois St John standards.'

Adam grinned sheepishly, 'Believe me, Lois tried to ban her from attendance, but Dieanna is not one to be told what to do. She dug in her heels, refusing to budge. She loved the Thursday evening Art Group and from all accounts, was one of the best artists in attendance.'

'I still don't believe any one person can be so influential where the medical profession is concerned,' Katie said, 'doctors form their own opinions.'

'That's true, however, Lois was on a crusade. She received full backing from Rosemary Scott-Thomas, who as you know, wields an inordinate influence in the local community, not to mention of course, her contacts in Westminster. Scuttlebutt going around is; Rosemary threatened to have Professor Clifford's funding cut in half if he didn't co-operate. We'd be talking rather a lot of money.'

'Very sneaky, that woman is like a serpent, using money to control others.'

'Yes indeed, but it certainly had the desired effect. Within one week of Clifford receiving the threatening phone call from 'The White House' as us locals refer to Rosemary's beachside property, Dieanna found herself locked up like a prisoner incarcerated in Tor Haven.'

'The poor wretch, she never stood a chance against such a strong bloc.'

'Precisely, although I wish I'd managed to do more to stop the admission.'

'You can't blame yourself,' Katie empathised softly, allowing him to top up her wine glass, 'Perhaps Dieanna's prognosis was cause for alarm. It's not uncommon for someone to appear placid when being examined by a doctor, five minutes later back in the community, all hell can break lose.'

Adam slowly swirled his glass watching the thin, purple coloured film run down the sides. 'Approximately two months prior to her admission there were episodes, when Dieanna became quite agitated. I put it down to a change in medications. Carl had decreased her anti-psychotics.'

'Well there you go,' Katie declared, 'Lois had good reason to worry about safety issues if Dieanna was displaying extreme anti-social tendencies. If a community feels unsafe, they have a right to do something about it.'

'Yes, but a person like Dieanna doesn't suddenly flip,' Adam defended. 'These things take time.'

'Surely, it depends on the severity of the incident,' Katie fought back. 'Perhaps Dieanna was always destined to have a nervous breakdown, anything's possible.'

'Sorry, I have to disagree. According to colleagues who worked with Dieanna she showed no signs of forgetfulness or stress prior to Daniel falling to his death. These are two classic signs of someone suffering from overload, yet Dieanna displayed none of these symptoms.'

Katie moved uneasily in her seat, 'Still not uncommon for someone to become mentally unstable from trauma,' she replied, 'what Dieanna witnessed that day at Portlemouth was pretty major stuff. I don't think many people would handle the death of a young child any differently.'

'There is another issue that concerns me,' Adam lowered his voice, casting a nervous glance around the restaurant, 'I have my suspicions Dieanna's husband tried to make her believe she was going crazy. It's not uncommon for a jealous husband to invent scenarios and it matches the profile I've put together. The concern he displays for his wife invariably resembles a façade.'

'What! You're suggesting Barry Payne played a part in his wife's mental breakdown? That's absurd.'

'It's possible,'

'Adam, you'll have difficulty proving anything,' Katie said officiously, 'you have so little to go on.'

Adam looked and sounded irritated. Almost unconsciously, he emptied the bottle into both their glasses. 'Dieanna Payne is probably saner than you and me put together Katie, that must mean something.'

'Still, you'll have difficulty proving it,' Katie reminded him.

'Why don't you visit Dieanna at Tor Haven and form your own opinion?' Adam suggested, tucking into a piece of Naan bread, 'I'd appreciate your expert opinion, and I won't have difficulty organising a visit.'

Katie signalled the passing waiter for the wine list. The way the conversation was going she needed more alcohol. If she consumed too much, she could always take a taxi home.

'Okay, I'll pay Dieanna a visit, so long as you accompany me?' then added as an afterthought, 'I think you've got this all wrong, Adam. No one's going to commit their wife to a long-term psychiatric unit without legitimate cause. What the hell would his motive be?'

'That's what I intend to find out,' Adam replied, leaning back in his seat looking satisfied he'd finally got Katie's support, 'God Katie, you're gorgeous. How about a night of sex, followed by more sex and perhaps even more sex?'

Katie was briefly amused, 'You're incorrigible Adam Finch. Ask me when you're not so drunk, and maybe I'll succumb to your wanton desires.'

'I am sober,' Adam implored, boldly reaching across the table and taking hold of Katie's hand, 'I'm serious, Katie Sinclair. Let's take things to the next level. At least agree to go out on a proper date with me.'

Katie stared blankly back, colour draining from her flushed cheeks. This was the moment she'd been dreading. After a moment's silence she finally mumbled, 'I'll think about it.'

****

Katie still hadn't agreed to Adam's proposition when they caught up the following week to pay a visit to Professor Carl Clifford; Dieanna's treating Psychiatrist. Something in her wanted to say 'yes' and something told her things wouldn't work out; she'd be heartbroken. Katie told him she would think over his proposition, but not right now.

Adam satisfied with a possible "maybe", happily piloted his Alfa Romeo saloon through the lush Devon countryside towards Aveton Gifford the locale of Clifford's primary practice. Greeted by narrow streets and frustrated by a dearth of spots Adam, much to Katie's amazement, ran the Alfa right up onto the pavement, leaving it parked directly outside the practice entrance.

'Professor Clifford, thank you for seeing us today,' Adam began, as they were greeted in the main reception area by the grey-haired gentleman.

'Not at all, always happy to help a fellow colleague, and don't worry about the official title. I'm happy for you to address me as

Doctor Clifford, Professor makes me sound old,' Clifford smiled graciously, showing them into a spacious sunroom facing South East with the English Riviera just visible on the horizon. For a man alleged to be mid-fifties, he looked much older, displaying a permanent, deeply creased brow and 'worry lines' around the eyes. Adam noticed his hands trembling when he sat down behind a large pine desk, wondering if it was the onset of Parkinson's disease, he displayed classic symptoms. As if reading Adam's shrewd mind, Clifford immediately placed his hands under the desktop, hiding them from his guests' view.

'What exactly would you like to know?' Clifford ventured, staring hawk-like at Katie, causing her to feel lightly uncomfortable.

'I'll come right to the point,' Adam replied, shuffling in a straight-backed chair, not designed for comfort, 'I struggle to understand why Dieanna Payne didn't respond to the initial treatment she received after Daniel Mercer's tragic accident. All my early reports were favourable she would make a full recovery.'

Clifford scratched his ear, pondering this question for an overlong period, 'Yes, a bit perplexing, I tend to agree with you there, Doctor Finch.'

'Then what went wrong?' Adam continued.

'My theory is the medications prescribed to Dieanna stopped having the desired affect resulting in a catastrophic turn for the worse,' Clifford explained, 'I guess none of us could have foreseen that.'

'I didn't notice any dramatic downwards spiral immediately after you decreased the anti-psychotics,' Adam remarked bluntly, 'I was seeing her twice a week and to me she appeared to be making excellent progress.'

'Perhaps I'm a little more experienced dear boy,' Clifford's tone taking on an icy edge, 'Not that I'm blaming you though. We don't always get things right, not in this profession.'

With Adam on the brink of outrage Katie stepped in and fired a question of her own. 'What medications did you prescribe to Dieanna, Doctor Clifford? I assume you kept to the normal treatment plans.'

'I'm sorry, I can't divulge such confidential information,' Clifford replied, a look of displeasure surfacing, 'What I can tell you; Dieanna Payne experienced severe complications to the medications prescribed. Like I said, none of us could have foreseen that occurring.'

'The community psychiatric nurse's report mirrored my own,' Adam continued, 'I find it hard to believe we both got it so wrong.'

'Like I said Finch, these things sometimes happen,' Clifford's voice carried a distinct air of arrogance.

'Would you mind if we popped in to see Dieanna?' Katie asked of the Professor, trying to prevent a blow up between the two men. 'I'd like to meet her if possible.'

At first Clifford looked irritated, before his features started to soften, 'Why of course. I'm sure she'd be delighted to see Dr Finch. Last time I met with Dieanna was a little over a week ago and she seemed in very good spirits. A familiar face would do her the world of good, I'm also aware she and Adam go back a long way.'

Although noting this was a curious comment to make, Katie brushed it aside. It appeared Clifford was deliberately baiting Adam to try and provoke a reaction. Fortunately, Adam knew better than to oblige.

'What sort of relationship does Dieanna have with her husband?' Katie asked, not sure how direct she could be with her questioning, but willing to give it a go.

Dr Clifford smiled. 'I'm hardly the expert on relationships Ms Sinclair. My wife left me after only ten months of marriage and I've never bothered to pursue any further permanent interactions with members of the opposite sex. However, I know Barry visits every week on a Wednesday between nine and ten in the morning. That to me shows some dedication and loyalty.'

'Or perhaps a sign of guilt?' Katie replied, nonchalantly.

'You need to be careful jumping to firm conclusions young lady. You and I are not in position to pontificate when it comes to other people's relationships. It is also dangerous to throw accusations about.'

'Not if there's a reasonable possibility they could be true,' Katie retaliated, 'my expertise as a forensic psychologist is to separate fact from fiction.'

'I dare say, but you must always remain professional Ms Sinclair. False allegations inevitably lead to all sorts of strife.'

Katie bit her tongue, tempted to make a vicious remark, but refusing to allow Dr Clifford the satisfaction. 'Who pays for Dieanna whilst she's residing in Tor Haven?' she enquired at last, 'I assume the government contributes something?'

'That's where you're wrong my dear, Dieanna is not state funded. As a private patient someone supports her stay in Tor

Haven. It's not cheap you know, each resident is billed over two thousand pounds a week.'

Katie shot a side glance in Adam's direction. From the astonished look on his face he clearly had no idea Dieanna Payne was being supported for her stay in the institution.

'Would Barry have that sort of money?' Katie's question was spoken aloud, but not meant for anyone.

'Perhaps,' Clifford replied, 'however, I'm afraid who forks out Dieanna's fees is confidential. Lawyers are quick to prosecute if clients' privacy is threatened. You can't meddle in affairs, which clearly don't concern you.'

Katie felt her cheeks redden, recognising an indirect threat. 'I'll bear that in mind. Adam, I think we're done here don't you, we'd hate to waste any more of Dr Clifford's precious time. He must be rushed off his feet with patients to see.'

Adam smothered a grin, knowing full well Katie was having a dig at Clifford whose waiting room was void of patients.

As the two stood up to leave Clifford manufactured a forced grin, 'Always a pleasure, I'll be in touch Finch with a suitable time for you and your lady friend to visit Dieanna. Good day to you both.'

'Lady friend, indeed!' Katie fumed, as they returned to the car, 'patronising prick.'

'Well, at least he gave permission for you to visit Dieanna,' Adam commented, fixing his seat belt, 'he could easily have refused our request.'

'What I'd like to know is why he decreased Dieanna's medications in the first place. It's obvious he's deliberately hiding crucial facts. How I'd love to get my hands on those medical files.'

'You know, there may be a way we can dig up the truth on Dieanna's treatment,' Adam informed her, 'it isn't a legitimate way, but right now I don't give a shit. That man is annoying as hell. I'm 100% convinced it's a cover up, I'm desperate to know what it is.'

Katie laughed, 'Adam Finch! It's usually me that'll try the unconventional way of doing things. My bad ways must be rubbing off on you.'

'I wish,' Adam replied, causing Katie to blush, 'oh, I wish.'

****

Two days later Clifford signed the form authorising Katie to accompany Adam on a visit to Tor Haven to meet Dieanna Payne.

The email came through shortly before midday. Katie got straight on the phone to Adam to arrange a suitable day and time.

'We can go this afternoon if you're free?' Adam advised, 'I have the afternoon off.'

'Perfect. Pick me up at two,' Katie instructed, before hanging up.

'I'll be in the vicinity should you need me,' Carl Clifford told Adam when he phoned to confirm the time of their visit, 'my mobile will be switched on.'

'I'm sure we'll be fine,' Adam reassured him, not appreciating the superior tone in Clifford's voice. Something about the man grated on his nerves. He exuded an aura of aloofness with arrogance, which Adam didn't like. It was almost as if Clifford either wished or knew something might happen during their visit, giving Adam an uneasy feeling.

Tor Haven was situated three miles from the town centre of Ivybridge, set in four acres of countryside. Low down and of dour brick construction its 'baronial' style of architecture blended well into the environment.

Announcing their arrival via an intercom at the front entrance Adam and Katie were met by a sour faced, disinterested security guard and ushered into a small, highly secure reception area. After signing the visitor's book and donning ID they were directed towards a set of glass doors. 'Through there, past the communal bathrooms, keep going until you come to a locked door. One of my colleagues will let you through.'

'They've moved Dieanna into a lock up facility,' Adam whispered to Katie, 'how many rent-a-cops do they have in this place? Last time I visited she was in the low security wing. Clifford didn't mention any of this when we were chatting on the phone.'

'I don't trust Clifford,' Katie whispered back, keeping close to Adam as they strolled along a narrow corridor lined with doors leading off in all directions. Few windows, poor lighting and abysmally low ceilings combined to create a "bunker" like atmosphere. On approach to the designated exit two metal doors swung open allowing them access.

'No doubt we're on CCTV,' Katie observed, as they once more found themselves walking along a narrow corridor. In contrast to the first corridor this area buzzed with activity; wards men and nurses hurried about with efficient determination.

Approaching another locked door, which didn't open instantly, Adam and Katie waited patiently for another burly security guard to appear, fumbling with a set of keys before managing to open the recalcitrant lock. 'Buzz for security when you're done,' he barked, heading down the corridor without a backward glance.

'How charming Tor Haven employees ensure our safety is kept close to their warm little hearts,' Katie murmured under her breath, spotting room 105, 'I couldn't work in this environment, reminds me of a maximum-security penitentiary.'

'With you there, could be one of those underground, nuke proof, Cold War command facilities you see in the movies,' Adam joked, 'I guess I'm a bit more used to these places, but to some, it can be quite daunting.'

Dieanna looked up and smiled as Adam and Katie walked in. She was sitting by an open French window dressed in jeans and a torn T-shirt. 'Hello Adam, how good of you to drop by. Is this your wife?'

Adam blushed, 'No, this is a colleague of mine, Katie Sinclair a leading forensic psychologist.'

'She'd make a pretty wife,' Dieanna smiled.

'I'll keep that in mind,' Adam replied, declining Dieanna's offer of a seat.

'Do you recall how long you've been in here now?' Adam asked, observing Dieanna closely, speculating on what thoughts were circulating through her mind. Her hands were clasped tightly in her lap, her face expressionless.

'No idea.'

'Do you remember much about your life before you came to Tor Haven?'

Dieanna started chewing her fingernails, 'God, I hate that bastard.'

'Who do you hate?' Adam asked.

'Him, of course,' Dieanna sounded cross, 'Don't tell me he's brain washed you as well. Not to worry, I shouldn't have done it, should I? That's why I'm being punished.'

'Why are you being punished?' Katie enquired.

Dieanna slumped forward in her chair exhaling slowly. 'Not you as well, can't you see what's happened? He has the money and the power to destroy anyone who gets in his way. I got in the old bugger's way, so here I am locked away for all my sins.'

'We'd like to know more, if you'd care to tell us?' Katie urged, 'whatever happened in your past is all over now.'

'It will never be over,' she mocked, 'what I did was unforgiveable, so many people suffered, and it was all because of me. As long as they all still walk this earth, there will be no justice.'

Katie was about to say something when Adam raised a hand to stop her. Dieanna drifted away into a ghostly trance. She sat deathly still, staring out the window, oblivious to her surroundings and visitors.

'Who the fuck are you?' Dieanna suddenly spat angrily, making Katie jump, 'Get out. Get out now before I beat the shit out of you.'

Adam sprung to his feet pressing the red button on the wall to alert security. Dieanna's eyes became wide portals, angry under sedated lids as she lunged forward.

'You bitch,' she screamed, staring menacingly at Katie, 'go to hell.'

Dieanna's right arm came within inches of striking Katie across the face as two male attendants bowled in to drag a kicking and screaming Dieanna through the side door.

Adam grabbed Katie firmly by the hand, leading her through another door to safety.

'That was a close-run thing,' Katie blurted out, her breathing slow and shallow, her complexion pale, 'I wonder what made her turn on us like that.'

'No idea,' Adam replied truthfully, 'Come on, let's get out of here. I need a drink, and I don't mean the caffeine type.'

'Who do you think Dieanna was referring to?' Katie asked, unwinding in the Frog and Toad an hour later, commiserating over a cold pilsner.

The visit to Dieanna had not gone according to plan. They'd learned very little, it had been a complete waste of time.

'Clearly a male, but I'm not sure who, Barry maybe,' Adam suggested.

'Yeah, I thought that at first, but I'm not entirely sure about that,' Katie replied, 'Dieanna seemed to be referring to someone who has influence and wealth, Barry doesn't quite fit the sketch. It wouldn't hurt to dig into Dieanna's background, who her parents are and where she grew up.'

'I've already researched her family,' Adam replied, 'Dieanna was adopted when she was only a few weeks old by a Mr and Mrs Short in Exeter. I've not been able to unearth any details on Dieanna's biological parents, but the Shorts hardly have two pennies to rub together.'

'Given the way Dieanna behaved today, I reckon it wouldn't be a bad thing to pay the Shorts a visit,' Katie concluded, 'clearly, someone has seriously ruffled Dieanna's feathers, and it would be nice to know who.'

'I rather like this investigation,' Adam jibed, 'I get to see a lot of you. I'll check if the Shorts are available. I'll drop by in the morning if they're free and report back with any interesting findings.'

****

'I'll be back around one thirty,' Liam informed Sonia, as she put the final touches on a leg of roast beef to go into the Arga, 'it's such a beautiful day, I wouldn't mind taking the GTV for a blast through the back lanes and blow the cobwebs away, maybe around Blackawton and into Dartmouth.'

'No need to rush back,' Sonia replied, 'we can eat around two or three. Give me a call before heading home, that way I can time the veg.'

Liam grabbed a set of keys for the vintage Alfa coupe, which occupied a special spot in the double garage next to the Spyder; recent opportunities to get behind the wheel of his beloved possession, proving a rarity.

The quintessence of classic Italian automotive design: the sleek 'pinoverde' two door was a cherished gift from his parents fifteen years ago, on his graduation with honours from Glasgow University. As such, the machine was lavished with the best care and maintenance money could buy, occupying a place in his heart, even more special than his family.

Almost by reflex, Liam sprung the bonnet and attached a portable jump start pack, knowing full well the battery was dead. After several pumps on the accelerator he pulled the choke and turned the ignition key. Without hesitation the 'jewel like' twin cam 'lump' fired into life, coughing and spluttering as it fought against the dual Weber carburettors dumping petrol down the inlet manifolds.

Reversing out he drove down West Alvington Hill rejoicing in the symphony reverberating off the high walls as the exhaust crackled and spat on the overrun, through Kingsbridge to the salutatory waves of envious tourists and along the Totnes Road at a heady pace, pushing inland.

It was the perfect day for a drive. A light breeze was blowing in off the coast, rustling gently through the golden fields of rapeseed. Liam put his foot down when the road ahead was clear, down changing with rifle bolt like precision through the gearbox at every opportunity and daringly overtaking any vehicle going at a slow jaunt.

He flew past California Cross, taking the bends with a measured precision, aiming to hit the apexes millimetre perfect, luxuriating in the exhilaration surge through his body as he accelerated out with just a hint of opposite lock.

"They don't build cars like this today," he conjectured, "all the fun has been engineered out in the so called 'safety' pursuit. No computer chips and servos controlling this beauty, everything you feel is real".

Classic cars were Liam's revolt against the daily dehumanising shackles of computers and cyberspace. More importantly he was alone, away from people, bloody people and the sordid reality of his existence.

Entering the approach to Dartmouth Hill his mind was far away, away from the hell of the Courts and legal system. Rather than slow to a prudent pace he changed down to fourth and accelerated, shooting past a tourist bus at speed before braking sharply, indignantly chopping back in front of it to the head shaking and gesticulating of the driver.

Plunging down the long, steep descent Liam instinctively grabbed the gear stick, dropping smoothly down into second gear while nudging the brake pedal ever so slightly, the car responded.

Attempting to overtake a delivery van Liam's blood turned cold when the steering suddenly and without warning turned into a dead weight. Jolting back to reality Liam wrestled the wood-rimmed wheel but to no avail. With a superhuman effort and adrenalin rush, he somehow managed to deflect the unresponsive Alfa back into the left-hand lane. Sighting the escape road rocketing into view, he summoned a last desperate attempt and wrenched the wheel hard over, spearing it into the run off. Applying careful pedal pressure, he judiciously brought the GTV to a gentle stop halfway up the escape road, his heart pounding and sweat pouring down his face.

For an eternity, he sat motionless inside the car trying to come to terms with the terrifying incident. The coupe was in top condition, no way could the steering suddenly fail. What took place was no accident. Someone had deliberately tampered with the car.

Chapter Nine

Removing his sunglasses, James reached for the yellow stick-it paper on the dashboard, once again checking the hastily scribbled note confirming Reg Applegate's address. A flashing message on the sat nav confirmed he was at "Primrose Muse", a small cottage in the village of Churchstow, an idyllic rural setting on the outskirts of Kingsbridge.

James had been trying to get hold of Reg for some time, only to be told he and his wife had taken an extended coach trip around Europe. Once James learned of their return to the UK he pounced.

Parking in the driveway behind an old Ford, he navigated up the cobbled path to a pale blue front door. He rang the bell, waiting patiently on the step for several minutes. As time ticked by James began to think no one was home, about to return to his 4WD and double check the address, the door slowly opened.

'James Sinclair?' Reg Applegate surmised, offering him a warm smile. 'Tom Markham mentioned you'd be dropping by sometime today, do come in, you'll have to forgive my sluggish gait. I suffered a stroke a few years back, thankfully a mild one, but it has been rather debilitating.'

James followed Reg into a small kitchen watching him ease gently into a high-backed chair, cushioned for support. 'I'd offer you a coffee, but we're all out of milk,' he apologised.

'That's fine. I've already drunk my quota of caffeine for the day,' James said truthfully.

'I used to drink twelve cups a day, partnered with two packets of cigarettes,' Reg volunteered, giving a shallow laugh, 'partly the reason I suffered a stroke; that and the pressures of being a high-flying journalist of course. Do you know the toughest job for a journalist, Sinclair?'

'Go on, tell me.'

'Determining fact from fiction,' Reg enlightened him, 'unless you're the infamous Tom Markham of course, who wouldn't know truth from fiction, he's so full of crap.'

'So I've heard. Now what can you tell me about Liam Mercer? I gather you were the journalist assigned to cover his son's death? I assume you met Liam on several occasions when attending press conferences.'

Reg nodded, 'What I can tell you is, it got messy. Liam Mercer was not an easy character to deal with, many a time I had to tread carefully. My Editor Lana Gibbs even offered me money to keep my mouth shut. Usually it's the other way around, we get paid to come up with the goods, but in this case the tables were turned, no one wanted me to report any juicy bits, especially if they directly related to Liam Mercer or his son.'

'Why do you think that was? The public would have wanted answers, considering the Mercers were big news.'

Reg shifted uncomfortably in his chair. He waited a few moments before carefully choosing his next words, 'I discovered Liam Mercer and Judge Malcolm Frobisher were involved in crooked art deals, some form of illegal activities taking place here and on the continent. I decided to do a bit of undercover work and low and behold when I came within inches of unravelling the whole murky business I was mugged, left with extensive bruises, one collapsed lung and several broken bones. I had to have my left knee completely reconstructed.'

'Do you believe Mercer and Frobisher were behind the mugging?' This line of questioning was more rhetorical.

'Definitely. I came within a hair's breadth of having my life taken away from me, ended up spending nine weeks in Derriford's intensive care unit. It was touch and go for a while, but I have to say Plymouth hospital is high priority on my Christmas list. The nurses and doctors were terrific, patched me up good and proper.'

'Good to know,' James replied, momentarily lost for words, marvelling at Reg's powers of resilience and ability to bounce back from a near death experience.

'Aye 'tis that me, boy,' Reg grinned, his Devonian accent coming to the forefront.

'How did the police handle events after you were attacked?' James probed, 'Did they take the initiative and follow up on these illegal activities?'

'No. They brushed it aside, practically told me I was a senile old fool who should know better than to try digging up dirt on Frobisher, one of Britain's top silks and a judge to boot. I was well and truly put in my place.'

'Now why does that not surprise me?' James responded wistfully, 'I expect Frobisher paid them good money to stay out of his private life. Tell me Reg, do you believe Frobisher is still dabbling in this line of work, illicit art works and the likes?'

Reg snorted indignantly, 'Why of course, there's too much money involved for him to give up that easily. Frobisher is all for making a quick quid, and he doesn't care how he does it.'

At that moment Pam Applegate appeared in the doorway, 'I'm sorry to interrupt Mr Sinclair but Reg needs to rest. Although he's in quite good health now, the doctor insists he doesn't exert himself too much. I get worried reminiscing about those dreadful events, could exacerbate his condition.'

'I'm afraid Pam is right,' Reg sighed, his eye lids looking heavy, 'I am feeling a bit tired, but I appreciate you dropping by and hope I've been of some assistance.'

'Yes of course, I am very grateful for the information you have provided me with today,' James replied, getting to his feet, 'I'll see myself out.'

James slightly disappointed, headed back to his car. He had only begun warming up with his questions, there was a whole lot more he wanted to find out about Mercer and Frobisher. Another visit to Reg was on the cards again soon, this time when his wife was out.

****

'What now?' Frobisher snapped, negotiating down the courtroom steps on short fat legs, with James close behind, 'Can't you lot leave me in peace?' The Judge was tired, clearly in a black mood.

'In case you've forgotten, I'm investigating a murder, the person in question being one of your colleagues,' James informed him, 'we won't stop asking questions until we get the right answers.'

'Well you're wasting your time with me,' Frobisher retorted, entering the confines of a local wine bar with James still in hot pursuit, 'I have no idea who killed Liam, so I suggest you take your investigation elsewhere. Go run a few fingerprint tests, you might get somewhere. Isn't that what you lot do best?'

James ignored this flippant remark, grabbing a vacant seat next to Frobisher who kept repositioning his large posterior on a bar stool to avoid overbalancing.

'Perhaps you can enlighten me on the Langham case?' James retaliated smoothly, 'I would have questioned you about it when we met at the gallery opening in Dartmouth the other evening but didn't feel it was the appropriate place.'

'How very gracious of you,' Frobisher jibed, using sign language to order his usual beverage from the scantily dressed female behind the bar.

'Yes, I thought so,' James replied smoothly, declining the offer of a drink, 'the thing is Frobisher, I'm curious to know why you handed Michael Langham such a hefty jail sentence. It seems a bit extreme.'

'All transcripts are available from my secretary,' Malcolm replied curtly, downing his drink in one go and ordering another, 'I suggest you contact her. Eileen will be only too happy to supply you with transcripts.'

James continued with his questioning, 'Neither you nor Liam would have been popular having produced that verdict. My understanding is, Michael Langham was a well-respected pillar of the community? I'm certain a few enemies would have surfaced for you when Langham went to prison.'

'I daresay,' Malcolm chortled, ordering another drink, 'however, I was only doing my job, Sinclair.'

'Yes, but a five-year sentence seems right over the top. People serve less for convicted rape.'

'Since when have you been an expert on the criminal justice system?' Malcolm questioned. 'You know nothing about Langham, or why that verdict was made. I have nothing more to say on the subject, so please leave.'

James watched Frobisher toying with his whisky glass, his mouth firmly remaining shut.

'I'll get those court documents like you suggest,' James threw back at him, anger crossing his façade, 'they may prove an interesting read. Enjoy the rest of your evening, your Honour, and don't drink too much. You could really do some mischief if you slide off that stool, ouch.'

****

'I was hoping I might catch you before you left for the day,' DCI Rose informed James, as he was shown into the lab through the airlock door by Fiona, 'I've managed to get hold of those transcripts and police files you requested in relation to the Langham case. Do you have some spare time to go over them?'

James, in the act of inserting thin layer coated glass plates into solvent tanks in the fume cupboard, nodded without looking up. 'No problem, I appreciate you bringing them over. Firstly, however seeing you're here, you may as well give me a hand spraying these plates.'

'Are you sure?' Rose spoke warily, events undertaken in laboratories were akin to the black arts in his eyes.

'You'll learn something,' James cajoled, indicating for the DCI to don a white lab coat hanging on a nearby hook. 'I'm running confirmatory thin layer chromatograms on the evidence samples your boys dropped over on Tuesday. All the stuff from that hush-hush lab raid in Plymouth you've been texting me about every five minutes.'

'The Khalil brothers,' Rose acknowledged, 'sorry for dropping that onto you without notice, but your lab was "Johnny on the Spot" and Bristol is snowed under, half their chemists are down with a virulent stomach bug. I'm been pushed for results. All of this is under strict confidentially guidelines, and please keep this under your hat, the heavies at the Yard are under direct pressure from the Prime Minister. I can't tell you anymore, but suffice to say, national security is involved.'

'I think I can give you something firm in about twenty minutes,' James checked his watch, a twinkle in his eyes. 'Oh, by the way I've run initial colour spot tests on all the seized materials and residues from the laboratory glassware. The Marquis Test indicated opiates in all the residues and powders.

I shot some of the residues through the GC/Mass Spectrometer this morning and there are a range of opiate alkaloids and derivatives present. I've already calculated the type and percentage breakdown of the derivatives in the samples. This is just about all I need, but I want the TLC results for peace of mind.'

'You mean these plates in the tanks?' Rose questioned, indicating with his finger.

'Yes, they're finished. What I need you to do Mick, is carefully remove the four plates and stand them upright in the fume hood so they can dry. Then you can give all four plates a light spray with this developing reagent. Imagine you're spray painting a car. The solution is Potassium Iodoplatinate Reagent. Opiates give colours from reddish blue to purple.'

Noticing a dubious Rose, James added, 'Don't worry it won't kill you.'

Mick Rose nervously followed the instructions given to him by James. While both men waited impatiently for the plates to develop, James delivered a rapid chemistry tutorial.

'TLC is a quick, inexpensive and reliable technique to separate and detect the presence of chemical compounds in mixtures, great for testing narcotics and most other illicits.'

'Looks a bit low tech,' Rose remarked.

'That's its beauty,' James chuckled, 'you don't need sixty grand's worth of ICP/Mass Spec for every test, and so far, they haven't found anything to replace it. In a nutshell, the unknown opiate sample solutions, as well as standard known opiates, are spotted onto the bottom of the plate. When placed in the tank each compound will move up the plate with the solvent as a distinct spot and be absorbed at different rates on the silica gel layer. The distance each alkaloid travels is characteristic for that alkaloid. All we need do is dry the plate and visualise the spots with a developing agent. The spots also fluoresce blue under UV light, but this is more dramatic. And I can photograph the plate for forensic reports.'

James paused momentarily, to double check the chromatograms.

'Here we go mate,' he exclaimed, pointing out purplish blue spot patterns on the plates and reaching for his scribbled lab notes. 'Exactly what I suspected, the Khalils were synthesising diamorphine, that's heroin to you. I've got crude codeine and crude morphine in two flasks, and a very impure heroin powder in assorted glassware and containers…quite a bit in fact.'

A relieved Rose stared at James intently.

'So, the caps?' he enquired, eager for confirmation.

'Never a doubt,' James grinned, 'they were using the hundreds of packets of OTC analgesics seized in the backyard shed as the source of codeine. The classical underground method for synthesising heroin by demethylation of codeine and acetylating the resultant morphine, hasn't been used in clandestine labs since the seventies to any large degree I believe. Also, if you look at the chromatograms, no thebaine or noscapine exists in any of the residues. This tells me the heroin wasn't made from raw opium, the usual method of illicit manufacture.'

'How did they get hold of that?' Mick asked, his full attention in play.

'Easy,' James continued, 'it's well documented in the literature, originally a 1951 paper I think, in the American Chemical Abstracts.

All you need to do is look it up on the web, it'll give you all the details. The idiot's bucket method is also there, a sure bet.'

'Then why would they use such a complicated and lengthy process?'

'Probably a shortage or long-term drought on the streets,' James explained, 'had any major heroin seizures lately?'

Mick scanned his memory bank, 'Half a tonne at Glasgow Docks in February from Pakistan concealed in the floor of a van and let me think… the big one: five hundred packets at Heathrow last summer from Turkey, invoiced as tile cement. It all ties in, and of course Boots reported a palette of codeine phosphate capsules missing from a warehouse break-in last April.'

'Touché,' James added, laughing at Mick's shocked expression, 'so, spill the beans Mick, what's going on.'

'I suppose it won't do any harm lifting the lid as it'll be all over the papers in a few days anyway.' Rose concluded, 'the Khalils have been under task force terrorist surveillance since Christmas. We now understand they were selling the heroin to fund illegal subversive activities, mostly for buying bulk quantities of ammonium nitrate.'

'Wow. Amatol hey.'

Rose reached for a lab towel, wiping his brow. 'It doesn't appear they were an isolated cell. The brothers spent six months towards the end of 2012 in Lebanon, training with the Hezbollah. I need to make a few quick calls, London are desperate to move quickly on leads. There must be at least a dozen charges they can hang on these guys. Good job James, I have to say I was counting on you coming through for us.'

'Looks like you nipped it in the bud well before they could do any harm?' James half guessed, hoping Mick would reveal more tantalizing details.

'Okay, I suppose I can trust you,' Mick joked, 'I owe you one anyway.

You don't want to know how close we came, Jim. We moved just in time. What I am about to tell you will never be released publicly. If this reached the media the political fallout will rock the nation. The potential damage it would do to our security services and government, not to mention NATO is incalculable.'

'Promise. Cross my heart and hope to die.'

'The brothers are part of a highly organised terrorist cell network spread over five counties with links to the top levels in the Iran regime. The Yard boys finally broke them after two days of intense questioning,' Rose paused to remove his lab coat and retrieve a glass of water from the cooler. 'Not pretty stuff; I was there.'

'I know; The Houses of Parliament? Westminster?' anticipated James, bursting for news.

'Nope, too obvious… although on reflection probably not such a bad idea,' the CI jibed.

'You've got me,' confessed James.

'Something more insidious,' Rose was having second thoughts.

'What? You can't leave it at that!'

'All right. The network had a Transit Van packed with 3 tonnes of Amatol at a warehouse on an industrial estate in a suburb of Newcastle. Fused up and ready to go. A short drive over the border.'

'There's nothing worthwhile in Scotland, is there?'

'The Vanguard Nuclear Submarine Base at HMNB on the Clyde,' Mick replied softly.

'Shit, no way. That's too well protected, isn't it?'

'We believe they have the inside contacts to get the van, posing as a defence contractor right into the heart of the complex at Faslane where the subs are moored and serviced. Sometime after 2am next Friday, just when the Navy will be servicing Trident missiles and reactors. They hoped to take out half the fleet, that's two.'

'Christ,' James' mind raced. *Mick was right. It would bring down the Government and destroy the Intelligence Services if the plot got out. If they succeeded, a lot worse. The blame game and finger pointing could start a major, full-blown conflict on NATO's Eastern borders.*

Iran would be drawn in. A nuclear holocaust was on the cards. Then there was potential radioactive contamination of the Clyde and Scotland in general. It didn't bear thinking about.

James pulled out a bottle of scotch from under the laboratory bench, grabbed two glasses and rubbed his eyes, the strain of the last few days etched into his face. 'Down this Mick, we've plenty of time to look at the Langham docs once our insides are warmed.'

With both men comfortably immersed in black swivel chairs in the front office, Mick Rose at last updated James on his findings pertaining to Michael Langham.

'According to the police report, Michael Langham was sentenced to five years in prison for brutally assaulting a security guard, this occurred down by the Barbican in Plymouth at the opening of an art exhibition. The report looks simple enough, states the crime and a clear arrest being made.'

'Let me look at that report,' James demanded, grabbing the thin A4 sheet from Rose. He read in silence for a few moments, before exclaiming in disgust, 'Why does it not surprise me the arresting police officer happened to be Rod Wetherill, back then of course, he was a Senior Sergeant.'

'That's interesting,' Rose said, taking another look at the police report to check out the signature. 'I must have missed that part, laid low with a stinking migraine all weekend, my concentration's been a bit off.'

James mumbled obscenities as he scanned the document a second time, 'This report's not only interesting, it's a corrupt self-indictment. Out of curiosity, what happened to the security guard whom Langham allegedly bashed, have you been able to track him down?'

Rose shook his head, 'He mysteriously disappeared not long after the attack, moved to an unknown address in Brighton. The trial continued with the guard's initial statement and photographs being taken by a police medical officer. Apparently, the guard didn't even front up at court and the medical officer in question has since retired and vanished overseas. I haven't been able to chat with either of them.'

'That's because no one is bloody well meant to trace any of these people,' James fumed, 'this whole fiasco was orchestrated by Mercer and Frobisher to get Michael Langham off their backs. They created enough false evidence to have the guy locked away. Frobisher was the one doing the sentencing, as far as this charade went, it was nicely sown up before the findings were made public.'

Rose blew out his cheeks, 'Then Langham was always behind the eight ball, even if innocent.'

'Which he was,' James replied bluntly, 'for some reason Michael Langham posed a considerable threat to Mercer and Frobisher, they needed him permanently out of the way. Whatever Langham had on them, needed covering up.'

****

James mounted the stairs two at a time to the third floor of Grays Law firm, going in search of Tabitha Fletcher. There were a few details he was anxious to sort out in relation to Liam Mercer and hoped Tabitha would be only too willing to oblige.

'James isn't it, nice to see you again,' Tabitha greeted him warmly, looking up from behind the reception desk. 'Are the police any closer to solving Liam's murder?'

'Getting there,' James replied, firmly clasping her outstretched hand, 'tell me Tabitha, how involved were you with Liam's court cases? Were you privy to inside knowledge?'

'I was never that involved,' Tabitha replied, 'I was mostly support, you know typing documents, raising subpoenas for witnesses, and liaising with court clerks and the like. I didn't play a major part in any cases he took on.'

'Do you have access to confidential files in the office, every case Liam ever worked on?

Tabitha gave a high-pitched laugh, 'Why of course. I was Liam's personal assistant after all. Having said that, I only occasionally got to sit in on client meetings, you need to speak with other partnering lawyers if you want more in depth stuff.'

James folded his arms, leaning forward to whisper in Tabitha's right ear. 'I hardly think Grays lawyers will confide in me Tabitha.'

Tabitha's pales eyes met his with a sultry expression. She became intoxicated by the smell of his full-bodied cologne, hanging on his every word.

'You and I both know they would always close ranks,' James continued, 'what I'm really keen to establish is the possibility of someone blackmailing Liam. Tell me, who else has access to company files?'

Tabitha, unsure of how much she should divulge, glanced furtively over her shoulder.

James, noticing her reaction placed his left hand on her knee, watching her blush as a warm tingling sensation swept over her.

'Liam's office was a thoroughfare for lawyers, judges and judicial personnel,' Tabitha explained a little breathlessly, making no attempt to remove his hand, 'a number of people could easily have been able to blackmail Liam.'

'Hypothetically speaking, if someone did blackmail Liam, any idea who that person might have been?'

'No idea at all, but here's the thing, James, has it not occurred to you, perhaps Liam was doing the blackmailing?'

James looked at her in surprise, 'Is this what you think was happening?'

Tabitha leaned forward, her mouth only inches from James' lips. 'Anything's possible James. Liam got himself into so much trouble he had a long list of enemies. If anyone could get one over on him, they would, but I'm inclined to believe Liam would have been the one with extortion plans. He is always one step ahead of all his rivals.'

Before James could reply, he felt Tabitha's sultry lips pressing against his. Her kiss was sweet, taking his breath away. Although wrong, he couldn't resist temptation, he had to have her…

Feeling lightheaded and completely satisfied, James left Tabitha buttoning her blouse as he headed up one more flight of stairs to the office of Sonia Mercer on the fourth level.

'Mr Sinclair, what brings you here?' Sonia questioned, gaze locked on a laptop, 'Do you have news on my husband's killer?'

James shook his head, 'Some progress is being made, but the real reason for dropping in is to ask you about the Langham Case. What do you have to say about Michael Langham and the obviously inordinate jail sentence he was served?'

'The Langham case is not one I'm familiar with,' Sonia replied sharply, switching her laptop to sleep mode and looking up to make eye contact, 'I'm sure you can get transcripts from reception on your way out, no court case is kept secret.'

'Let me refresh your memory,' James responded as he edged nearer, his voice slow and deliberate, 'Your late husband was heavily involved in the sentencing of Michael Langham, who spent time freelancing as an art critic for a leading art journal. I'd like to know more about that case, if you don't mind?'

'I honestly don't know what you're talking about,' Sonia insisted, nervously fidgeting with a brief on her desk.

'Yes, you do know what I'm talking about,' James dug in, pulling up a chair to sit opposite Sonia, 'I need to know what happened during that investigation. The Langham case could well be linked to Liam's death.'

'I cannot provide you with any insight,' Sonia replied, through clenched teeth. 'Now please leave.'

'You can play games all you like,' James told her firmly, 'sooner or later, you'll have to tell me the truth. Why make life harder for yourself, tell me what you know, and I'll leave you alone.'

'I know very little,' Sonia conceded at last, breaking off eye contact and slumping back in her chair.

'Ah, you admit knowing something,' James said triumphantly, 'go on, I'm listening.'

'Liam was dabbling in illegal artwork trafficking, paintings I believe. Michael Langham discovered what was going on and Liam had him put away, I suppose to stop him from talking. A few months later Michael Langham committed suicide, in the Scrubs I think, but I'm not sure why. That's all I know, I promise.'

'Am I right in assuming he was jailed for alleged assault, an assault which never took place?' James fired back at her, determined to get the full story.

Sonia nodded, 'It was the easiest way to get a conviction, to make him out to be some kind of monster.'

'Did you ever meet Langham's widow?' James asked, thankful never to have had any involvement, business or otherwise with Liam Mercer.

'Yes, I saw her during the trial, but we never spoke.'

'How would you describe her during the trial, was she angry? Could she have enough hatred to have killed your husband?'

'I guess so,' Sonia reached into the top drawer of her desk producing an unopened packet of cigarettes. 'Look Sinclair, where is this line of questioning taking us? You need to find Liam's killer, not waste time on every bloody criminal matter Liam worked on over the past few years. The Langham trial was an isolated event, it has no bearing on Liam's death.'

'Yes, I expect you're right,' James replied, getting to his feet, 'oh, before I forget, we've uncovered a few interesting facts connected with your son's death. The evidence that's surfacing might help bring your husband's killer to justice. If you happen to think of anything relating to Daniel's death which may help with my enquiry, do let me know.'

Sonia's face turned ashen, 'As I keep reminding you, Mr Sinclair, the death of my son was an unfortunate accident, totally unrelated to Liam's death. I wish you lot would realise that, instead of continually dredging up the past.'

'We'll see,' James replied, moving towards the door.

He stopped and turned before exiting, watching Sonia light up a cigarette and exhale slowly, staring up at the ceiling. 'Sonia, I will uncover the truth eventually, it's only a matter of time.'

****

'Sinclair, I hear you've been running around throwing half-baked accusations at people again. It's not on. You can't go around falsely accusing people of things,' Superintendent Ashcroft informed James, his tone frosty, 'this is your last official warning. I don't want to have to read the Riot Act again. Another error of judgment, and you'll land yourself in serious trouble.'

'Aren't you asking yourself why Sonia Mercer phoned to complain?' James shot back at him, 'Sounds like a cover up to me, otherwise why would the re-opening of her son's inquest or the Langham Case upset her so much?'

'Perhaps your constant badgering is upsetting her,' Superintendent Ashcroft shot back crisply, 'let it go Sinclair. Channel your enquiries elsewhere. The woman has just lost her husband for Christ's sake, she's a grieving widow.'

'Surely, you're not buying that,' James scoffed, 'Sonia could win a trophy for her acting skills.'

'I'm not buying anything,' weariness creeping into the Super's narrative, 'this line of enquiry is not getting you anywhere. Stick to forensics, which is what you know best.'

James sat opposite the Superintendent wondering why he was coming up against so many brick walls. He was even beginning to wonder if the police were involved in a conspiracy.

'I'm convinced Sonia Mercer is hiding something,' James fired back crossly, 'if only I can find out what, we might have a chance of bringing someone to justice.'

'For God's sake back off,' Ashcroft ordered, testily, 'there is no evidence linking Sonia Mercer to the place or time of her husband's death. You continue in this way and I'll refer Moorlands contract to the Deputy Chief Constable for review. There are plenty of other good forensic scientists out there desperate for a job. Push me any further Sinclair, and you'll give me no choice.'

****

Concerned by the lack of any fresh, hardcore forensic evidence, James met up with Matt for a drink to vent his anger and aggravation. The Mercer case was turning into a veritable Chinese puzzle, every time a new lead surfaced it fizzled out like a damp firework on Guy Fawkes Night.

'This may interest you James,' Matt said, flicking a piece of paper over to James who was drowning his frustration in a pint, 'I've managed to retrieve this from Liam Mercer's desktop computer. The one you requisitioned from his office.'

James adjusted his reading glasses, casually perusing the document on offer. 'This is just his weekly pay slip,' disinterest in his tone.

'Take a closer look,' Matt urged, 'it indicates Liam's weekly salary was divided into two payments. May be nothing, but on the other hand it could be a credible lead.'

James pulled out his mobile, dialling in the phone number shown on the top of the pay advice. At 7pm on a Friday night he doubted he'd get more than a voicemail, but it was worth a try.

In the act of hanging up a woman's voice came down the receiver, 'Grays accounts department, Vicky Lowe speaking, can I help you?'

'Ms Lowe, my name's James Sinclair, I'm with government forensics looking into the death of Liam Mercer. Sorry to disturb you, I've got one quick question I'd like to ask.'

'I'll help if I can. What would you like to know Mr Sinclair?'

'Would you mind confirming the method of payment for Liam Mercer each week?'

'By electronic transfer into his bank account, it's the same for all employees,' Vicky replied.

'Do you recall anything unusual about the transfers?' James pushed.

'Not off hand. If you hang on one moment Mr Sinclair, I'll fetch Liam's file.'

James waited patiently for the accountant to return to the phone.

'Each week Liam requested for one thousand pounds to go into a separate account,' she announced over the sound of papers being shuffled.

'Is that unusual?' James questioned.

'Not necessarily. People often split wages to pay off loans or a mortgage.'

'Can you tell me where the one thousand pounds was deposited Ms Lowe?'

'Yes, the money was to the account of *Preastly Holdings*, it's all here on the payroll spreadsheet; each week we deposited the money directly. At least that's what it looks like, my predecessor set up the regular transfers, and unfortunately, Mr Lack's writing skills were pretty abysmal.'

'Are you familiar with this organisation *Preastly Holdings*?' James enquired.

'Can't say I am, my job is to process the B-Pay every week as instructed, not ask questions.'

'Thank you for your time, you've been most helpful,' James remarked, pressing the "end call" button.

James dialled another number. 'Tabitha, James Sinclair. Have you ever heard of an organisation *Preastly Holdings*?'

'It doesn't sound familiar,' Tabitha came back, 'perhaps they trade under another name.'

'Yes, quite probable,' James agreed, 'if you recall the name, could you contact me?'

'Yes, of course,' Tabitha gushed, remembering her excitement from the other day, and hoping it wasn't a one off.

'Thanks, I'd appreciate it. I can always count on you to deliver.'

James turned to Matt, 'Job for you: I need information on a company called Preastly Holdings. Apparently, Liam Mercer paid them a grand each week, not a sum to be sneezed at.'

'On to it right away Gov,' Matt grinned, 'well, perhaps not right away. It's your shout, make mine a double. By the way, good, was she?'

James looked at Matt blankly, 'Come again.'

'I picked up on the undertones when you were speaking with Tabitha Fletcher.'

'God, I'm losing my touch if it's becoming that bloody obvious,' James smiled, slightly embarrassed.

Matt patted him firmly on the back. 'Elementary dear Watson, Elementary.'

Not wanting to spend all night drinking James finished his beer, before heading back to the lab to attack a backlog of overdue maintenance schedules. Late in the evening the call he was waiting for came through.

'Sorry mate, Preastly Holdings does not want to be unearthed,' Matt informed, supressing a yawn, 'I've conducted every search imaginable, but it keeps coming up with no listings. Are you sure you've spelt it correctly?'

'I can't be certain, I'm going off the information Vicky Lowe gave me at Grays,' James said, sounding disgruntled.

'Well, I've thrown as much inside computer information I can your way, but everything draws blanks. Maybe you need to start directing your enquiries elsewhere.'

****

Liam headed to the old boat yard keeping in the shadows, avoiding passers-by. It puzzled him why a rendezvous had been arranged after all these years. Of course, they'd met on occasions through social functions, but until now the request for a meeting had never arisen.

'I thought it was about time we met to discuss our options, Liam,' the smile was warm but didn't quite reach the eyes, 'I apologise for what happened to Daniel, I didn't quite mean for him to die in such a way.'

Liam felt sick to the stomach, he was facing his son's killer, who was not showing any remorse, merely an apology for how the execution had been carried out.

'Liam, you do realise more deaths need to take place, don't you?' The words devoid of all emotions, 'God knows I've tried my best to rationalise everything, but the future looks very bleak with all that dead wood floating around. I blame myself of course, although, I'm not entirely at fault. Your affair with Dieanna Payne was unforgiveable. The branches on the trees became distorted.'

Chapter Ten

Balancing a glass of cheap Chilean pinot in one hand and a cheroot in the other, Matt began copying some of Frobisher's files from a USB. Once completed, he made a start on deciphering the codes. The next step was an attempt to login remotely to the Law Firm's main server and sift through stored company files.

It had only taken Matt ten minutes earlier that afternoon to gain physical access to Malcolm's office computer. The young woman on reception, completely absorbed in gossip magazines, didn't seem bothered when Matt turned up to fix a loose connection on Frobisher's computer. It was the easiest scam he'd undertaken in a long time.

'Ah! Now this is interesting,' Matt commented out loud, as he topped up his glass, 'our honourable judge was also paying a sum of one thousand pounds each week to Preastly Holdings. Who the hell is this mob?'

Matt picked up the landline and dialled James, 'I know it's late, but can you come over? I'm digging up some interesting stuff and think you should be in on it. You're not busy, are you?'

'Me, I'm never busy,' James teased, 'I was just checking some rather boring Home Office invoices, which need emailing to Bristol, nothing of great importance. Give me till eleven.'

True to his word, in a little under an hour, James was heading onto Dartmoor driving decidedly recklessly over Cadover Bridge to join Matt in his nineteenth-century farmhouse. 'I see the farm gate is still longing for its hinges,' James jibed, crossing the threshold into a fifties vintage period kitchen, also in need of major restoration.

'It endows that little bit of extra charm,' Matt replied sarcastically, 'besides, the vast amount of work you lot throw my way doesn't allow for domesticity.'

'The farmer needs a wife,' James smarted, taking up residence at the kitchen table alongside Matt, 'so, what is this "interesting stuff" you've unearthed?'

'James, I've found what you're looking for,' Matt said, smugly. 'It's not Preastly Holdings Limited, it's P.R. Eastly Holdings. Separate the first two letters and there you have it: P.R. Eastly, not Preastly.'

James was now wide awake, avidly perusing the website brought up on Matt's laptop. 'Excellent work buddy, you've earned a few pints for this one.'

'I'll hold you to that. Anyway, P.R. Eastly Holdings are listed as a propriety limited company, their head office is domiciled in Exeter. The focus of their business is Mergers and Acquisitions. I'm inclined to believe the weekly cash transactions Liam and Malcolm made were related to dodgy deals the lads had going, but perhaps not linked at all with the murder enquiry. I'll do further checks if it helps.'

'Nice work uncovering this much,' James said, visibly pleased, 'I still think we need to delve deeper, can't leave anything to chance. What else have you dug up on our beloved Judge? Are there any juicy secrets locked away in the dark corners of his computer?'

'I'm afraid not. According to accountant reports, the Salcombe wine bar nets a healthy sum each year, especially during the summer months, but there isn't anything to provide us with connections to Liam's death. Mal Frobisher was clever not to store much on his computer or laptop.'

'Too bad.'

'Oh, there was one more thing,' Matt added, 'a file completely devoid of information titled "Rembrandt". I get the feeling it would have made fascinating reading, unfortunately, the contents were erased. Not worth the time and effort to recover.'

'Well, if Frobisher is a killer, he's bound to slip up somewhere.' James concluded, helping himself to some wine. 'With or without computer files we could still nail him. In the meantime, we need to research more on P.R. Eastly Holdings, find out who runs this company and pay them a surprise visit.'

****

The warm, oppressive atmosphere of a late August night enveloped the house. Sonia tossed fitfully in bed, realising sleep would never come under such stifling conditions.

The last vestiges of an early evening thunder storm rumbled and flashed twenty miles away, venting its fury on unfortunates further down the Coast. Resigned to the fact resistance was futile, Sonia threw off the one sheet covering her naked body, and reached for a lightweight throw over, hanging off the end of the bed rail.

With Luke away on business, not due back for another three days; Sonia decided to sort through Liam's belongings. They couldn't be kept forever, and she needed to make a fresh start.

She padded quietly along the landing, stopping outside the closed door. Her hand rested momentarily on the brass door handle, until she gathered courage to turn the key. Inside, the spare room reeked of stale aftershave and mildew. The essence of Liam still lingering.

Sonia moved to the small East-facing window, opening it a fraction to drink in the country smells, and eavesdrop on the primeval sounds drifting up from the ancient woodland, across the field. Away in the distance, just above the horizon, a new crescent moon sat in a sky abundant with stars. After standing staring at the moonscape for over half an hour Sonia finally moved over to a rustic pine wardrobe, where she sifted through Liam's clothes, throwing them into an empty suitcase, before making a start trawling through his antique writing desk. Rubbing tired eyes, she subconsciously probed the confines of a thin drawer, gliding her fingertips gently through various nondescript items until her hand came to rest on a small book wrapped in a silk scarf. Retrieving a brown, Moroccan bound vintage edition of "East of Suez" she flicked through the lavishly illustrated pages intrigued, knowing Liam detested Kipling's poems. About to cast the slim volume on to the bed, her focus was drawn toward a small, green envelope falling out from inside the rear cover, coming to rest silently between her feet. Picking it up Sonia sat down on the bed and extricated the three-page letter folded inside.

Now fully awake, her eyes scanned each word, taking in the full meaning of the sentences. Liam had kept the letter hidden for very good reason; the author could hold so many people to ransom with the secrets it revealed.

Captivated by the paragraphs, the identity of Daniel's mother was revealed, causing Sonia's stomach to churn, the puzzle pieces coming inexorably together. Turning the page, she discovered her son's death had not been an accident, but a deliberate murder, to keep forever hidden the truth of a shameful past.

Unable to endure the pain any longer Sonia fumbled for her lighter, determined to destroy the poisonous words, clearly maliciously written. As the paper started to burn so did Sonia's eyes, warm tears trickled down her flushed cheeks. The tip of her index finger seared, the ashes falling onto the diamond-patterned bedspread.

How long Sonia sat transfixed she had no idea, finally easing herself up off the bed to step into the narrow hallway, her mind mulling over the contents of the letter, until she finally knew what had to be done. She picked up the phone, placing it back in the receiver five times, before eventually dialling the number.

'Yes,' questioned a sleepy voice at the other end.

Sonia looked at her watch, it was three in the morning, and she had woken them up.

'I've read the letter,' Sonia blurted out, 'I know you killed Daniel and I know why.'

A gasp came down the line, then an unnerving laughter, then an uncontrollable cough. 'You're quite the detective. I wondered how long it would take you to figure it out. So, what happens now, will you confront me about it, or will you keep your distance, in case something bad happens to you?' Further laughter followed, this time more sinister.

Sonia gripped the telephone, desperate to steady her nerves. 'Either you hand yourself in to the police, or I'll pay them a visit,' she threatened, trying to instil fear, although inside she felt sick.

A few seconds passed, before the voice on the other end responded, 'No, I'll tell you what you'll do, you'll wait for me to send you a text specifying a time and place we're to meet. I have no intentions of harming you Sonia, you're nothing to me. I will pay you money, enabling you to go away, no one needs to be any the wiser. I also did you a favour getting rid of Liam, look at all the women he bedded, to say nothing of the one who fell pregnant. No, you won't split on me Sonia, you're too smart for that.'

****

Sonia Mercer clad in an old pair of dungarees, loose fitting turquoise top with brown hair neatly tied up in a ponytail, slowly opened the door to James. Spread through the reception rooms were packing boxes, lying next to large quantities of bubble wrap.

'Have I caught you at a bad time?' James asked, edging himself through the door, to stand in one of the few clear floor spaces.

'No, now is as good a time as any,' Sonia replied, weariness in her voice, 'do you have time for a cuppa? I could do with a break.'

'Please. Are you going anywhere nice?' James asked, following Sonia into a half empty kitchen.

She smiled, 'The Western Isles. Luke and I have decided to get away from all this sadness, to make a fresh start in Scotland. We're leaving at the end of next week.'

'A lovely part of the world,' James commented, pausing momentarily, struck by the emptiness in her words, 'I'm sorry we don't have any fresh news on who killed your husband Mrs Mercer, but we will do everything in our power to uncover the truth and bring the perpetrator to justice. Unfortunately, these things take time, working through all the scientific evidence.'

'I have every faith in you,' Sonia replied, dropping tea bags into a teapot, 'and please call me Sonia. Gone are the formalities, James. I know our last meeting was a bit harsh, but tempers do flare during difficult times. If I came across as unhelpful, or keeping information from you, I apologise.'

James and Sonia sat at the kitchen table with a view across an adjacent field, watching the sun setting in a hazy, crimson-streaked sky.

'Over the years Liam and I drifted apart,' Sonia volunteered, pouring two cups, 'I suffered from leukaemia as a young child, and due to the invasive treatment, it rendered me sterile. Liam knew we could never have children together, yet it didn't seem to bother him. Well, at least that's what I thought when I married him. It came as an almighty shock to discover he'd been sleeping around and an even bigger shock to learn he had fathered a child. We officially adopted Daniel when he was a few weeks old, so technically, I guess, he was always my son.'

'Did you know who Daniel's biological mother was?'

Sonia toyed with her teacup, 'I begged Liam to tell me, to understand him better, but he wouldn't divulge that information.'

'Have you any ideas? Surely, you must have a slight inkling?'

'It doesn't matter anymore,' Sonia told him, her eyes beginning to water, 'for everyone's sake, the past is best forgotten.'

'You do know you have been cleared of being a suspect in Liam's murder, don't you?' James said at last.

'Yes, I received confirmation from the police a little over a week ago. I should have been relieved, yet I felt an overwhelming sadness, coupled with grief. Liam and I may have experienced differences over the years, but he didn't deserve to die, James.'

James acquiesced.

'I have a confession to make, I kept some facts from you James, and I'm sorry. I panicked when Liam was killed and didn't want to become embroiled in a lot of additional emotions.'

'What sort of info?' James quizzed, dipping a ginger nut.

'For several months prior to Liam's death, terrible things happened to him, which at first we assumed were unfortunate events. Over time, I realised this was not the case, but didn't want to alarm my late husband, so I kept secrets hidden from him.'

'Go on,'

Sonia took a large breath, 'Late February, Liam was rushing to the courthouse in Exeter, stepping out onto the road he was hit by a speeding car, the vehicle impacting with his thigh, causing pain and bruising. A week later I think it was, Liam found himself locked inside the courthouse, receiving a disturbing phone call. Then there was the night his laptop was stolen, and another time when someone deliberately left a rusty wheelbarrow along our pathway, causing a nasty gash to Liam's right leg. He also received a strangely worded poem in the post, clearly hand-delivered. All of these events took place over a three-month period, quite scary with no known origin.'

'This is serious stuff,' James told her, his voice smarting with irritation, 'having those facts to hand, could have saved effort and time into the investigation of your husband's death. Did you report any of these incidents to the police?'

Sonia meekly shook her head, 'No, because I think I know who was behind it all.'

'Even more reason to tell the police,' James replied, 'they could have laid charges. Would you like to tell me who you think tried to harm your husband?'

Sonia poured a second cup of tea. 'Michelle Langham.'

'Are you certain it was her?'

'Yes. She called our home phone one evening, telling me Liam would pay for the death of her father: Michael Langham.'

'When was the call made?'

'Exactly three days prior to Liam's death.'

A hushed silence reigned, then Sonia spoke again, 'James, I don't believe Michelle Langham killed my husband. She may have caused injury on several occasions with these outrageous attacks, but she strikes me as a confused young woman, seeking solace by way of petty revenge.'

James dropped a sugar cube in his tea. 'A hit and run is not a minor offence,' he reminded Sonia, 'intentional or otherwise, whoever rammed a car at Liam could easily have killed him or maimed him for life. I also very much doubt you can be one hundred percent certain Michelle Langham didn't kill your husband. She had the ideal motive.'

'I'd better give you this,' Sonia handed over a small, cream envelope.

James took out the typed note from inside, reading it quietly to himself: *Roses are Red, Liam is Blue, Oh shit! You've stopped breathing. What happened to you?*

'When did you receive this?' James demanded, reading the note again, letting the words sink in.

'The day after Liam's body was discovered at the bottom of Portlemouth cliffs,' Sonia replied submissively, 'I found it on the welcome mat in the hallway. There was no stamp or postal mark, so it must have been hand delivered. I recently discovered an identical note, sent to Liam two months earlier.'

'I'll take the note back to the lab for examination,' James told Sonia, carefully placing it in his shoulder bag. 'Before I head off, is there anything else you'd care to share with me?'

Sonia shook her head, 'No, that's all, James. Please try to understand the complexities of Liam's death. I understand you have a job to do, but life is never easy. Perhaps whoever killed Liam needs to be given a second chance.'

James rose to his feet, thinking there were a million responses he'd like to give Sonia Mercer, but none of them would suffice. Instead, he quietly drove home, wondering if Sonia's instincts were right and Michelle Langham was not the one to murder Liam Mercer, although the new evidence Sonia brought to light clearly put her in the running.

****

Liam opened the door, encountering Tabitha standing with a manila folder tucked under her arm. 'I need you to sign these court documents for the Arnolt Subpoena,' she dutifully informed, stepping over the threshold to follow him into the living room, 'Is Sonia about?'

'She's retired to bed over an hour ago, complaining of a migraine. Come on in, I'll get a bottle of bubbly from the cellar. It's been an arduous day and I for one, need a drink.'

'Sounds lovely,' Tabitha replied, entering the hallway and making her way into the living room.

Liam disappeared, returning moments later with two champagne flutes, a chilled bottle of Spanish Brut and a bowl of prawn-flavoured crisps.

Tabitha drained her glass in one rapid motion, waving it at Liam. 'Fill her up Lee, there's a good fella, I can always catch a cab home if necessary. Don't forget those papers, best do it now before we both forget.'

Liam obliged on both accounts, topping up Tabitha's glass and signing the documents.

'My, this is cosy,' Tabitha remarked, motioning again for the wine bottle.

'Are you okay, Tabs?' Liam enquired, resting his arm on the side of the settee, studying her flushed features. 'In the few years I've know you, you've never been a heavy drinker.'

'People change,' Tabitha replied stoically, 'actually, some people change more than others. I'd say I've altered quite a bit over the years. What do you think Lee, have I changed?'

'I can't say I've noticed,' Liam answered, reaching for the near empty bottle to top up his own glass.

'Ah, yes, but that's because you don't really know me,' Tabitha laughed, unintentionally slurring her words, 'go fetch another bottle, and I'll tell you why I've changed.'

Liam amused by Tabitha's drunken state did as he was told, this time fetching a bottle of red.

'Oh, bloody good Chateaux Cinq-Neuf, my favourite, not a cheap plonk,' Tabitha giggled, unscrewing the top to slop the contents into her empty glass, half of it spilling onto the white flocked rug. 'How clumsy,' Tabitha apologised staring at the red stain, 'Sugar will fix that, or is it salt, maybe pepper, ha whatever, that rug needed a bit of cheering up. White is such a boring colour. Now where was I, yes, guessing who I am, go on, Lee my man, who am I?'

'You're a very drunk Tabitha Fletcher,' Liam jibed, 'I think I should ring you a taxi.'

'That's where you, yes you Lee is wrong, I am not Tabitha Fletcher, I am not the Queen, I am not a bird or a plane, I am actually Michelle Langham, ha there's a surprise.'

Liam turned grey, every facial muscle tensing as the words struck home.

'But you can't be,' he stammered, 'I was told you'd moved permanently to Australia, was it North Queensland or the Outback?'

'Do I look the red desert type?' Tabitha retorted, swallowing more of her drink and waving the glass in the air. 'Fancy me having a drink with the man who killed my father,' Tabitha's eyes

156

narrowed, *'you're the bastard who fucked my life and now I'm about to destroy yours. Watch out Lee, it won't be a pretty sight.'*

Tabitha swayed onto her feet, precariously heading to the front door. 'Bye bye, Lee old boy. Mind how you go, it would be awful if you met with a dreadful accident. I'd be looking over my shoulder if I were you. Cheerio.'

Chapter Eleven

'Intriguing read?' Katie enquired, turning to James engrossed in the four lines printed on the creased piece of paper.

James refrained from comment, tossing the paper in her direction.

'Interesting little ditty,' Katie remarked, placing it on her desk, 'I'd assume a young creative mind had fun putting that together.'

'What makes you think they're young?' James quizzed.

'Oh, it's easy deciphering that one,' Katie replied casually, 'the words are uncomplicated, it strikes me as something a less worldly individual would come up with, not a person with years of erudition. I could be wrong of course, but I doubt it. I'd be keen to hear where you found this poem extraordinaire?'

'Sonia Mercer gave it to me,' James dutifully informed his sister, 'she believes Michelle Langham was the author, this ties in with acts of violence Michelle may have orchestrated against Liam. Tell me Katie, in your experience, could someone who wrote such a note possess a lethal streak?'

Katie laughed at her brother's direct questioning, 'Anything's possible, but nothing's definite.'

'Sonia is convinced Michelle Langham's not the murdering type,' James continued, 'how she comes to that conclusion I have no idea, especially as I believe Michelle once tried to run Liam over.'

Katie listened as her brother detailed the recent assaults on Mercers' physical and mental wellbeing, spanning several weeks.

After he'd finished, Katie came up with her frank response, 'I tend to agree with Sonia Mercer. Although, Michelle demonstrated bursts of anger, she could merely have been seeking attention.'

'Are you serious?' James shot back, scratching his left cheek, 'the woman sounds like a certified nutcase.'

'If Michelle Langham really wanted to kill Liam Mercer, she would never have failed on her first attempt,' Katie slowly replied,

'No, I believe Sonia's right, Michelle Langham does not profile as a cold-blooded murderer.'

****

James and Mick Rose lounged in the opulent foyer of P.R. Eastly Holdings waiting for Preston Eastly to conclude a conference call to New York.

'Mr Eastly will see you now, gentlemen,' Rising to their feet, the duo followed the immaculately groomed blonde into the board room, where they were directed to a large oval table crafted from rare, exotic rainforest hardwoods.

'If it gets too warm in here please let me know,' she advised, leaning forward to adjust the thermostat, revealing a large pair of breasts.

James dragging his eyes away, glanced out of the window to take in the Exeter skyline.

Preston's suite, occupying most of the top floor, was dominated on two walls by four large abstract paintings as decreed by latest interior design fashion. By contrast, placed at intervals around the room were examples of the early twentieth century decorative arts standing on plinths, securely displayed behind Perspex cases.

Preston Eastly strode purposefully into the room, hand outstretched in greeting, 'Detective Rose and Mr Sinclair, welcome. Sadly, gentlemen I can only spare a half hour for our meeting today, I have a flight booked to Paris at three.'

'This won't take long,' James replied, slowly diverting his gaze from an impressive, hand worked silver presentation cup centre-place on the table.

'An early piece of Jugendstil from the Wiener Werkstatte,' Preston exclaimed, easing into a chair, 'are you a fan of Art Nouveau Mr Sinclair?'

'Ah…yes,' James replied truthfully, 'Unfortunately, I covert English Arts and Crafts jewellery and prices are way out of my reach.'

'I know what you mean, it's a weakness of mine; have a look at that Guild of Handicraft silver and amethyst casket before you leave.'

For someone edging towards sixty, Preston was in good shape. The dark blue Italian designer suit without doubt tailor made, his crisp white shirt immaculate, complemented by a pale blue tie and gold cufflinks.

James sat staring at the man for a few moments. He looked very familiar, yet he was certain they had never met.

'I believe gentlemen you'd like to discuss Mr Malcolm Frobisher and the late Liam Mercer; God rest his soul. At least that's what Mr Sinclair allured to when we briefly chatted over the phone this morning.'

Rose nodded, 'As you'll be aware Mr Eastly, with all suspicious deaths we need to thoroughly check out the business and private affairs of the deceased. It has been brought to our attention Liam Mercer and Malcolm Frobisher were paying your company the sum of one thousand pounds on a weekly basis, why was that?'

Preston Eastly leaned back in his Barcelona chair casually placing both arms behind his head, 'Both men were investing in a subsidiary company of P.R. Eastly Holdings in particular, a retail property development venture in Truro, the centrepiece a cutting edge, art exhibition space and gallery.'

'Do you have documents supporting this claim?' Rose enquired.

'Most certainly,' Preston replied, 'I can have my chief financial officer courier across all relevant paperwork.'

'May I ask how you met Frobisher and Mercer in the first place Mr Eastly?' Rose continued.

Preston paused to pour a glass of water, 'I believe we were introduced at a function hosted by Lady Scott-Thomas back in November 2009.'

'What about Grays legal firm, which the men shared equity in; did you utilise their services for any legal matters? Your company must surely use lawyers from time to time.'

Preston shook his head, 'P.R. Eastly Holdings has a long-term arrangement with Trent Thornton Partners in London. They handle all our legal work.'

'What happens now Liam has passed away?' James stepped in with a question of his own, 'Does his widow Sonia inherit Liam's share of the gallery?'

'It's a little more complex, I'm afraid,' Preston replied, 'from what I recall; Clause 3.5 of the contract states as Sonia Mercer didn't actually contribute any funds to the project, she is not eligible for any equity or profit share. However, as a good will gesture, I am recommending she receives a lump sum of fifty thousand pounds. My legal team will have this finalised by the end of the month, with the money deposited directly into Sonia's HSBC account.'

'That's a very generous offering,' James commended.

'Sorry gentlemen, but if that's all, I'll have to wrap up our meeting to ensure I get my Heathrow connection. I'll have my secretary show you out. I hope you manage to enjoy the rest of this fabulous day. Too bad the forecast for Paris is not so inviting, 12 degrees and occasional showers.'

'What do you make of all that?' James quizzed Mick, as they exited the building opting to use the fire stairs rather than the lift. 'He seemed pleasant enough.'

Rose pulled a face, 'I felt he was a bit too slimy. He told us all but nothing of what we really wanted to know.'

****

'What have we got here?' James enquired, heading over to where the body lay face down on the rocks, the tide already starting to wash over sandaled feet.

'Not so much what, but whom,' Nick corrected him, 'Sonia Mercer to be precise, it looks like she met the same fate as Daniel and Liam. Although on this occasion, our killer decided to bash her about a bit. Not for the squeamish.'

'Good God, I was only speaking with her yesterday,' James remarked in horror, 'What the hell is going on around here? Everyone's dropping like flies, and we are no nearer uncovering the truth. What has Sonia Mercer done to upset our killer, there has to be some association we can't seem to reconcile.'

Nick pulled back the sheet covering Sonia's face, allowing James confirmation. One side of her skull was badly crushed, indicating repeated impact with a sharp, heavy object.

'Shit,' James gasped, not about to choose his words carefully.

'I'll requisition a post mortem as soon as possible, but I'm betting it won't indicate much,' Nick's voice wavered slightly, 'Mick and I are coming under fire from The Divisional Commander as to why it's taking so long to catch this bastard. The media's already circling. He wants a full report on his desk by tomorrow, now Sonia turning up in this way will really spice things up.'

'I can already envisage the headlines of the local paper when it goes to print,' a visibly worried James concurred, 'the Star's not going to let this one slip by without demanding scalps.'

'Buggar what Tom Markham has to say, I'm shit scared of the nationwide TV and press getting hold of it. I already had to deflect enquiries from two major tabloid journos yesterday. Our killer is a psychopath hell bent on creating maximum chaos, we desperately need that break through before we have a major crisis on our hands.'

'Agreed. Unfortunately, that's easier said than done, and in the meantime the whole thing's turning into a French farce.'

'And, there's something else you should know,' intimated Nick, signalling a nearby SOCO for the removal of Sonia's body. 'The same print we discovered under Liam's body "Falling Memories" was also found with Sonia's. But that's not all. Guess what day it is today?'

'Don't tell me, Sonia's birthday,' James ventured.

Nick nodded.

****

'I don't understand why our psychopath is turning serial,' Fiona spoke up, again scrutinising the white board with all the latest lab reports and crime scene results, 'they seem to strike randomly, yet there has to be some common denominator linking all our victims.'

'Don't worry, we're not alone, Mick Rose's team is hitting the same brick wall. All their leg work has produced a host of dead ends,' Nick concluded, trying to make sense of the complex victim relationship diagrams stuck on the lab partition.

'They keep going because they don't feel their mission is complete,' Katie informed her colleagues, 'typical signs of a killer's frustration.'

'Katie, can you put together a more detailed analysis on our killer?' Nick pleaded, 'Perhaps, if you go over each murder more thoroughly you can create a better picture, something that stands out.'

'It's worth another analysis,' Katie acknowledged, moving over to her desk, 'there has to be a prototype emerging, lying just under the surface. Your choice of words was interesting Nick; you mentioned the word "picture". Here's an interesting fact, so far four people in *Falling Memories* have died: Liam, Sonia, Daniel and Louise.'

James coming to join the group clapped his sister firmly on the back. 'Good deduction, Katie. You know what else this means don't you: Mal Frobisher and Dieanna Payne are the only two in the painting still alive.'

'It's not looking good for either of them,' Nick confessed, throwing a worrying glance in Katie's direction.

'Right, but we need to look at things from outside the box,' Katie remarked, 'either one of them could be our killer, or possibly the next victim. The trouble is, we don't know which.'

****

'You have no idea how I feel about you,' Lauren screamed into the phone, 'why are you doing this to me James, to our son? You need to make a commitment, we can't continue this way. I am not a sex object for you to screw on demand.'

James was frustrated, 'When we first got together Lauren, I told you I didn't want strings attached. I was happy for us to have a casual relationship, which I thought suited both our needs. How the hell did I know you would get yourself pregnant?'

'Oh, so this is something I did on my own, was it?' Lauren shot back, momentarily taking one hand off the steering wheel to run fingers through short blonde hair, 'Conceiving a child is not one-sided, you know.'

'I never wanted a child,' James retaliated, 'I'm not a kid person.'

'Yeah, well tough, the end result is Jason. There's no going back. At least, can we please meet up to talk about our son?'

'No,' James was being stubborn, not planning on backing down any time soon.

'I feel you owe it to Jason to at least see him, hold your son in your arms.'

'It's over Lauren, there's nothing more to say,' James told her firmly.

' Oh no, it's not over,' Lauren yelled back, her anger rising to the surface as she negotiated a series of "S" bends, her mind 100% focused on her conversation with James she wasn't watching the speedometer, 'So long as I have breath in my body, I will fight for you to acknowledge Jason is your son.'

James' reply was cut short by the screeching of brakes, followed seconds later by Lauren's petrifying screams exploding through his brain. The next noise was an almighty metallic thud, as the car impacted side-on with a tree.

****

James felt physically sick seeing Lauren slumped behind the steering wheel of the crumpled, gold MG saloon. He didn't need to touch her, from the pall of her skin and the way the body was twisted, he knew she was dead.

'You okay, Sinclair?'

James was slammed back to reality at the SOCO's direct question. 'Yeah fine,' he stammered, 'It would appear speed was involved.'

'That's what we're suspecting, but it also looks like she's another cell phone statistic. Do you want the body now?'

'Er, no, my colleague Nicholas Shelby is on his way to take over. I know the deceased, which is a possible conflict of interest.'

'Right you are. What about the kid?'

James took on a puzzled look. 'Kid?' he questioned.

'Yep the one gurgling in the front seat of the forensic van. I'm surprised you missed the baby seat in the rear, mind not on the job today?'

James looked over into the adjacent van as the SOCO shaking his head, moved away.

Adrenalin surged through James' entire body as he stood staring at the infant, whose large eyes reached into his very soul. There was no doubt the child was Jason, instantly recognisable from the photograph Lauren had recently sent. For a moment he was unable to move, he stood staring at the small child uncertain what to do.

Finally, he stepped forward picking up his son to cradle him in his arms. The smell of baby oil combined with lemon scented washing powder filled his nostrils as the infant's soft cheeks brushed against his two-day stubble.

James was overwhelmed with emotions as he held his son close. It was a magical moment as he realised he had created such a perfect human being.

Whilst the rest of the accident response team stood several metres away deep in muted conversation James seized the opportunity and did something out of character. Cradling Jason under his left arm he quickly reached into his jacket pocket to retrieve a glass vial. Practiced, trained precision saw him gently swab the inside of Jason's mouth, gaining a small amount of saliva. James couldn't take Lauren's word for it, he had to be certain, he needed to know if Jason really was his son.

****

'What you're doing is not on,' Fiona informed her brother, 'you should only use our automated DNA test equipment for government business, or our other contractual client arrangements. It's unlike you to act unprofessionally.'

'What, on my own son?' James objected, 'Lauren's dead for Christ's sake, and I'm hardly going to seek permission from her husband.'

'I know it's not strictly illegal, so instead why don't you get a DNA profile check through third party channels,' Fiona fought back, 'It's commonplace procedures these days. Gina can send off your samples to a commercial paternity lab and have a confirmation back in ten days.'

'No way am I involving my GP. Do you think I'm stupid?' James retaliated, 'I need to find out the truth. Besides, you don't know the first thing about my character. Siblings we may be, but that doesn't mean we know everything about each other.'

'Okay, okay, so what if you do discover Jason is your son, what then? I very much doubt Lauren's husband will give him up without a fight. This could turn messy, James. Besides, when will you have time to look after a young baby?'

'Don't preach Fiona, it doesn't become you. Now I suggest you finish that report I asked you for two days ago. If the Environmental boys don't get the numbers on the Malborough pesticide poisonings, I'll know who to blame.'

Fiona was about to up the ante, before deciding against it. She rarely fared well when she and her brother got into a feud. Regardless, the atmosphere in the office remained tense for the remainder of the morning. Everyone got on with their work in silence, not bothering to make each other cups of coffee, as was the norm.

'Are you going out?' Fiona enquired of James as she saw him reach for his car keys, shortly before midday.

'Yep, I won't be back until tomorrow. I have an urgent errand to run.'

'Can't it wait?' she urged, 'You promised to help me with the DNA testing on the Baxter murder evidence.'

'I didn't promise, I said I'd help if I had time,' James corrected, 'besides, you're more than capable of running that show on your own. Perhaps Katie could help? She's getting proficient in the lab.'

'Sorry, no can do,' Katie interjected from behind her desk, fingers flying swiftly over the keyboard, 'I've got a psychological profile due at the Home Office by two. The rate I'm going, they'll be lucky to receive it by five.'

165

'Well ladies, I'll leave you to it,' James announced, heading for the door, 'I'll be on my mobile for urgent calls, and I mean urgent.'

As James swiftly exited through the emergency side door Fiona banged her in-tray hard on the desk, 'Ever since he's discovered Jason might be his son, he's become unbearable.'

'It'll only get worse,' Katie mumbled, 'the best we can do is weather the storm.'

****

'Katie, it's Adam Finch. I've just received news Dieanna Payne has passed away from a drug overdose.'

Katie sank down in a chair to absorb the shattering news. 'Oh Jesus, Adam I'm sorry to hear this, what happened? How on earth did she get hold of the drugs?'

'I'm not entirely sure,' Adam replied, sounding distant, 'I'm heading over to Tor Haven for a case conference with Clifford. Not for one moment do I believe Dieanna took her own life. From what I've been told so far, it sounds as if someone deliberately forced her to take those tablets.'

'If you can give me a few minutes to get ready, I'd like to come with you,' Katie pleaded, 'Can you pick me up on your way through town?'

'Sure, but once we arrive at the centre let me do all the talking. If Dieanna died under suspicious circumstances, no one's going to want to discuss anything with a forensic psychologist.'

Driving in to the sanatorium car park Katie spotted Barry Payne sitting on a wooden bench in the clinic grounds hands behind his head, a look of anguish covering his façade.

'I'm sorry for your loss,' Adam began softly, as he walked up to Barry, placing a comforting arm upon the man's hunched shoulders, 'have you spoken with Carl Clifford?'

Barry managed a brief nod, 'Yes, he believes Dieanna got hold of a bottle of temazepam, carelessly left in her room by one of the nursing staff. She was discovered in the early hours of this morning, slumped over a chair. I only hope she didn't suffer.'

'I'm sure she didn't,' Adam replied, hoping his words rung true, 'you do realise there will be an autopsy? This won't be an open and shut case given Dieanna's complex history.'

Barry nodded, 'I can't believe she took her own life. Why would she do such a thing?'

'We'll try to find those answers,' Adam reassured him, 'right now, I need to go and see Professor Clifford.'

Adam and Katie made their way to Clifford's office, where he was finalising a statement for the police. He looked up and scowled when the pair walked in. 'What?' he snapped, 'Finch, this is not good timing, can't it wait until tomorrow?'

Adam shook his head. 'Nope, in case you'd forgotten, Dieanna Payne was also one of my patients. I'll need to type a lengthy report for presentation to the Coroner, so now is as good a time as any for us to have our discussion.'

Clifford visibly stressed from lack of sleep, manifested in heavy bags ringing his eye sockets, reluctantly beckoned for Adam to take a seat.

'I wasn't aware Dieanna had any recent suicidal tendencies,' Adam questioned, note book and pen at the ready. 'Apart from a small outburst last time I was here, nothing seemed out of the ordinary, which in my opinion doesn't render her suicidal.'

'Whether you or I like it, Dieanna Payne swallowed those damned pills,' Clifford replied, 'if you go suggesting this was not an act of suicide we'll have police crawling all over the place, prying and probing, what good will that do anyone?'

'If Dieanna was murdered it can't be brushed aside,' Adam replied curtly, 'what do the nurses on duty say? Is anyone admitting to carelessly leaving the pills within Dieanna's reach?'

'Annie Pink, the nurse on duty at the time of Dieanna's death, has been employed here for over fifteen years and has never made this sort of mistake in the past. She assures me all medications were safely locked in the drug cabinet, as per standard protocols.'

'And you believe her?' Adam fired.

'Yes, I do. This is a classic suicide Finch, I don't know why you're trying to point the finger of blame. Dieanna was depressed, we both know that, somehow she managed to get hold of those wretched pills.'

'When did you last appraise Dieanna face to face?' Adam enquired, contempt present in his eyes. He had little time for the likes of Clifford who only ran places like Tor Haven to line their pockets.

'I met her yesterday, she appeared fine, quite settled in fact,' Clifford answered, turning a paperclip around in his fingers.

'I take it the Police have arranged a full investigation?' Adam questioned.

'Yes, I chatted with Doctor Nicholas Shelby half an hour ago,' Clifford scowled, 'he's been asked to carry out the autopsy. His initial reaction on examining the body was to suggest someone forced Dieanna to take the pills, he mumbled something about marks on her face, which suggested a third party. What rubbish. These scientific boffins don't know what they're on about.'

Adam was appalled, 'You mean someone literally rammed the tablets down Dianna's throat?'

'That's one pathetic theory. His other suggestion is, someone entered her room carrying the bottle of pills, wound Dieanna up about something, knowing this would have a catastrophic effect, and bingo; thirty pills were downed with a glass of water. In other words, whatever this person allegedly said, or did, resulted in Dieanna ending her own life.'

'Surely, the CCTV cameras will provide the answer?' Adam questioned.

Clifford gave a wry smile, 'Yes, if they were working. Unfortunately, all cameras in the wing where Dieanna resided, were removed last week prior to modern cameras being installed.'

'A bit coincidental,' Katie remarked, speaking up for the first time, 'and even if the autopsy proves Dieanna did ingest the whole bottle without assistance, it will be hard to establish what triggered it all.'

'I'm afraid you're right,' a reluctant Clifford concurred, 'we're going to speak with all the staff, quizzing them in relation to visitors sighted throughout the day, and any irregularities.'

Leaving Adam to continue his arm wrestle with the Professor, Katie slipped back into the garden to chat further with Barry. He was still seated on the bench, mumbling quietly to himself as Katie approached, sitting down next to him.

'I understand you and Dieanna never had children?' Katie remarked, trying her best to make light conversation.

'That's right,' Barry replied, without bothering to look up. 'Dieanna suffered from endometriosis, rendering her infertile.'

'Doctor Finch tells me Dieanna was a very talented artist,' Katie continued.

Barry smiled, looking up for the first time, 'Yep, for a number of years she taught at Plymouth Art College, her still life drawings picked up a lot of prizes; later on, she took up a teaching post at Salcombe Primary School.'

Neither spoke for several minutes. Instead, they sat listening to birds in the trees and the sound of a stream close by coursing under an ornamental bridge.

'I can only begin to imagine what you must be going through Mr Payne,' Katie said at last, breaking the long silence, 'if you want someone to talk to I'm happy to arrange one on one counselling sessions.'

Barry accepted the business card she slipped into his hand. He sat staring at it for a few minutes, before tucking it away in the breast pocket of his suede jacket.

'You know it was Dieanna's birthday today,' Barry enlightened Katie, 'she would have been thirty-eight. I used to think Dieanna could no longer remember specific dates, yet I was wrong. Why else would she decide to kill herself, today of all days?'

Katie stared at Barry as if she'd been shot. Daniel, Liam and Sonia Mercer had all died on their birthdays and now Dieanna Payne. This was more than coincidental.

'They also found a print of a painting in her room, which I swear was never there before,' Barry continued, 'I remember that particular photo being taken, the day Daniel Mercer died. It had some silly title: Falling Memories, I believe.'

'Are you ready to go?' Adam directed his question at Katie, joining her in the garden.

Katie was lost for words, unable to utter a response.

'Are you ready to go?' Adam repeated.

In a semi-trance Katie stood up, stuttering a brief goodbye to Barry then following Adam across the lawn to the car. They drove most of the way back to Bovey Tracey in silence, only chatting briefly when they turned off the motorway. Adam didn't question her lack of conversation, putting it down to a long harrowing day and although Katie trusted Adam, she wasn't quite ready to enlighten him on the bombshell news Barry Payne had divulged. Instead, she needed to call an urgent meeting of the forensics team to review all new evidence. It was now almost conclusive the deaths of Daniel, Liam, Sonia and Dieanna were related. It was no longer circumstantial that all four had died unceremoniously on their birthdays, there was also the added complication of the painting, which obviously played a leading role in all four murders.

Katie conjured up an alarming picture in her mind, realising there was complete certainty they were dealing with a serial killer. Each murder had been carried out with precision timing, characteristic of a psychopath.

****

'We've checked the tablets and caps found in the bottle next to Dieanna Payne,' Nick Shelby informed his colleagues, providing them with an update one week after Dieanna's death, 'full analysis confirms the proprietary description of all the drugs. Only a handful was 5mg valium, the rest a mixed bag of digoxin, endone and paracetamol. My initial assumption was an overdose, but now that seems highly improbable.'

James looked amazed, 'Well that proves the bottle wasn't left in the room by a careless nurse. Obviously, some unknown outsider planted the cocktail there.'

'Not necessarily,' Nick replied, 'who's to say one of the medical staff didn't do the deed, perhaps wanting to do away with Dieanna Payne, anything's possible. They could easily have thrown the deadly concoction together, deliberately leaving the bottle of pills within Dieanna's reach, most of the time Dieanna didn't even know what time of day it was, she was hardly going to question actions of the medical staff.'

'Okay, I suppose maybe a slight chance.'

'Now here's another interesting fact,' Nick continued, 'According to Katie, Dieanna was unable to fall pregnant, having suffered from endometriosis; yet, from a quick examination of the deceased, there is evidence she underwent a caesarean section. Something which will definitely need following up.

I have the time of death narrowed down to between 7am and 11am on the morning of the 24th, which we have since learned was Dieanna's birthday. The central doors of Tor Haven are unlocked at 8am allowing easy access for staff and visitors. This widens the possibility of the person who placed the drugs in Dieanna's room being an outsider, not necessarily one of the medical staff, which James of course has already proposed.'

'What time did Dieanna have her breakfast that morning?' Katie asked, jotting down notes.

'This is where things start to get atypical,' Nick told them, 'on the morning of Dieanna's death, she was due to have fasting bloods. Essentially, she was not permitted to eat or drink anything, anyone with access to Dieanna's medical notes would be aware of this fact, hence further opportunity to commit the crime.

We also need to keep in mind it's not only medical staff in the know, but kitchen staff as well. To complicate things further, Doc Clifford informed me all appointments and procedures are written

170

down in the red communication book kept on the central reception desk. Anyone walking past reception would have access to the book.'

'Hardly a source of confidentiality and highly unethical,' Fiona scoffed.

'Yes, I tend to agree with you on that score,' Nick said, 'however, as the book doesn't detail medical information as such, the facility is not crossing any illegal boundaries. The main point to make is, on the morning of Dieanna's death any number of people would have known there would be no delivery of a breakfast tray, creating an open invitation for our killer.'

'When are you doing the autopsy?' Katie enquired.

'I've not scheduled a full autopsy as I don't feel it's necessary,' Nick responded, 'instead, I've completed full blood pathology, which will confirm the cause of death. My final report will be presented to the Coroner this Friday, but sadly it won't provide any other information in relation to Dieanna's death. Her body will be released for burial and the rest will be up to the police.'

'Do we know what possible link there could be between all four victims?' Katie prompted DCI Rose, who had so far remained silent during the briefing.

Mick Rose cleared his throat, 'I don't have much information to hand. I did discover Dieanna Payne taught Daniel Mercer when he attended Salcombe primary school back in 2007. According to school reports, Daniel was a gifted artist, showing a lot of talent and flair for his young years. The headmistress also claims Dieanna had several heated arguments with Liam Mercer, over the course of many months. Liam complained art was a waste of time, Dieanna, in her capacity as an art teacher, naturally disagreed.'

'Where do you think the painting "Falling Memories" fits in to the scheme of things?' Katie enquired, 'after all; it appears to have a strong connection with our victims.'

'Not sure,' James broke in, 'although, there is one important thing to remember: Malcolm Frobisher QC is now the only one in the painting still alive.'

****

Katie reached for her mobile to make a call, 'Matt, it's me, what are you doing tomorrow night?'

'Is this a date?' Matt enquired, a flicker of eagerness creeping into his husky voice.

'Sort of,' Katie acknowledged, 'let's just say our entertainment for the night involves a break and enter, a bit of night time fun.'

'Ah... I think not. The last time I carried out this sort of narcissistic deed for you I aged ten years.'

'I happen to like older men,' Katie teased, 'come on, where's you sense of adventure?'

'It disappears whenever you have one of your mad ideas,' Matt replied coldly.

'I rather enjoyed my dream the other night,' flirtation creeping into her voice, 'the sex was extremely inventive; perhaps, we could do it again sometime. That is, if you're prepared to help me with my little plan.'

'Resorting to blackmail,' Matt said crossly, 'I really didn't think you'd stoop so low.'

'Oh, I can go as low as you like,' Katie laughed, 'be a sport and help me out, just this once.'

'What did you have in mind?' Matt asked, noncommittal.

'Ah, now that's more like it. I need to get into Dr Furlong's Salcombe surgery after hours, and gain access to a patient's file. Shall we say around eleven? It'll be dark by then, less chance of being caught.'

'The answer is no,' Matt told her bluntly, 'besides, what are you looking for? Surely, Furlong will give you what you want if you show a bit of leg.'

'He's the limp-wristed variety. Anyway, I know he'd flatly refuse, and I don't want to alert him to the fact I'm after confidential records. We haven't got enough time or hard-core evidence to go through the hassle of a subpoena.'

'Who's the patient?' Matt enquired, a tad curious.

'Dieanna Payne,' Katie responded, 'I want to find out more about the alleged child she bore, delivered via a C-section. The medical notes are bound to hold key information. So, are you with me on this one, or not?'

'I don't suppose I have much choice,' Matt sighed, 'if I don't go along with this crazy plan of yours I know you'll go it alone, which means more chance of you being nabbed, then I'd never forgive myself.'

'You're an angel,' Katie laughed down the phone, 'I knew you couldn't resist my sensual charm.'

Matt hung up, before he made a comment, he'd later regret.

****

The Salcombe surgery was shrouded in darkness, except for a small LED desk lamp shining through the shuttered window of the reception area.

'Are you sure there's no one about?' Matt hissed, duffle bag over his shoulder, walking quietly along the front path to the main steps.

'Stop badgering me, I've done my homework. Last ones out are the cleaners at 8:30pm. Have you remembered the security code I emailed through to you?'

'For fuck's sake, that's the tenth time you've asked me. Wait here till I switch off the alarm and cameras. I'll whistle when it's safe to head around to the back door.'

Entering the old house was relatively easy. Using his smart phone Matt logged onto the security company and accessed the supposedly secure client files by uploading one of his favourite decryption programs, having already checked it was possible earlier in the day.

Quickly noting the time, Matt remotely disabled the surgery alarm system using Katie's code, before entering the house to let his accomplice in via the back door.

'No lights and turn off your bloody pencil torch,' Matt warned, 'keep it quick, in twenty minutes the system automatically reboots and is fully enabled. We have to be out in fifteen.'

Katie as usual was full of bravado, enjoying the thrill of her twilight escapade. She knew exactly where to locate the patient files so strolled into the surgery with an abundance of confidence. Matt found her brusque attitude irritating as she hummed softly to herself, sifting through the unlocked filing cabinet. He kept glancing out into the gloomy corridor and checking the luminous hands of his diver's watch, afraid at any moment they'd be busted.

'Another five minutes,' Katie instructed, seemingly in no hurry to speed things up whilst Matt impatiently tapped his fingers on the office divider.

Katie carefully removed the loose pages from Dieanna's file before heading over to the photocopier, positioned on the other side of the room. Her eyes becoming accustomed to the subdued light of the desk lamp, Katie quickly scanned through the pages absorbing the information.

'This is all very interesting,' Katie relayed back to Matt, 'I think we may be on to something here.'

'Shut up and keep photocopying,' Matt hissed through clenched teeth, 'in case you'd forgotten, it'll be the devil to pay if we're sprung.'

'Shame you seem in such a rush,' Katie replied casually, 'I was about to suggest we make wild passionate love, right here next to the filing cabinet, my treat.'

Matt shot her a murderous glare, 'You are incorrigible, how much longer?'

'All done,' Katie replied, slipping the folder back into its rightful place, 'come on let's get out of here. You're beginning to make me nervous with your sighing and twitching.'

Hastily heading back down the corridor towards the side entrance Katie snared her plimsolls on the hall runner, instinctively reaching out to steady herself. Simultaneously, her silver charm bracelet caught on the handle of a small hall table. Katie fought to release the catch to set herself free.

'Shit, now the damn thing's fallen off,' she exclaimed loudly, 'I'd better look for it.'

'No time,' Matt cautioned, 'if we don't exit the premises immediately, the alarms will trigger. Don't risk it.'

'Yes, but the bracelet belonged to my late grandmother,' Katie wailed, 'it means everything to me.'

'Katie we've got to make ourselves scarce. Grab the file, let's get moving.'

Katie, visibly upset about the bracelet took a wrong turn, only to find herself opening the door to an old storeroom. Fumbling for her torch she switched it on, chillingly confronted by a person slumped over an old wooden luggage box. Her feet unable to move, Katie let out a high-pitched scream, bringing Matt bolting in her direction.

'Oh my God, a dead body,' Katie cried, 'Matt what are we going to do?'

'Make them a refreshing cup of tea, with a dash of lemon,' Matt replied in a dry tone.

'It's not funny,' Katie spat back, 'this is no time for joking. What if we get accused of their murder?'

'Impossible,' Matt told her, scorn in his voice.

'Anything's possible,' Katie replied, her complexion pale, 'Perhaps we should contact James, he'll know what to do.'

'That won't be necessary. If you'd stop panicking you might realise it's just a manikin, one of those resuscitation dolls used for

CPR. For goodness sake Katie, pull yourself together and let's get out of here.'

****

Chapter Twelve

Armed with documents obtained by Katie from Dr Furlong's clandestine surgery bust-in, James spent the best part of the following afternoon ensconced in a Totnes street side bistro comparing them with notes he'd borrowed from Professor Clifford and Dr Adam Finch. According to the last page of the report, Dieanna had undergone an emergency caesarean section at Torquay hospital, carried out by the high-profile obstetrician Professor Bruce Branson, one of Devon's best-regarded medicos. His Kingsbridge private rooms occupied the bulk of a discreet Regency terrace right on the promenade, with views along the town estuary. It was the date Dieanna gave birth which held fascination for James, it was a million to one coincidence.

James picked up his phone to dial Branson's number, desperate for answers. He got through to the obstetrician's over officious secretary who refused to put the call through to her boss. Eventually, after making several threats about obstructing justice, an angry Branson came on the line.

'I suggest in future you make an appointment like everyone else. Now say what you've got to say Sinclair, I have a room full of patients.'

James, ending a decidedly interesting call with Branson, drove over to Nick Shelby's lab bent on requesting some urgent DNA testing.

'What if you're wrong with your assumptions?' Nick enquired, removing labelled vials of blood and body fluids from James' portable dry-ice container.

'I won't be,' James replied with confidence, 'get them through as quickly as you can, I'm heading to Cardiff later today to guest speak at a National Law Enforcement seminar. When I return late Friday afternoon, I'm hoping you'll have come up with the goods.'

'Four days is really pushing the boat out, mate,' Nick scorned.

'I know, I know, but you have the qualified staff to do it, surely you can crack the whip. Fiona and Katie are flat out, at the moment it would take us at least ten days. There is plenty of sample DNA there and you have the latest automated diagnostic equipment. You won't have to run many, if any, complicated PCR multiple replications and there is no contamination or degradation. Easy Peasy.'

'You drive a hard bargain,' Nick sighed, gently shoving James out the door, 'go on, leave me in peace. The time you spend waffling is valuable minutes I can use on the tests.'

James laughed, 'I'll have my mobile switched on as often as possible whilst I'm away. Make sure you ring me immediately when the results come through. If I'm right with my assumptions, all these findings could just solve the case.'

****

Nick stood next to a female staff chemist staring at the polyacrylamide gel chromatograms in an Ultra Violet light viewing cabinet, the fluorescing blue DNA fragment pattern clear and defined. It was a classic electrophoresis separation, the complex ladder pattern for standard nucleotides of known molecular weight, contrasting with the simpler DNA human profiles, inherent in each of James' samples.

'I don't believe it,' Nick murmured, double checking his notes against his biochemist's and again cross matching the bars on the electropherograms. The DNA maps were unambiguous.

'You were right,' Nick's voice came through the speakerphone, confirming the results. 'I must say I was…'

James hung up, wrung out from his return drive from Wales. However, there was no time to lose. Climbing into the muddy Land Rover he reversed out of the service station at break neck speed, oblivious of horn blasts and rude gestures from other motorists. Driving as fast as he dared, James headed back to Moorland Forensics, taking the quickest route possible. Using hands free, he put in a few late-night phone calls before contacting his siblings, summonsing them to an urgent meeting.

'This had better be important,' Katie protested, splashing cold water on her face in a half daze, 'what sort of hour do you call this?'

'Two in the morning to be precise,' James mocked, 'if you arrive at the office before me, I'll have a strong black with plenty of sugar.'

Katie fought back a few unsavoury words as she hung up the phone.

The disgruntled sisters sat waiting impatiently as James drove through the security gate, pulling up at the rear of the office building. They watched him on video monitors step out of his car, then enter the building through the emergency side door.

'What's so urgent it can't wait until morning?' Fiona quizzed, clad in dressing gown and slippers.

'Interesting business attire,' James teased, taking a sip of scalding coffee handed to him by Katie. 'My apologies for interrupting your beauty sleep, but what I've discovered is breaking news; Dieanna Payne and Liam Mercer had an affair, Dieanna fell pregnant, giving birth to a healthy baby boy: Daniel Liam Mercer.'

'Hardly a crime,' Katie remarked, not feeling this piece of news was particularly earth shattering, 'lots of people have affairs, resulting in a love child.'

Her eyes locked keenly with her brother's as she made this poignant statement.

'You're not looking at the bigger picture,' James said, sounding fractious. 'Who do you think would be most impacted by this affair? Barry Payne of course, and if my theory is correct, Barry Payne is our killer. It all fits. A jealous husband will stop at nothing, even murder.'

Katie shook her head in disbelief, 'No, no, no…I don't think Barry is capable of murder.'

James stared at her blankly, 'Everything points to the man, and he certainly had good reason to hate Liam.'

'Yes, but Payne doesn't match the profile I've created on our killer,' Katie remarked, biting down on her lower lip. A habit she'd got into when she didn't agree with someone's comments.

'Your profiles are sometimes wrong,' James replied stubbornly, 'we're all allowed to make mistakes.'

Katie kept quiet whilst James continued with his theory, building a case against Barry Payne.

'According to Sergeant Smith at Kingsbridge Police Station, whom I happened to chat with less than an hour ago, he remembers several domestic violence reports being recorded on Barry and Dieanna Payne. Hardly a match made in heaven. It's obvious, Barry Payne would have held a grudge for years after discovering Dianna and Liam Mercer were carrying on behind his back. I believe Barry's anger grew until he hatched a plan to destroy the two people he resented most in the world. He was cunning with his moves, Dieanna had become traumatised from witnessing her son fall to his death, it was then an easy progression for Barry to have her

178

scheduled into Tor Haven. Once Dieanna was safely locked away, Barry had the time and opportunity to kill Liam Mercer.'

'That's nonsense James,' Katie protested, 'you're simply going on pure conjecture and what you want to believe. You don't have a strong case to back any of this up.'

'There's certainly credible reason to connect Barry Payne to Liam's murder,' Fiona reminded her sister, 'what we need to fathom, is why Barry waited so long to kill his victims? Barry could have murdered them ages ago and be done with it. Why wait years to seek revenge?'

'He needed time to plot a successful killing,' James replied, 'perhaps find the courage.'

'Bullshit, sorry it doesn't add up,' Katie retorted defiantly, standing firm with her belief, 'it seems too contrived and our killer is not always methodical. They act irrationally. I have a hunch you're wrong about this one.'

'Then prove it,' James snapped, heading out the door, closing it firmly behind him.

****

'You're both insane, I didn't kill Liam Mercer,' Barry protested, when James and DCI Rose turned up on his doorstep throwing their accusations around. James was relying on adrenalin to get him through the day, he'd managed a two-hour catnap following his return from Cardiff, severe fatigue clearly visible on his face.

'Then who did?' James shot back, framed in the doorway.

'How the heck do I know?' Payne retaliated.

'Can you at least admit you didn't like the man very much?' James continued, following Payne into the sitting room, where all three men took up residence on the three-piece suite, 'After all, not many men like their wives having an affair.'

'Yeah, I hated the bastard, but that doesn't mean I killed him,' Barry spat back.

'Bet you would have liked to have, perhaps you didn't even mean to kill him, was it an unfortunate accident?' James was pushing hard to get a submission.

'Oh, very clever,' Barry mocked, 'I see what you're trying to do, trick me into a false confession.'

179

'Let's try another way,' Rose instructed, stretching over the coffee table to come within inches of Payne's face. 'What can you tell us about Liam Mercer?'

'I detested the moron,' Barry replied with venom, 'he always got what he wanted: women, money, exotic cars, you name it, he had it all. I'm glad someone finished the prick off.'

'So why didn't you kill him?' James broke in.

'I couldn't be bothered,' Barry replied stoically, 'his life was a lost cause.'

'Did you ever threaten Liam?'

'Oh, yeah all the fucking time, every waking hour of my day was dedicated to making that man's life hell. It gave me a cheap thrill.'

'Don't mess with us, Payne,' James fired back, 'you're in enough trouble as it is. The toxicology report confirmed Dieanna had ten times the therapeutic dose of Temazepam in her blood stream, coupled with other illicit drugs, and your finger prints were found all over the bottle. I'd like to see you worm your way out of that.'

'Yes, but that doesn't prove I killed her,' Barry rising to the good-cop-bad-cop routine, an air of confidence creeping into his voice, 'you prove I killed my wife Sinclair and I'll take my hat off to you.'

'Oh, I intend to, and you know what else, Dieanna had a fine needle mark in the side of her neck; with modern forensic techniques I can discover exactly who was holding the needle and I sure as hell suspect it was you.'

James was bluffing but he wanted to see a reaction from Barry. His statement got the desired effect, but not the one he was expecting. A fragment of doubt crept into James' mind; perhaps, Barry hadn't been the one to kill his wife or her lover.

'You're losing your touch, Rose,' Barry shot at the DCI, 'you really want to know why Dieanna's affair with Mercer angered me. Well, I'll tell you. Purely on the basis he was an arsehole, and she could do better, no other reason.'

'Whatever,' Rose snapped.

'No, I'm serious, not that it's any of your business, Dieanna and I were never in a sexual relationship. We got together in order for her to provide financial assistance with the small hardware business I was setting up. Dieanna has a healthy trust account provided by her biological parents. I needed money and Dieanna offered to help.'

'You expect us to believe that?' Rose snorted.

'Believe what you like. My partner Graeham can verify quite readily that I'm homosexual. Grae and I have been in a solid relationship for a number of years and his brother happens to be the Area Police Commissioner. I hardly think Commissioner Cole will lie under oath if you put him on the stand.'

Rose and James exchanged glances. The tale Barry Payne was spinning seemed vaguely plausible and he was right; Acting Commissioner Cole would be a credible witness.

'Oh, and another thing,' Barry added as an afterthought, 'the day Liam Mercer fell off the cliff, I happened to be attending a trade fair in Munich, that's Germany. You should do your homework better, Rose. Surely, a reliable alibi is first base with any murder enquiry. Anyway, thanks for dropping by, and sorry to have wasted your precious time.'

'There's still the small matter of Dieanna's death,' James remarked, not moving from the couch. So, you may not have murdered Liam, but we still need to know where you were when Dieanna was murdered.'

'Nowhere near Tor Haven,' Barry replied. 'I would imagine the CCTV footage could confirm all that.'

'Yes, if it was in working order,' James replied sharply.

'Not my issue,' Barry mocked. 'Good day gentleman. You can see yourselves out.'

****

James located Gwyn Lacey sitting outside the art gallery, wine glass in one hand, cigarette in the other. 'Both bad habits,' Gwyn smiled, as James came to join her on the stone wall, 'if you've come to visit Lois, I'm afraid you've missed her. She's driven to Dartmouth for a meeting with her accountant. Can I help you with anything?'

'This is a social call. I'm here to purchase a painting,' James told her, 'a friend of mine is getting married later this month, and I thought a nice framed work of a local landscape would make the ideal present. Any chance you can help with my quest?'

'I'd be delighted to,' Gwyn smiled, stubbing out her cigarette, placing the butt into a nearby bin, 'let's get off this cold wall and go and see what might suit the happy couple.'

'Now I like this one,' James declared, glancing swiftly at the price tag to make sure it was within his budget.

'I can offer a discount,' Gwyn informed him, 'shall we say, three hundred pounds?'

'Sold,' James replied, shaking Gwyn's hand to seal the deal.

'I'll wrap it for you,' Gwyn carried the painting over to the counter, before reaching for some elegant silver paper with matching bow.

'Excuse me a moment,' James apologised, retrieving his mobile from the pocket of his jeans, which was persistently ringing. 'Yes, James Sinclair speaking. Who did you say the victim was; Tabitha Fletcher? How bad are her injuries?'

Gwyn, bubble wrap in hand listened in on the one-sided conversation, the wrapping completely forgotten. Her face looked anxious, her skin almost transparent.

James finished the call, turning to Gwyn, 'Sorry, I have to dash, there's been a shooting in Exeter. A young woman has been seriously injured.'

Gwyn remained silent for a few moments, before quietly asking, 'The injured woman, will she be all right?'

James looked at Gwyn, surprised at her intense concern, 'I won't really know until I get to the crime scene. My understanding is they are transporting her to Exeter hospital by ambulance accompanied by a Consultant Paramedic.'

'Then it must be serious,' Gwyn mumbled, collapsing into a chair.

'Sorry I really have to dash,' James said, heading to the door.

Gwyn's reaction to Tabitha's injuries puzzled him somewhat, but he didn't have time to mull over it.

****

Greeting the DCI in the Exeter Hospital foyer, James was taken aback by his friend's gaunt, pale complexion and dark sunken eyes, but more so by an uncharacteristic weak handshake, he refrained from comment.

'There's a forensic team at the crime scene, which includes Nicholas Shelby,' Rose began, 'I've informed them you'll drop by after our brief, to go through the primary evidence.'

James rubbed his chin, listening intently as Rose continued to update him.

'Tabitha Fletcher sustained a superficial gunshot wound to her right shoulder, coupled with a more life-threatening injury to her upper chest. I've spoken with the chief of surgery, who intends operating within the hour. I've tried contacting Tabitha's next of kin without success, there appears to be no listing and she has been placed in a drug-induced coma. I'll keep trying. The surgeon tells me Tabitha has a good chance of survival, but it will be a delicate operation, lasting several hours.'

'Do we know exactly what happened?'

'Not really. She'd mounted the first set of steps leading up to the court when she was confronted by a bloke shouting demands. There was only one witness, an elderly woman whose eyesight and hearing are not the best, not much to go on. Tabitha momentarily turned around to face the attacker, and that's when she was shot, pretty much at point blank range. Luckily for her, the bullet fired at her chest ricocheted off the large brass button of her jacket, otherwise the shot would have proved fatal.'

'Any idea what the man was after?'

Rose shook his head, 'Nothing was found at the scene, expect Tabitha's handbag. No crucial evidence. Not even the spent cartridge.'

James, surprised to hear someone calling his name, looked up to see Gwyn Lacey rushing towards him. 'James, I need to know if Tabitha's going to be all right,' she panted.

'I'm afraid we can't divulge that information,' James replied, his words measured and slow, trying to work out why Gwyn Lacey would be seeking him out at the hospital to ask this question.

'I'm an old family friend,' Gwyn piped up offering an explanation.

'Well in that case you can tell me where I might track down her next of kin,' Rose said, stepping forward, 'the surgical team intends to operate on Tabitha within the hour to remove a lodged bullet, it would be good if we can contact her family to let them know what's happening.'

Gwyn hesitated, 'Yes, I'll contact them to save you the trouble.'

'No need, I can do it,' Rose replied sternly, 'write down their details for me on the back of this card, and I'll see to it straight away.'

Gwyn looked distressed before starting to sob in an oversized handkerchief. 'You can't contact her father, he's dead,' she wept.

'What about her mother?' Rose enquired, his pleasant demeanour about to disperse. He had little patience with sobbing females.

James, having a bit more sympathy for Gwyn Lacey, put his arms gently around her sagging shoulders. 'Tabitha's mother really should be told about her daughter's condition, Gwyn. Please let us get in touch with her.'

Gwyn stopped crying, her face turning upwards, so her eyes met with James' pale blue ones. 'Tabitha's mother already knows,' she replied softly, 'that's why she's here.'

Gwyn managed a watery smile, 'James, I'm Tabitha's mother, only her real name is Michelle Langham.'

James had been struck by lightning, his expression competing with stunned silence, 'So that means you are…'

'Yes, Claire Langham.'

****

James reached in his pocket for his phone. 'Reg, James Sinclair here, when you were unearthing information in relation to Frobisher and Mercer, by any chance did you discover how they were shipping the suspect artworks?'

'It's only hearsay, nothing concrete mind you, but indications from a number of sources kept pointing towards a yacht which is moored on the Salcombe-Kingsbridge estuary,' Reg replied, 'on the last Sunday about every two months at high tide, without fail, weather permitting, that same yacht would sail to Cherbourg to off load the paintings.'

'The yacht's name?'

'Don't know. I never delved any further. I didn't want to end up on a slab. But I do believe it was an ex-classic ocean racer, a forty-footer, at least?'

'When we met you mentioned this information was passed on to the police, but they refused to do anything about it, is that right?'

'Yes, I told DI Wetherill, but nothing was ever followed up.'

'So, he was dismissive?'

'Shifty more like it. I don't even think he filed an official report.'

'I don't suppose you've had the chance to read today's Star, but on page seven Tom Markham has penned quite a scathing article implying in a roundabout way, that Lois St John has something to do with a couple of small Post-Impressionist fakes turning up at a Paris auction house, any idea why he'd suddenly decide to print this?'

'Beats me,' Reg replied, clearing his throat, 'perhaps she's pissed him off in some way. When a person annoys Tom Markham, he usually fires back by placing unsavoury annotations in the Star.'

'Thanks,' James hung up, then made another call, this time to DCI Rose.

'Okay, I'll see what I can do,' Rose replied, 'I can't promise I'll have much success. Wetherill guards his personal computer like a spider over a hole, all his paperwork under lock and key.'

****

Michelle Langham was sitting up in bed reading a paperback when James and DCI Rose entered the private ward in the newly renovated hospital wing. Two windows overlooked a small ornamental garden with a view facing north to the Dartmoor escarpment. The charge nurse on duty permitted a brief visit, warning the men not to exert or excite Michelle in any way.

'Michelle needs to rest,' the nurse informed them curtly.

For a brief few moments James was caught in a surreal place, puzzled who Michelle was, for so long he'd known the injured woman as Tabitha Fletcher.

'How are you feeling?' James enquired, pulling up a chair adjacent to the bed.

'Yeah, fine,' Michelle answered, putting down her book, 'a bit sore in places, but the Chief of Surgery is confident I'll make a full recovery.'

'We need to know exactly what happened that morning,' James urged, 'we understand how events may be sketchy or distorted, however it's vital we try to piece together fundamental details.'

Michelle took a deep breath. 'I woke up early, I was scheduled to present documents to the Clerk of Court before eight o'clock. It was a case Liam had been working on for several months and the legal argument was scheduled in Court No 4 that morning. Prior to his death, Liam briefed me on the matter and what needed to be done, he was quite specific. I knew where to find the supporting paperwork, hidden behind a large picture frame, no one apart from myself knew where it was kept. Liam reiterated the sensitivity surrounding the case.'

'Did you not think to relay any of this information when we initially questioned you about Liam's death?' James asked, slightly annoyed.

'I'm not a police woman or a forensic officer,' Michelle punched back, 'what might seem important to you, could quite easily shoot right over my head. Liam dealt with a lot of complex cases. If you examined them closely, a good percentage could be linked to his death.'

'Well, it would have been nice if you'd provided this snippet of information when the young female constable dropped by this morning to grab an official statement of the shooting,' James continued harshly, not for a moment thinking he'd crossed the line.

Michelle looked at him in disbelief. 'Given the fact I've suffered a severe traumatic experience over the past thirty-eight hours, supposedly I've got something known as Post Traumatic Amnesia, I think I'm doing pretty well under the circumstances providing you with any information, thank you very much.'

'Point taken, but what can you tell me about this particular case?' James softened his tone a notch.

'Details of a large quantity of amphetamines, "Ecstasy" I think, being shipped to Rotterdam in a container had come into Liam's possession. A senior Dutch Policeman by the name of Fred Van den Dolder I recall, contacted Liam advising they had arrested an English national for manufacturing the drugs, a Heath Mortimer from Padstow. The Dutch prosecutors were pressing charges against Mortimer and had a subpoena ordering Liam to surrender the documents. If found guilty, Heath Mortimer could be looking at a healthy stint in a Netherlands prison. I can remember someone mentioning eight to ten years.'

'Where are those documents now? I assume the proceedings didn't go ahead after what happened to you?'

Michelle forced a wry smile, 'I understand the committal hearings in Rotterdam were to be put on hold without those documents, and as you probably guessed, they were not in my bag when it was brought with me to the hospital. I'm assuming the gunman ran off with them.'

James grimaced, 'Honestly Michelle, I wish you'd relayed this news earlier.'

'Right now, I'm concerned about my well-being, not bloody court papers,' Michelle retorted.

James looked apologetic, 'Yeah, sorry, look I don't suppose you had the notion to photocopy those papers, did you?'

Michelle still angry, nodded, 'Actually, I did. After what happened to Liam, I didn't want to leave anything to chance. The file is safely locked away in a safety deposit box at my local bank.'

'Good work, if you can provide us with the particulars and an authority, DCI Rose here will pick them up first thing in the morning.'

Rose took the instructions from Michelle, stowing them away in his shirt pocket.

'So, what's the next step for you?' James asked with empathy, 'have they said when you can go home?'

'I am hoping I'll be discharged by the end of the week,' Michelle replied, 'I'll need physiotherapy on my shoulder and sessions with a psychologist to help me through the Post Traumatic Stress. In fact, your sister Katie has been recommended to me, she's meant to be an excellent trauma psychologist. Hasn't she authored some articles on PTS?'

'Yes indeed. And she'd also tell me off for asking this next question: can you describe the person who shot you? Did they say anything, before firing the gun?'

'I can do one better than that,' Michelle smiled, 'pass me that note book and pencil. I'll rough out a facial sketch.'

James hesitated for a split second, unsure how far he should push Michelle into submitting. He didn't want to be responsible for conditional relapse. With Michelle pointing unwavering to the items requested James eventually obliged, then sat back and watched quietly as her slender fingers danced effortlessly over the paper. Seemingly satisfied, she briefly nodded, before flicking the assailant's impression onto the side table.

'That's some talent you've got,' James remarked, glancing at the drawing. He then studied the sketch in more detail. 'Michelle, the man you've drawn is a police officer, Rose, have a look at this, will you.'

The DCI, who'd spent the last ten minutes idly gazing out the window, moved over to James, peering at the drawing. 'It can't be,' he stammered, 'Michelle, you've drawn an exact replica of one of my senior police officers.'

'That's the man who shot me,' Michelle insisted, pointing at her handiwork, 'I'd remember those sinister eyes anywhere.'

'Michelle, can you remember what the bloke said to you before opening fire?' James asked.

'Not word for word I can't, it was something along the lines of "Where in Christ's name are they, give me the damn, bloody documents or I'll blow your brains out". I turned to run up the Courtroom steps and that's when he opened fire. First in the left shoulder, where it felt as if I'd been punched hard, next thing I felt my chest explode, copping a bullet which narrowly missed my heart. After that, I must have blacked out. The next thing I knew I was being treated by two paramedics.'

James remained quiet for a few moments, pondering how to tackle the next subject, 'Michelle, my next line of questioning may seem unjust, but I have to ask, why did you try to kill Liam Mercer?'

'I didn't try to kill Liam,' she protested stunned, 'I only wanted to punish him for what he did to my father. I was angry. You both have to believe me, I'm not a murderer.'

'But you admit to carrying out carefree acts of violence towards Mercer, some more serious than others?' The DCI added.

Michelle nodded, before turning her face into the white hospital pillow.

'Time's up gentleman,' the smiling assassin broke in, standing guard at the door, 'I hope you haven't been upsetting my patient.'

'We'll be in touch. I'll get a full statement next visit,' Rose reminded Michelle, as they exited the room, heading along the hospital corridors to the main entrance.

'What do you make of all that?' Rose turned to James, stepping outside into a sultry evening.

'I feel sorry for her,' James replied, 'it can't have been easy coping with what Mercer did to her father.'

'Is she a murderer?'

'Hell, no.'

'What about my officer, do you think he's capable of murder?'

'Hell, yeah.'

****

'Jim Sinclair, I won't pretend this is a pleasant surprise,' Frobisher mumbled, opening the door to find James standing on his front door step, 'What do you want? If it isn't bad enough you frequently pester me at work, you're now stalking me at home.'

'I'd hardly call it stalking,' James told him, keeping the tone soft, 'this is not a business call. I'm here to ask a personal favour.'

'Of me, wow, you'd better come in,' Frobisher laughed, heading off down an expansive hallway waving for James to follow, eventually ushering him through a locked door and into an intimate study at the rear of the residence.

'I've recently unleashed a fine Bordeaux from the cellar,' Frobisher announced, 'just letting it breathe. Can I tempt you with a drop?'

'Sounds good.'

'You play golf?' Frobisher enquired of his unexpected guest, retrieving two red wine glasses from an imposing Regency Revival bookcase.

'Very badly,' James replied, savouring the woody taste of the vintage wine filling his palette.

'We must have a game sometime Jim, at Thurlestone Course next door, my club, help blow away a few unwanted cobwebs.'

'I'll check my calendar,' James politely responded, 'I've had dinner there on occasions, but never played a round. It's a pretty impressive location above the cliffs and beach, old smugglers coves and the like.'

'Right, that's the good part,' Frobisher continued, 'need to watch your step in the wind though, especially when a gale strikes, one wrong step and you can easily follow your wayward tee shot onto the rocks below. Now enough of my prattle, let's get down to business, what's this favour you require of me?'

James took a deep breath, 'I need a court magistrate to provide me with custody of my young son, his mother recently died in a car crash.'

'Surely that would automatically happen,' Frobisher replied, looking confused, 'You don't need special provisions for that.'

'It's complicated,' James continued, 'the mother of my son was married. Her husband unfortunately is a commissioned officer in the SAS. The relationship I had with the child's mother would be classed as an affair. In her husband's eyes, she would have committed adultery.'

'You do like to complicate things, don't you?' Frobisher muttered, more to himself than to James, who sat patiently waiting for a response. 'It's possible I can come up with something plausible, but this fella won't fair too well out of it. We'd need to make it look like he's been heavily involved in drugs or some other underhand activity.'

'But it can be done?' James pressed for clarification.

Frobisher leaned back in the armchair, inspecting his cut crystal wine glass. 'Ah yes, most definitely. Leave it with me and I'll set the wheels in motion.'

****

'I don't care what you think,' DI Wetherill shouted into the mouthpiece, 'I have kept your shady business under wraps for a couple of years now. I'm more than happy to continue doing so, but my price has just gone up.'

Wetherill remained silent whilst the other party spoke. After a few moments he continued his ranting, 'Look Frobisher, if you don't start paying at least two thousand pounds a week, I'll blow the whole operation wide open. I want the cash deposited into my personal bank account by ten o'clock every Friday, or you might find yourself falling from a very great height.'

Wetherill hung up, oblivious to a shadowy figure eavesdropping in from behind a pot plant screen in the foyer. Smiling, Mick Rose picked up his document satchel and stole quietly out of the office.

Chapter Thirteen

Wetherill sat with his arms folded, a picture of impatient anxiety. On his right-hand side, Arthur Hyde-Brown shifted uneasily in his chair, periodically glancing at a gold Cartier tank watch. James, an interested spectator, watched from behind a two-way mirrored wall with a female uniform sergeant, hoping Wetherill would crack under pressure.

'I hope this isn't going to take long,' the solicitor enquired, 'I'm due in sessions this afternoon. If you aren't going to charge my client, you have a very limited time before you need to release him.'

'I know all that,' Rose snapped, 'it'll take as long as it takes. Now I suggest your client starts talking. Detective, where were you on the 3rd of September around 7 o'clock in the morning?'

'I was out walking my dog,' Wetherill replied effortlessly.

'Are there any witnesses to this?'

'Nope, unless Laika, my faithful Keeshond can engage in the art of human conversation,' Wetherill laughed, 'she's a clever soul, I guess anything's possible.'

'Do you own a .45 Colt Automatic?' Rose continued, ignoring Wetherill's dry humour.

He shook his head, 'Nope, I'm not into guns, too messy if anything goes wrong. An American service pistol? You're kidding me, it's not even police issue. I'm a law-abiding citizen, that's why I joined the force. You, of all people, should know that Rose, how long have we been colleagues, five nearly six years.'

'Too long,' Rose muttered, not loud enough for anyone to hear.

'This is ridiculous,' Wetherill continued, 'I'm a senior police officer, why would I go around shooting people?'

'That's what I intend to find out,' Rose replied, 'I believe you knew the woman in question: Michelle Langham?'

Wetherill looked stunned, 'My understanding is the woman who was shot has been identified as Tabitha Fletcher, Liam Mercer's personal assistant.'

'They happen to be one and the same,' Rose replied triumphantly, 'you haven't done a very good job of protection if you allowed Michelle Langham to be shot now, have you? From all accounts you were the lead officer assigned to keep her out of harm's way after her father's demise. I'm guessing you took the job on to earn extra cash, not because you felt any loyalty.'

Wetherill raised an arm attempting to lash out at Rose, but his lawyer restrained him. 'He's not worth it Rod. They've no concrete evidence to charge you with anything, we'll be out of here soon.'

'I'm like a Pitt Bull Terrier when I get going,' Rose warned, 'if I don't charge you with anything now Wetherill, I'll get you sooner or later, that's not a threat, it's a promise.'

'Look, I'm due to have lunch with my wife in half an hour,' Wetherill informed Rose, pointing to the clock on the wall, 'I won't be popular if I fail to turn up. Now if we're done, I'd like to leave.'

Rose dismissed his plea for clemency, 'Have you ever had affiliations with Liam Mercer, other than those which were work related?'

'No, can't say I have. You know, I pity you Rose, you'll have egg on your face when all this blows over and I get the promotion I'm after. How embarrassing for you, accusing a fellow officer of attempted murder.'

'I don't recall mentioning the word murder,' Rose replied, 'but was that what you were trying to do?'

Wetherill yawned, 'Look, I'd love to stay and chat, but I'm afraid I can't help with your enquiry. You've brought in the wrong man. I'm on your side, I'm the good guy.'

'Quite the comic, aren't we?' Rose mocked, before turning to the burly officer standing by the door. 'Let him go. Perhaps when DI Wetherill's lapsing memory comes back, we can continue this conversation.'

'It would be a pleasure,' Wetherill eased to his feet, his lawyer doing the same. 'In the meantime, Mick, I look forward to seeing you back at CID first thing in the morning. Would you like your usual coffee brought to you, strong with three sugars? I'd hate you to think we'd be sworn enemies after this little spat. I'm happy to let bygones be bygones.'

Rose inwardly fumed, knowing he'd been beaten. Unless ballistics came up with some rock-solid evidence, they could pin nothing on Wetherill. They lacked a weapon and the evidence to raise a warrant for a search of Wetherill's house. So far, no eyewitnesses had come forward. Michelle Langham had been shot in the full light of day, and the assailant was still at large.

'Good day, gentlemen,' Wetherill remarked, standing by the door of the interview room, 'I hope you find the man you're looking for. He sounds dangerous, and needs locking up if you want my opinion. Best of luck.'

****

'Ah there you are Rose, you got a minute?' Wetherill grinned, striding up to stand directly in front of Rose, 'Firstly, I'd like to apologise for the stress I've caused you lately. I understand you were only doing your job, so I shouldn't bare a grudge. In fact, I have some information I think you'll find rather interesting.'

Rose wasn't impressed being cornered by Wetherill this early in the morning in the Police HQ car park, barely allowing time to reach the main steps. 'What's up?'

'Listen to me, it may be nothing, but I thought you should know, I've heard on the grape vine Malcolm Frobisher is up to his neck in some sort of dodgy, international artworks operation. What hard facts I've got to hand could well see this pathetic specimen behind bars.'

Maintaining a relaxed composure, a blasé Rose immediately realised the DI was trying to stitch up Frobisher, 'I'm certain "His Honour" has his finger in a lot of unsavoury pies, but I'm not sure what I can do about it,' Mick responded, all his suspicions instantly confirmed, Wetherill was not only a bent cop he was a back stabbing, snake in the grass, a poisonous one, possibly of the lethal variety.

'Fine, if you're not interested, I'll take things to a higher level,' Wetherill threatened, smugly. 'I'm sure the Commander will be prepared to listen.'

A few police officers walking through the car park appeared interested in the conversation taking place between Rose and Wetherill, lingering longer than usual as they made their way into the building.

Rose, knowing he was beaten, exhaled long and slowly, 'You'd better come inside, where we can discuss this in private.'

Wetherill, sitting comfortably in Mick Rose's office, unwound. 'I've been carrying out some covert surveillance on Frobisher during my off-duty time,' he began, 'I have it on good authority Sunday night at high tide, a boat will sail from Salcombe, en route to Cherbourg with a load of paintings stowed away in the hold. If you can gather a group of officers together, I'm confident you'll catch the Judge red-handed.'

****

'Everyone knows what they're to do?' Rose briefed his men, gathered in the modest tea room at the back of the station. He rubbed his pounding temple subconsciously, annoyed the raid on Frobisher's old boat shed had come about through Wetherill's referral, hidden behind deception and lies. He had to play the game, pretending he knew nothing of Wetherill's involvement, if anyone found out there would be lengthy interrogation.

With everyone nodding readiness, Rose gave the command to step outside and into the three, unmarked waiting police cars. Mercifully, when they arrived at the Salcombe boatshed, they would catch Frobisher in the act, arrest him and make it home just in time for a late supper. Rose was tired of chasing unruly citizens, he longed for retirement.

****

'Why do we have to hang around for the boss to arrive?' Phillipe Le Magnion grumbled an aside to his English counterpart. 'I want to get back to France and how do you say. Paint the town green.'

Alan Skelly smiled, 'Red, we paint the town red, not green.'

'What difference do it make, my friend, a colour is a colour. Read, popple, blue, green, they matter not.'

Phillipe stood up, moving outside the boat shed to light up a Gitanes. 'You English are so loyal. Me, I am happy to stick up the fingers and tell this boss…'

'Quiet, someone's coming,' Alan warned, 'get rid of your cigarette. You've already been warned to cut out the fags around the paintings. You'll get a kick up the arse.'

Phillipe muttered a few swear words in French, casually tossing his cigarette into the water.

'Is this what I pay you for?' Malcolm Frobisher bellowed, standing full framed in the doorway, a stubby finger pointing to a sleek ocean racer moored on the boatshed pier. 'Get the rest of those boxes loaded onto "Fool's Paradise" and don't let me catch you slacking off again.'

Frobisher pulled the folded sheet of paper out of his jacket and for the fifth time that evening methodically went over the type written notes, illuminated by the faint yellow glow from the boatyard office:

- Eugene Boudin –2 x Small Oils on Panels–"Bridge at Deauville", "Fishing Boats, Honfleur."
- Albert Marquet–1 x Small Oil on Canvas –"Ferry on Seine."
- Edouard Vuillard – Gouache on Cardboard–"Children in Garden."
- Louis Valtat– Large Oil on Canvas –"The Surfers."

Nodding slowly, he mentally ticked off each item against the list, which included another four large works by top and middle rank French Post-Impressionists. He scanned down confirming the three, medium size, marinescape oils by well-known painters from the Newlyn School, and two beautifully rendered English School landscapes.

'Excellent, all there,' he murmured to himself, happy with the quality this time. He knew Bentoit would have no complaints from this shipment, but they might need to look at reducing the frequency and quantity; there was no use flooding the market, one had to be very subtle and careful.

The pickings were rich, and the market for good names was rising in line with the dearth of quality alternative investment opportunities. Maurice's contacts with the Swiss dealers was a Godsend, there was always the opportunity to sell to a greedy collector, anxious to pick up a reputed work, or launder some funds at a discount, provenance or no provenance. He also fed them discreetly into the Parisian auction houses; when queries arose often falling back on the by-line… *'It's been in the Hermitage, Leningrad since 1935.'*

'I'll take over from here,' a muffled male voice broke in from across the opposite side of the yard, competing against the background cacophony of halyards banging against masts out on the moorings.

Frobisher squinted in the limpid light of a new moon hidden behind cloud, trying to make out the dark shadowy figure. 'What are you doing here?' he enquired, momentarily surprised as the person came into full view, 'I wasn't expecting you tonight.'

'In case you've forgotten this is my operation Frobisher. I give the orders and you obey,' his shallow laugh echoing loudly across the dark harbour waters, 'Oh, and Judge?'

'Yes?'

'I'm still waiting for the deposit of two thousand pounds to go into my bank account each Friday. Best you take care of it soon, there's a good chap.'

****

Frobisher annoyed at being told what to do, made no immediate plans to leave the boatshed, instead he bumbled around outside tossing up whether or not to sabotage the precious cargo. Used to getting his own way, his anger reached boiling point watching the boxes being loaded aboard the yacht.

After a fretful half hour pacing back and forwards on the sea wall, Frobisher finally witnessed "his boss" jump into a black Audi convertible and drive at speed through the open gates. Remaining in the shadows his temper gradually cooling, Frobisher systematically grafted out a plan aimed at revenge. A few photographs in all the right places and wham, he'd be framed.

Frobisher smiled at his prohibitive thoughts and choice of words. Pondering a next move, distinct voices drifting softly through the yard alerted his senses, unease raising goose bumps.

'Everybody in pairs and keep the noise down,' Rose whispered to his squad, as they exited the police vehicles to gather outside the boatshed yard, a few paces from the main doors. Buttoning up jackets to combat the chill of a light northerly, they waited the order to move, barely visible in the pale moonlight.

'We could have chosen a better night,' Senior Constable Dean complained, 'we're almost two hours behind schedule. Let's get on with it, or we'll catch pneumonia hanging around here.'

Rose checked his watch, ignoring the officer's grumblings. 'It's almost midnight, we move in at twelve ten precisely. I want everybody in there arrested and the crates carefully placed inside the police van due here from Kingsbridge in half an hour. We don't believe the men are armed and dangerous. If they are let the tactical response group take over, shooting is an absolute last resort. I want these people apprehended, with a minimum of fuss.'

'Any idea how many villains we're talking about?' Dean asked.

Fighting debilitating double vision Rose blinked to readjust his sight. 'Half a dozen max,' he replied, a wave of nausea sweeping over him, 'Sergeant Fletcher, please take over, I'll join you in a few minutes.'

Without explanation Rose disappeared to an old outbuilding near the wrought iron gates before throwing up. Damn headache was starting to get the better of him. Perhaps, it was time to get it checked out. Straightening up to re-join his colleagues, Rose jumped feeling someone tap him firmly on the shoulder. He turned around fearing the worst.

'DCI Rose, what a surprise. Am I glad to see you, I popped down here to check I locked up after my visit this morning, I have my suspicions something patently illegal is going on in my yard.'

Rose stood staring at Frobisher for several minutes, listening to him prattling on. He didn't seriously consider for one moment Frobisher had co-incidentally turned up at the boatshed. He must have been inside, spotted the arrival of the police cars, before coming outside to invent his little story.

'Excuse me, but I must re-join my officers,' Rose informed Frobisher, gently shoving him aside, 'I suggest you go home, I'll call you in the morning with an update.'

Frobisher broke out in a broad grin, 'Yes, mustn't get in the way of a police operation. Cheerio.'

Rose, anger building, re-entered the boatshed to witness his officers clamping handcuffs on two men. One protested loudly with a volley of French, most of which Rose understood.

Enduring the solo night drive back to Exeter, Mick Rose's frustration peaked as the realisation of Frobisher's clever ploy to make out he knew nothing about the inside operation hit home, an Oscar winning performance indeed.

Valiantly resisting lethal micro sleep, Rose for the umpteenth time fought off a wave of nausea, his eyes resolutely focused on the road ahead. Maybe he really did need to consider early retirement, his head continuing to pound away.

Night vision worsening, Rose fumbled in the glove box for an aspirin. What should have been a relatively quick trip back to the station, was taking an eternity.

****

'A very rewarding evening,' Rose informed James, passing him a cup of industrial strength coffee, the wall clock showing a little after three in the morning. Sitting in his office, summarising results from the boatyard "bust", Rose swallowed three strong painkillers, washed down with a large nip of rum. 'All up, my team has recovered fifteen works from five packing crates, all oil paintings save one,' he revealed, now suitably fired up after the night's escapade. 'We've been in contact with Professor Peter Wilder, a local art expert based in Honiton. He's the best we could get at short notice and he's advised for us before, but I'm reliably informed he knows his stuff, consults for a major London auction house. Should be here within the hour.'

James stifled a yawn, fingers massaging tired eyes, longing to head home and get some sleep. This was the third night in a row he'd managed on only a few hours' kip, the effects already starting to manifest themselves.

'I'm amazed to learn Wetherill was part of this whole scam,' James remarked, 'you have to be commended for flushing him out of the undergrowth. The long hours your boys spent on this operation eventually paid off. Undoubtedly Wetherill hit the panic button, hence the reason for speaking out.'

Rose laughed, 'Too right, Wetherill knew we were getting close to unravelling what was going on. He was cunning to turn the tables; dobbing on his own mates, divorcing himself from any involvement. It's just a pity we didn't catch Frobisher QC in the act. I've a feeling this was actually his brainchild, but as usual "His Honour" manages to extricate himself from the deepest hole.'

'Getting me out of bed this time of the night, it's uncivilised, bloody lunacy,' Professor Wilder complained loudly, bursting into Rose's office dressed in mandatory hound's tooth jacket, black skivvy and tan cords, his dishevelled appearance enhanced by a two days stubble and unruly long grey hair. 'I might have known you'd be behind this Rose, you bastard.'

The DCI laughed as the eccentric Professor whipped wide rimmed glasses off the bridge of a patrician, aquiline nose, staring intently with keen blue eyes at the two men seated before him. 'Now where in hell are these so-called forgeries, you're pestering me about? I sincerely hope this has not been a wasted journey. I'm not giving an appraisal on the bloody "Antiques Roadshow".'

Rose exchanged smiles with James as the three men strolled along the corridor to a locked room presided over by a uniform constable.

The paintings, free of the crates, were carefully stacked along the walls still clothed in protective bubble wrap.

Wilder positioned himself strategically in the middle of the secure storage area, his face lighting up as he surveyed the bounty laid out before him. He then moved slowly from painting to painting, in turn carrying out a cursory examination from a distance and close up.

'Remarkable,' the Professor uttered softly to himself, then turned to the other two observing the ritual with interest from the other side of the room. 'What we have here are works of consummate quality. Stunning paintings. I'd be happy to hang any of these on my walls.

My area of expertise is coincidently, the French Post Impressionists, and the four examples here are as good as any originals out there. Most of them purporting to be middle rank painters of course. However, the Marquet and Boudin are in the top rank and two exceptional paintings. I need a stronger light source; can you get me something?'

The constable hurried off, returning with a low voltage quartz desk lamp which Wilder used to closely examine the backs, frames and overall appearance of each oil, concentrating in particular on the brush strokes, surface appearance and colours.

Forty-five minutes and three cups of tea later, Wilder removed his reading glasses and delivered a preliminary verdict.

'The Newlyn School works are very, very good. As for the English School landscapes, not my domain strictly, but masterful attempts regardless. These are the best forgeries I've seen in a long time. Definitely up there with Han Van Meegeren.'

'Who's he?' interjected James now wide awake, soaking up every word like a sponge.

'You don't know the best forger of the 20th Century? His copies of Old Masters baffled the best experts and still do. Whoever executed these works I'm already willing to bet has most likely employed the same fundamental forging techniques. But in some ways, he or she whoever it may be is better; because they have succeeded in almost pulling off the painting techniques of three markedly different period styles.'

'You've lost me,' Rose stated, muffling a yawn.

'Well, to start,' Wilder continued, slightly irritated, 'you have to use original canvas, wood panels and cardboard materials from the correct period. Then the frames must be right, not to mention the paint pigments and varnishes in common use at that time. Van Meegeren went to those lengths. These paintings would, without question, fool a lot of my colleagues. The frames are correct and typical for the period, probably recycled from old unwanted paintings, and I reckon lab tests will confirm they used 100-year-old canvas duck, and stocks of cardboard. Someone went to a lot of trouble, almost fanatical attention to detail.'

'In conclusion,' he added putting on his jacket, hands in pockets, 'there is nó evidence of antiquing or artificial ageing used anywhere on these pictures. They undoubtedly ground their own pigments to the 100-year-old formulas.'

'So that's it? No UV or Infra-Red lamps like in the movies,' James queried.

'Nope. That's my opinion, more than sufficient. I wouldn't even bother wasting time and effort on X-Ray and laboratory examination. These guys did their homework.'

James and Rose swapped looks whilst Wilder threw one final distant glance over the artworks.

'You know, you have to hand it to them. I don't think I've seen a truly convincing Newlyn forgery before this…for twenty minutes I thought I was looking at a lost Stanhope Forbes,' he declared with authority, pointing to a large marine oil of fishing boats, 'very clever to boot, aping works by painters represented in the Hermitage Museum archives. High value artists also chosen, but not too high, essentially the lower to middle dollar bracket. They were onto a good thing, could have been getting away with it for a long time, very smart, very intelligent. Now if that's all gentlemen, I'll be off. I'll invoice as usual, my fees don't come cheap. Goodnight.'

****

Malcolm Frobisher hurried along the narrow country lanes, periodically slowing to check the surrounds, his face mirroring mild concern. Why tonight of all nights did his car have to break down; especially after a full service two months prior that cost him a fortune, the Porsche allegedly receiving a clean bill of health.

Reaching into the back pocket of his trousers Malcolm retrieved his mobile punching in the numbers for a local mechanic. After five rings the answer machine kicked in advising the garage was closed until eight o'clock the following morning. With little chance of a taxi reaching him any time soon and cursing the expired AA membership, Malcolm plugged resolutely on towards his Thurlestone property one and a half miles away, anxious to reach safety before the building clouds opened up. His short fat legs drove him on, his breathing more laboured and irregular with each passing step.

Stopping to press hard on a recurring stitch, Malcolm looked behind and to the sides, sensing someone or something, close by, in the darkness. For the first time in an eon he felt fear, foreboding muddling his brain.

You're being silly Frobisher, the phrase going over and over. *There's no one around. It's just a colourful imagination playing tricks.*

Fifty-five exhausting minutes later, a relieved Malcolm rounded the last bend, praising God when the two storey Edwardian property hove into view. Already gripping the front door key, he turned it in the lock stepping inside and away from the cold inhospitable evening. Flicking on the hall light and disarming the security alarm he ambled into the lounge to fix a very large brandy; a deserved reward after his forced march. The plasma television was switched on in the kitchen to catch the evening news whilst he warmed up a plate of left-over pasta.

From a tray balanced on his knee he devoured the meal with gusto, eventually dozing off at the start of a movie. He was woken an hour later by a persistent front door chime.

'Damn and blast,' he cursed aloud, slowly forcing his portly figure upright, urging stiff limbs into motion. Visitors weren't on the agenda this late on a Friday night, on odd occasions when Lois decided to pay a visit she always phoned well in advance. Lois knew Malcolm hated surprises.

'Who is it?' Malcolm called out from behind the closed door, not about to open it to a complete stranger.

'Malcolm it's only me, sorry to call around so late at night but I'm keen to get your estimation on an item of Art Nouveau art glass I picked up at auction this afternoon. May I come in?'

Malcolm undid the security bolts on the door before opening it wide to allow access for his visitor.

'What a pleasant surprise,' he smiled warmly, 'I'm just having a night cap, care to join me?'

'Count me in.'

Malcolm ushered his caller into the lounge room, letting out an unexpected sneeze. 'I think you've been a bit heavy handed with your toilet water tonight,' he chuckled, 'What's your poison?'

'Poison, what a lovely choice of words, I'll have a Martini on the rocks, a double.'

'Wise decision, now where's this lovely piece you've come to show me. Knowing your impeccable taste, I am only expecting the finest.'

'All in good time, I feel we have some unfinished business we need to attend to first.'

'You always were one to spoil a good moment, what can you possibly want to talk about at this time of night?'

'The reason so many people have already needed to die,' Malcolm's visitor smiled, 'of course, I blame you as much as I blame myself. It seems so long ago now, but it has caused lots of heartache, wouldn't you agree. We were foolish Malcolm, we didn't think about the consequences. God knows we could have prevented it all if we'd not been so young and foolish.'

'Now hang on a minute, that's rubbish and you know it,' Malcolm retaliated, gesticulating with his wine glass, causing a few drops to spill onto the carpet, 'stop living in the past and look for the future, that's my motto.'

'Oh no, I can't do that. It's far too late. Those who are responsible must die.'

'What the hell are you doing? Put the knife down, are you crazy?'

'I expect I am, but it's too late to ask questions. I'm sorry Malcolm, I really am.'

'Oh shit, no, for God's sake put the knife down, stop, I beg you to stop…'

****

In a state of shock Katie placed the phone gently onto the console and turned to her brother. 'That was Mick Rose, Mal Frobisher's been found dead in the study of his Thurlestone home; stabbed several times in the chest with a six-inch knife.'

James looked up from his laptop disbelief in his eyes, sitting motionless for about ten seconds staring straight ahead. Snapped back to reality by the phone ringing on his desk he suddenly jumped up and sprinted for the side emergency exit, grabbing his jacket, keys and forensic kit in the process.

'If that's someone asking about Frobisher, hang up. Our Judge is big news, the calls will be coming in all day.'

He disappeared out the door, slamming it forcefully behind him.

'Frobisher dead,' Fiona exclaimed, sinking into a chair, 'wow, who'd have thought it?'

'If you want my honest opinion, I'm surprised it's taken this long,' Katie said, 'I never liked the man. I doubt he had many friends.'

'All the same, no one deserves to die so traumatically,' Fiona commented, cringing as the phone again burst into life, 'I bet that's Tom Markham looking for the gory details. Come on, let's get out of here, before we're driven insane.'

Katie followed her sister out of the office and started up the High Street, heading for the nearest café.

'Hey, wait up girls,' Tom Markham shouted from across the street.

'Oh shit,' Fiona cursed under her breath, 'there's no stopping that rat. Quick, hurry, we might outrun him.'

'Not in these shoes,' Katie proclaimed, as Tom Markham caught up with them, panting slightly.

'What do you want?' a livid Fiona asked, not slackening her pace.

'Is it true the honourable Mal Frobisher has been murdered?' Tom enquired, his eyes flashing with excitement, 'Rumour is, he was extensively dissected with a six-inch filleting knife. Can you confirm that?'

Fiona spun around, 'No comment.'

'Ah, so it is true, come on Fi, give us the gossip,' Markham pleaded, stepping in her way so she couldn't escape, 'I have a newspaper desperately in need of a good juicy scoop.'

Fiona rubbed her chin, appearing to be deep in thought, 'Okay, I suppose on this occasion it won't hurt to give you some details.'

'Are you mad Fiona, it's not acceptable giving the likes of Markham confidential information,' Katie broke in, grabbing her sister's arm, 'James would kill you.'

'I doubt he'd do that, or he'll be up for manslaughter,' Fiona chuckled, 'no Katie, I understand Tom has a job to do. The public wants to know what's going on, and morally we can't stand in the way of a good story. It's the least we can do for a desperate journalist and his struggling rag.'

Katie stared speechlessly whilst Tom produced his mobile phone ready to record the conversation. For a split-second Katie wondered if her sister was suffering from mild heatstroke, after a lunchtime spent in the office courtyard.

'Fire away,' Tom instructed to Fiona, phone at the ready, 'Give me what you've got.'

'Only if you promise to keep this exclusive, for the Star only,' Fiona warned, 'you can't allow leaks or sweetheart deals with the large tabloids, we don't want them getting wind of this just yet.'

'Mum's the word,' Tom shot back earnestly, trying to conceal excitement. Finally, he'd won over Fiona Sinclair, she was putty in his hands.

'Right, well what I can tell you is this, it was Colonel Mustard, in the Library with the Candlestick,' Fiona blurted out, before bursting with laughter, 'come on Katie, forget the coffee, why don't we go for something stronger. See you around Markham. I look forward to reading tomorrow's Star. I've always thought Mustard was the one to watch.'

The women strode off arm in arm, leaving an angry Tom Markham in their wake, mouthing obscenities.

'That took the smirk off his face,' Fiona grinned, entering the confines of the pub, 'I'll have a large gin and tonic, ice and lemon.'

****

Chapter Fourteen

The news of the high profile Judge's untimely demise had already spread like a forest wildfire through the immediate community by the time Nick and James arrived at the residence sited on the cliff tops overlooking Thurlestone.

Nick swung his vintage 280SL into a reserved spot between a Sky News OB van and a patrol car. Fighting their way through a media scrum, the pair flashing ID, gained immediate access through police cordons.

Nick cornered the senior crime scene officer: Ridley Kemp, whom he vaguely knew by sight. Kemp a "no nonsense" sort of guy knew his stuff, gained from years spent working alongside some of Britain's top criminologists. He patted Nick firmly on the back, moving aside so the lads could officially enter the crime scene. 'I'd appreciate assistance moving off some of the buffoons,' Ridley remarked, pointing to a few junior police officers lingering by the side of the house, 'half these guys here have never worked on a crime scene investigation before. They belong shuffling papers behind a desk, not here getting under my feet. Work some of your magic Shelby, before all evidence is wiped clean.'

'I'll see what I can do. Might get them to do a walk around the surrounds, what do you think?' Nick replied, heading towards the front door of the imposing Edwardian two storey, and showing his ID badge to the two senior officers guarding the entrance. They raised the yellow tape to let him pass, James closely following behind.

'Take a look at this,' Nick whispered, shooting an initial cursory look at Frobisher's corpse, slumped awkwardly in a blood soaked and splattered lounge chair, 'See here James, there's a large contusion on the side of Malcolm's forehead. Someone took something heavy and gave him a few good whacks.'

'A burglary gone wrong?' James suggested, taking a closer look at the indicated bruising.

'It's possible, but somehow you've got to doubt it,' Nick replied, removing a tape measure from his forensic case, 'whoever did this knew where to deliver a strike to cause maximum damage. I'm almost certain the initial blow rendered Frobisher unconscious, he was then stabbed repeatedly in the chest and any subsequent blows would have nicely finished him off. It's my guess the assassin held the blunt instrument in the left hand, the knife firmly in the right. There's every possibility Frobisher only saw the knife coming towards him, so the blows would have been unexpected.'

'Any sign of a murder weapon,' James continued, scouting around before checking in with a junior tech on the scene, 'no, it's as we guessed, no weapons and no signs of forced entry. Let's have a look in Frobisher's study it's through this door, second room on the left.'

Nick looked questioningly at James, 'How on earth do you know that?'

'I, er, well, instinct I guess,' James replied meekly, his cheeks reddening as he frantically tried to invent a plausible excuse.

Nick twigging James was lying turned on him. 'You've been here before, haven't you? Fuck James, what are you playing at? If anyone finds out you've entered the premises of a murdered man, you'll be an immediate suspect. Exactly when were you here? On official business I hope, which will at least give some credence.'

'The night before last,' James answered, lowering his voice, afraid they would be overheard by forensic officers in the immediate vicinity, 'I had some private business with Frobisher, nothing that concerns you, or anyone else for that matter.'

'It bloody well does concern me if there's evidence of you being here,' Nick rebuffed, 'you're a complete idiot, James. You were here only a day or so before Frobisher was murdered. What possessed you?'

'Well, for a start I had no idea he was to be bumped off,' James fired back.

'Yes, that's as maybe, but you've really compromised your position. I've a good mind to report it to Rose.'

'Be my guest. The point being, if you turn me in, I'll happily do the same to you.'

Nick came within inches of his friend's face, his features tense, anger surging, 'Meaning what exactly?'

'Meaning, it's amazing how the cocaine you were meant to be testing for me miraculously disappeared. We both know what really happened, don't we?'

Nick forced his hands behind his back, afraid of what he might do, 'You wouldn't dare.'

'Wouldn't I? Why would I let you destroy me, when I can easily do the same to you?'

A bleak silence descended for several moments, then Nick spoke, 'Let's forget we ever had this conversation Jim, it won't do either of us any good. We've a job to do, so I suggest we do it.'

'Suits me.'

James, his tongue guarded, ventured outside, anxious for fresh air to regain composure. It wouldn't do for a dispute to erupt between the allies, he valued Nick as a friend and long-standing colleague. After ten minutes James re-joined Nick in Frobisher's study, where they continued the probe in silence before Nick finally spoke.

'Now this is interesting,' he remarked, moving over to a small drinks cabinet sniffing the contents of two glasses covered with dusting powder. 'One was drinking Scotch, the other a dry Martini. I assume we've already tested for finger prints?' The question directed at Ridley Kemp, scouting around outside the study.

'We've only managed to lift prints from the Scotch glass,' the SOCO confirmed, 'those may be Frobisher's paws. The Martini glass is void of any prints, a clear indication the owner either didn't touch the glass, wiped them or they were wearing gloves, I'll put my bet on the latter. We can't even find any lipstick marks around the rim, so at this stage we will need to take the evidence away for further testing. We may be wrong thinking the guest was a woman, but I have a suspicion they might have been.'

'Did Frobisher die almost immediately?' Nick quizzed.

'You'll have to ask Ingalls, the duty forensic pathologist. He just left in a patrol van, been here for a couple of hours, I think he had an urgent appointment or something,' Ridley advised.

'Did he give you a preliminary?' Nick asked.

'Yeah, he ran me through it. The blow to the head didn't actually kill him. Indications are he suffered a massive heart attack during the knife attack. Again, that's something Ingalls can't be certain of until they conduct a full autopsy, although there is tale tell signs around the lips to support the theory.'

Nick and James left Kemp and two others setting up for photos whilst they conducted a tour of the rest of the house.

'It's big enough to double as a guest house,' James acknowledged, taking in one of seven spacious bedrooms, most en suites, 'Why on earth would one person want to rattle around in a place of this size?'

'That, we may never know,' Nick replied, picking up an opalescent, designer glass bowl decorated with parrots, sitting on a bedside table. 'Nice piece, must be worth a bit. Somehow it doesn't quite fit in with the rest of the furnishings. It may not be important, but just in case I'll have someone bag it, so we can take a closer look when we return to the lab.'

'You sure have a keen eye for detail,' James remarked with admiration, 'to me, the bowl is just an ornament, looks like early Lalique, expensive I must say, but nothing unusual about it at all.'

Nick laughed, 'I think I've spent too many years working at the Home Office. It tends to get you thinking along different tracks. At times it's useful to be pedantic, other times I find I keep chasing my tail. Come on, let's see what else we can discover in the old boy's den.'

'We've found this note sir, thought you should know,' one of the SOCOs informed Nick, holding out an outstretched hand.

Nick carefully took the folded piece of paper in his gloved hands.

'It appears to be from Claire Langham,' Nick enlightened James, quickly scanning the contents, 'hardly a love letter, it contains a fair bit of hatred and the desire to cause Frobisher serious harm.'

'Well it makes sense, seeing Frobisher was a major contributor to her husband's suicide,' James replied, 'come on Sherlock. Let's get out of this elaborate address with its vast rooms, for some reason it's giving me the creeps.'

****

'How did everything go today?' Katie enquired, keen to get the inside on events at the Thurlestone property.

'Okay,' James answered, helping himself to fresh coffee from the machine, and easing a weary frame onto the reception settee. 'Got some evidence, possibly implicating Claire Langham in Frobisher's murder. Essentially from stuff in a rather nasty letter found at the Judge's house. Mick Rose will need to bring her in for questioning. If she was intent on seeking revenge for her husband's suicide, she's our killer, armed and dangerous.'

'Her profile doesn't match,' Katie informed James casually, 'from the picture I've drawn already on Gwyn Lacey or rather Claire

Langham, she's not your typical passive aggressive type which our killer patently is. Claire using a knife? I don't think that's in her makeup.'

'Motive and opportunity are what we're really looking for,' James said stubbornly, not in a mood to entertain reason. Katie had proven his theories inaccurate in the past but this time he hoped his sister was wrong with her assumptions. James finally wanted to nail someone for the recent spate of murders, time was running out and he needed a breakthrough. 'Besides, how well do we really know this woman?' he questioned, 'Up until now we never thought her to be hiding under another persona, leading a double life. A person capable of such deception could well be capable of murder.'

'The two don't necessarily go together,' Katie continued, strident passion showing in her voice. Confidently relying on an in-depth knowledge of psychology, she was always up for a good banter when she felt passionate about a cause.

'I would type our killer as someone more conservative, disguising their true colours,' she informed her brother, 'in my opinion if Claire Langham was a killer, she'd quite happily shout it from the rooftops. Sorry, but I think you're wrong on this one, Brother.'

****

'Hello James, you're the last person I expected to bump into on this fine summer morning. You've strayed a fair few miles from home. Opting for water scenes, rather than rugged moorland?'

James smiled, 'I often like to revisit a crime scene as it helps me to stay focused.'

'I don't envy your line of work,' Rosemary Scott-Thomas remarked, adjusting the orange silk scarf around her head to keep off the sun, 'it's hardly upbeat.'

'On the contrary, it can be very rewarding when things fall into place, especially when we catch the villain,' James responded, 'forensic science can be fascinating, the simplest tests can toss up the results we're after.'

Rosemary laughed, 'Yes, I guess there is that aspect. Are you in a hurry James, or would you like to join me for breakfast?'

'I've a meeting in Plymouth at eleven-thirty,' James replied, glancing at his watch, 'breakfast might be pushing it, but I've time for a coffee.'

'Perfect.'

Within ten minutes James and Rosemary were sitting once more in Rosemary's drawing room, taking in the panorama of the estuary.

'I never asked where you lived prior to your move to Devon,' James remarked, stirring his coffee with a delicate silver spoon, 'I'm guessing London.'

'Then you guess wrong,' Rosemary laughed, 'we moved from Warwickshire. The only difficult part for me was leaving behind family and friends.'

'I don't suppose you get much time to enjoy the Devon countryside with all the entertaining you do,' James remarked, allowing Nancy to replenish his cup.

'That does have its drawbacks,' Rosemary answered, 'But I enjoy being a social butterfly. As a youngster I was constantly exposed to the whole social roundabout, you know, garden parties, cocktail evenings, polo and such.'

'Quite a privileged upbringing,' James laughed.

'Yes indeed. How about you James, tell me about your family.'

'Quite boring by comparison, a typical middle-class adolescence I suppose. Saying that however, as a result of dad's thoroughbred concern, the family has developed strong contacts and friends in the establishment over the years, especially within the equestrian and racing elite. Lord and Lady Allingworth and the Earl of Newbury are often around at the family house. I recall as a youngster, the Aga Khan dropping by on the occasional, unofficial flying visits in his jet to our stables.'

'How impressive,' Rosemary beamed, 'you underestimate your refined connections, dear boy. There's nothing common about you Jim Sinclair, I instantly recognised your fine qualities the moment we met. You need to hold on to your upper-class status, make sure you marry a sophisticated woman, preferably a rich one. Once the bloodline gets compromised all sorts of failings occur. Common is to common and all such things.'

'Can I ask you a personal question, Rosemary?'

'You can try. I may not provide you with an honest answer,' her laughter was sweet, intoxicating.

'I'm intrigued to know how you became Daniel Mercer's godmother.'

'Oh, that's an easy one to answer,' a bemused Rosemary turned her gaze back to the waterfront, 'I initially came across Sonia when I was on the organising committees for local charities in Somerset. From there a friendship developed. Chatting one morning I was shocked to learn young Daniel had not been christened, so I took it upon myself to arrange a service. Sonia naturally asked me to be godmother and I readily agreed. Between the two of us we arranged a lovely service at St Winwaloe's Church up the road. I enlisted the Archbishop for the ceremony, the dear old boy owed me the odd favour, from memory there were over two hundred guests at the Church and later back here. I even decorated the church myself as I wanted to make the occasion very special.'

'You seem to always place other people's wants in front of your own, very commendable,' James said, declining a third cup of coffee, 'I assume you don't have children of your own Rosemary, I never hear you speak of any?'

'That's where you are wrong,' Rosemary replied softly, her eyes misting over, 'I had two children, a boy and a girl, sadly both have passed away. I often tell myself they were taken to the Kingdom of Heaven as God's need for their love, was greater than mine.'

James felt a lump forming in his throat. 'I'm so sorry,' he muttered not sure what else to say.

'Sometimes smiles on the outside can be sadness on the inside,' Rosemary stated, staring out of the window, 'remember James when you go through life, not every happy face is a picture of bliss. Now, I hate to break up our intimate little chat, but if you don't get a move on you'll never make it to Plymouth before lunch. If you miss your meeting, I'm sure you'll be blaming me for keeping you here so long.'

James got to his feet. 'Thanks for the coffee Rosemary, it's been nice chatting.'

'Anytime, hopefully next time our paths cross, you won't be in such a rush.'

****

Claire Langham's mid-morning cleaning assault on the bathroom of her two-bedroom Salcombe townhouse was rudely interrupted by firm, repeated knocking on the front door. Hastily checking her appearance in the vanity mirror, and discarding bathrobe for light grey tracksuit, she hurried to the glass-panelled door, cursing the premature halt in her Tuesday morning routine.

'What time do you call this?' Claire laughed, genuinely surprised to see the unsmiling faces of James Sinclair and Mick Rose before her. Quickly throwing a furtive glance up and down the street, wondering if any inquisitive neighbours were behind twitching curtains, she opened wide the door and motioned the pair to come inside, 'I've not been up long, and I've certainly not had time for breakfast. A cup of tea?'

'This is not a social call,' Rose began, stepping over the threshold and following her into the kitchen, 'we have more questions, this time they concern the hostile note you penned to Malcolm Frobisher, which he received only a matter of days before his murder. You were thoughtful popping the date in the top left-hand corner, you didn't think about that when you dropped it through the letterbox, did you? Now what can you tell us about that letter?'

'It was a letter, that's all,' Claire replied stubbornly, dropping tea leaves into a china teapot.

'Not a nice letter,' DCI Rose remarked, 'in fact, I'd go as far as to say quite threatening.'

'I wrote it in a moment of despair and anger,' Claire told him, opening a cupboard to retrieve three glass mugs, placing them onto the work bench, 'I'm not the first person to write idle threats, yet not carry them out.'

'You must have hated Mercer and Frobisher, possibly enough to kill them?' Rose casually said, 'After all, ultimately they were responsible for the death of your husband.'

'Oh yes, I despised them,' Claire replied, her face tense, the colour in her cheeks deepening to crimson, 'I won't deny, on several occasions I wished them dead.'

'So, after years of grief you finally decided to seek revenge, by first killing Liam Mercer, then Frobisher,' Rose alleged, 'I'm still working out why Dieanna and Sonia had to go but I imagine there's a simple explanation.'

Claire ignored Rose, instead turning to James for answers, 'Do you really see me as a serial killer, James? If you do, you don't know me very well.'

'I hardly know you at all,' James remarked, 'shall I keep calling you Claire or would you prefer Gwyn? It's up to you.'

'Claire will do nicely, thank you,' her tone curt, eyes full of disdain, 'for the record, I didn't kill anyone. Sure, I came close to thinking about it, but what would be the point? A life in prison is no way out. Let me tell you a little story James, my marriage to Michael was not always picture perfect, we argued like most married couples. There were times Michael would drink heavily, the end result often physical. As much as I loved my husband, I was not about to seek the ultimate revenge for his memory. I've also done a lot of things I'm not proud of, but to take life from another person is not one of them. Michelle and I deliberately sought out Frobisher and Liam, in order to get inside their heads, mess with them a bit. We wanted to destroy them as they had destroyed us, but the truth is James, neither was worth it in the end.'

With her brief heartfelt outpouring over, Claire turned her attention back to the serious business of morning tea.

James leaned back in his seat, running fingers through unruly hair. He had been so convinced Claire was the killer, now tangible uncertainty had surfaced. He took a punt with his next question, 'How did you get involved with Frobisher's art fraud scheme in the first place? Was that co-incidental or another of your little schemes to mess with his head?'

Claire let out a long drawn out sigh, 'One night I was working late with Lois in her studio. We were mucking around copying early expressionist paintings. Frobisher walked in, and soon spotted my freakish talent as a copy artist. A few weeks later he blackmailed me into working for him, forging paintings to be sent abroad. He and his associates on the Continent arranged all the old materials, frames, what pictures to paint, by who and even the fake titles. They also ground the period pigments and oils, would you believe.'

'In what way did he blackmail you?' James asked, downing a coconut cream.

'By threatening to divulge my real identify if I didn't go along with his shenanigans,' Claire replied quietly, 'Malcolm Frobisher was a shrewd man, I doubt many people got the better of him. You may have also guessed, he used me for sexual favours.'

Both men were silent as Claire buried her head in her hands.

'How did Malcolm know who you were, I mean your true identity?' James enquired, as Claire slowly regained her composure.

'He'd seen me during the trial of my husband,' Claire replied wistfully, 'however, I had no idea I'd run into him once I commenced working for Lois, who assured me her relationship with Malcolm was estranged, advising their paths rarely crossed. I was meaning to use Lois to get back at Malcolm but sadly it backfired. In the end, I was the one being manipulated. Look Inspector Rose, arrest me if you must, but I categorically state, I am not a murderer.'

'The Police will need you to provide them with a statement and we'll also need to undertake some DNA testing,' James responded, rising slowly to his feet, 'DCI Rose here will expect you at Exeter police station by two o'clock this afternoon. We'll see ourselves out, no need to bother about the tea.'

'You do believe I'm innocent, don't you?' Claire said, reaching for James as he moved towards the door.

'For now,' he replied, firmly brushing aside her hand, 'whatever innocent means.'

****

'We're running out of suspects,' DCI Rose announced, hustling the Jaguar saloon through the back roads to North Bovey, both men deflated from another false lead. 'Who else do you know with possible links to Liam Mercer and Malcolm Frobisher?'

'The only person I can think of is our yachtie mate Leicester Scott-Thomas,' James replied, bracing his feet against the floor as Mick accelerated round a convoy of harvesters.

'It's worth a shot,' Rose replied, 'I can run a background check on Leicester, but probably won't get the full story until next week. What concerns me Sinclair, is the killer is still out there, and we don't have a bloody clue to their identity.'

****

Seated at a stool, the seconds ticking by, James impatiently drummed fingers on the bar, and once again checked his wristwatch, twenty minutes late. Drinks were already ordered. He was about to call the DCI on his mobile when the stocky policeman walked in through the swinging door, greeting James with a half salute.

'This Leicester chap has quite a history,' Rose began, pulling up a bar stool and stretching for the pint of bitter, 'I nearly got locked in the office, I was that pre-occupied reading through the file. I had to yell out to the cleaner only moments before he locked the main door. Don't fancy spending an hour in there when the air conditioner goes off.'

James tried to push Rose along, desperate to know what he'd discovered. Rose getting the hint, started to divulge information.

'Back in 1980, Leicester was heading south from Bristol along the M4 near the Weston-Super-Mare Junction when he lost control of his dark-blue Merc, ploughing headfirst into a telegraph pole. Leicester walked away with only a few cuts and bruises, but his five-year-old son Warwick, died on impact. Leicester returned a blood alcohol level three times over the legal limit.'

'What happened?' James pressed, 'Did he go to prison for manslaughter?'

214

Rose shook his head, 'Nope, he got off with a good behaviour bond, coupled with eighty hours of community service.'

James shook his head in disbelief, 'What Magistrate would be so lenient?

'Ah, well I thought you might have guessed that one,' Rose replied, 'none other than our Honourable Judge: Malcolm Frobisher, at the time a newly appointed junior magistrate'

James gave a low whistle, 'Are you sure about this?'

'Absolutely,' Rose reached into the lining of his jacket removing folded pieces of paper, 'Now, whatever you do mate, don't let anyone get hold of these documents. If you do, I could lose my job. It's all here in black and white, every detail as to what happened that night, and in the weeks which followed.'

James took the papers, shoving them into the back pocket of his jeans.

'I've also managed to obtain copies of national newspapers around the time of the accident,' Rose continued triumphantly, 'here are headlines from a few of them: *Son of rich socialite dies in car crash. Father's drink driving, results in death of child. Heartache for lady of the manor.*'

'Rosemary Scott-Thomas mentioned she had two children who died, could there have been a second child caught up in the crash?' James questioned.

Rose shook his head, 'Nope, there is no mention of anyone else being involved.'

'Quite a sorry state of affairs to lose two children on two separate occasions,' James said, downing his beer in one go, before ordering another. I suppose we'll need to quiz Leicester on exactly what happened the night of his son's death, not a job I relish.'

Rose nodded, 'I'll leave that pleasurable act to you. I'm not officially allowed to quiz Leicester on a matter thirty-five years ago when recorded as "not guilty" of criminal charges. You also need to be careful James, technically the death of Leicester's son is none of our damn business.'

****

Over the next two days James spent his spare time away from the lab going over the newspaper cuttings and court documents supplied by Rose in relation to the death of Warwick Scott-Thomas. The coroner's report was unequivocally damning in its findings, clearly stating at the time of death Leicester's young son had not been wearing a seat belt.

James, finally plucking up enough courage to visit Leicester, took the long drive down to Salcombe the following Sunday afternoon, quickly tracking him down at Tindall's Yard positioned on wooden scaffold planks putting finishing touches on his restored thirty-five-footer. A light breeze blowing in from the French Coast ninety kilometres away, found its way under the yard hoardings and into the boat shed providing welcome relief on an unseasonably warm early October day. Leicester humming softly, blissfully absorbed in hand painting the name of the yacht on its transom, wasn't aware of James' presence, until he was standing directly below him.

'Nice day for it,' James remarked casually, looking up at the wiry figure, 'you must spend several hours here each day.'

Leicester looked down, grinning, 'It gets me away from the nagging wife, but don't tell her I said that.'

James laughed, 'Your secret's safe with me.'

'This place grants me peace and solitude, I would quickly go insane without my boats,' Leicester continued, 'I'm forever having to meet boring entities at the functions Rosemary throws, some who wouldn't even know a cutter from a ketch, sacrilege. Any bit of freedom I can get sees me pounce.'

'Yes, you must tire of so many parties,' James acknowledged.

Now it was Leicester's turn to laugh. 'I am not one for pomp and ceremony at the best of times. I could do without all the frills and formality, black tie every night, special cutlery for every course and such. I'm happiest sitting on the beach eating fish and chips out of an old newspaper.'

'Have you always been swept up in the well-to-do socialite whirl? I would guess life would have been different prior to your retirement, less time for all the social engagements.'

'My work in the legal system provided me with income, independence and stability, certainly little time to relax,' Leicester replied, placing the brushes in a tin of turps and standing back to admire his work, 'there were some aspects of the job I really enjoyed, but it was a very stressful life, one I don't miss.'

'I'd like to ask you about your son, I understand he was killed in a car crash back in 1980,' James knew this line of questioning was risky. All the time he kept his eyes fixed on Leicester's face for any hidden clues.

Leicester turned to watch a small fishing boat drifting slowly to its mooring. James standing two metres below the walkway looking up, waited patiently for him to continue the conversation and when he finally did, his voice held an element of fury.

'My son's death is not up for discussion. Now if that's all you've come to chat about, I'd like you to leave.'

'What I don't understand is why you weren't charged with drink driving,' James continued stoically, not put off by Leicester's icy manner, 'surely you would agree, you were in the wrong and should have been punished?'

'I suffered enough. I did not deliberately kill my own son.'

'I'm not accusing you,' James retaliated, 'I'm merely trying to discover the truth behind your son's death.'

'For what purpose?' Leicester shot back, 'dragging up the past is not going to achieve anything. Besides, I don't see what this has to do with you or an investigating team, it's a private matter.'

'My understanding is Malcolm let you get off with a minimal sentence, why was that?' James knew he was pushing boundaries but wanted answers.

'How the hell should I know, we were mates I guess, he wanted to give me a chance. Legal tendencies and practices were different in those days, less political correctness.'

'I thought you and Frobisher didn't really get along,' James remarked flippantly.

'Perhaps I appealed to his better nature,' Leicester politely informed him, 'you're wasting your time, Sinclair. My son died at a young age, I spent nearly six months in a rehabilitation centre and since the accident I have not touched a drop of alcohol, every day I live with what happened. What more do you want from me?'

'The truth, the honest truth,' James said cynically.

'I've told you all you need to know,' Leicester replied, in barely more than a whisper, his face a blank canvas, 'as the Lord is my witness, there's no more you need to know.'

****

Chapter Fifteen

'If only we can make Leicester talk,' James sounded out to Katie, recapping their notes in preparation for compiling Rose a detailed report, 'he has to crack eventually.'

'Perhaps he has nothing to hide,' Katie remarked, heading into the kitchenette to rustle up a salad sandwich, 'you seem to want him to be guilty of something, but he may well not be. What actual evidence do you have so far from the surveillance Rose has been working on?'

'Apparently every morning, regardless of the weather, Leicester strolls up to St Winwaloe's church in East Portlemouth, spending over an hour walking through the graveyard.'

'Hardly riveting stuff,' Katie mocked, 'lots of people amble around churchyards, but it doesn't mean they have sinister thoughts or have something to hide.'

'Yeah, you may be right, but it's something we need to check out, care to join me? We can squeeze in a bite to eat at the pub on our way back, that sandwich looks archaic, must be fifty varieties of flora on that cheese.'

Katie tossed the bread and salad pieces into the pedal bin, washed her hands, grabbed her coat and joined her brother out in the courtyard confronting the Land Rover with two flat tyres.

With no other option they jumped into the Fiat, Katie the designated driver sitting proudly behind the wheel, secretly praying the Punto would make it to the Coast. James in the passenger seat kept up a pleasant banter, their recent differences brushed aside.

'This will do nicely,' Katie announced, gliding to a halt on the grass verge directly outside the church gates, 'Come on James, prove me wrong and find some sinister motive to all our murders right here amongst the dear and deadly departed.'

'You may well mock,' James countered, heading off along a rickety stone path meandering in and out amongst the headstones. Katie not a fan of coercing with the long gone, stayed at a comfortable distance, keeping her brother in full view as he went from grave to grave reading inscriptions.

'This must be the grave of Leicester's young son,' Katie called out to James, as she knelt to study the poignant words: *Warwick Scott-Thomas–Now with God, dear sweet child, eternally rest in peace.*

Katie felt tears welling up inside as she read the words. She couldn't begin to imagine what it was like for a man to lose his son.

'According to Mick Rose, Leicester visited more than one grave during his visits,' James informed Katie, as they turned to head along another path, this one overgrown with noxious weeds.

'Good luck, it could be any bodies, pardon the pun,' Katie replied, making sure her feet always stayed firmly on the narrow path. She had a thing about stepping over dead bodies, feeling it was disrespectful. James not sharing the same view, stomped irreverently around with little obvious respect for the deceased.

After a tedious fifteen minutes James shouted, beckoning his sister over. 'This could be what Leicester visited. It's the resting place of Daniel Mercer, come take a look at the inscription.'

Katie joined her brother, reading aloud the words printed on the headstone: '*Daniel Liam Mercer–now with God, dear sweet child, eternally rest in peace.*'

'It clearly means something,' James replied, 'there must be a connection between Warwick Scott-Thomas and Daniel Mercer. Now all we need to do is find that connection.'

'Good, can we go now?' Katie asked, not enjoying their dalliance with the departed.

James shook his head, 'Nope, one more grave to go, hurry up, get searching.'

Katie pulled a face, as she aimlessly headed off along another path, this one leading into a more recent section of the graveyard. It was by accident she stumbled upon what they were seeking. Stopping to free a pebble wedged in her sandals she leant against the nearest headstone. Her eyes inadvertently set upon the inscription as she freed the tiny pebble.

'James, here, I've found it,' Katie yelled out breathlessly.

James bolted over to his sister, reading the inscription: *Dieanna Marie Payne–now with God, dear sweet child, eternally rest in peace.*

'Have you the faintest idea what all this means?' Katie quizzed her brother on the drive back towards Moorlands Forensics, 'Why would all three graves have the same inscription?'

'A special discount,' James chuckled, 'three for the price of one.'

'Even by your questionable standards, that's low,' Katie responded, pulling up to a set of traffic lights at the top of Totnes hill. She had opted to take the lanes and B roads back to Bovey, avoiding the busy motorway, 'What possible connection could there be between Warwick, Daniel and Dieanna?'

'I haven't a clue, but I intend to find out. Wake up sleepy, the lights are green. The quicker we get home, the quicker I can solve this mystery.'

****

James ventured along to the next Artisan meeting with a copy of "Falling Memoires" tucked away in his jacket pocket. The painting had been almost forgotten over the past few weeks, but now he wanted to bring it back to life.

'James, this is a surprise,' Lois beamed, greeting him at the Gallery entrance with an endearing hug, 'what brings you to our humble art group on this wet and windy evening? Get in out of the deplorable weather, before you catch your death. I presume you're here on official business? Can I get you a peppermint tea, or perhaps something a little stronger?

'Yes, and a tea will do nicely,' James replied, rubbing his hands together and removing a damp flak jacket.

'The assembly will be packing up in a few moments,' Lois told him, lowering her voice, 'we'll wait for them to leave, before we have our little chat.'

With zealous clatter the small art group packed away easels, paintbrushes and other art supplies, James musing at the interminable, organised chaos required to return the studio space to a semblance of normality. Finally, with the last artist waved off, Lois turned the key in the lock pulling down the security shutters in the front display windows.

'I love these art sessions, but they can be very draining,' she remarked, moving over to the couch, 'come, sit down, how I can help you with your enquiries?'

Obliging he took a seat next to Lois on the couch, retrieving the copy of Falling Memories from his pocket, 'Can you explain Lois, why all five in this painting are now dead?'

Lois reacted slowly, caught off guard by his direct line of questioning, 'Heavens, it didn't even register until you mentioned it,' Lois stuttered, gazing down at the print, 'James, I honestly have no idea.'

'Lois, I need you to think carefully and tell me what all these people have in common. Surely you must know? There has to be a connection.'

Lois firmly shook her head. 'I'm sorry I have no idea. Ah... maybe just pure coincidence?'

'And still no recollection of who the artist was?'

Again, Lois shook her head, 'No, I really haven't the faintest.'

James deflated, rose to his feet, 'Thanks for the tea.'

'It's always a pleasure,' Lois looked up at her visitor, slight concern in her voice, 'James, I know you didn't always think highly of Malcolm, but I'd appreciate you attending a memorial service for him this Saturday at St Mary's church in West Charleton, if you can spare the time.'

He took a moment to reply, 'Yes, of course.'

****

DCI Rose knocked forcefully on the door of Estuary View, waiting impatiently for someone to open it. As soon as Nancy appeared, he pushed her aside, marching straight into the drawing room where Leicester and Rosemary sat enjoying a light supper.

'What is the meaning of this?' Leicester exploded, jumping to his feet, 'You can't barge in here unannounced.'

'Looks like I just did,' Rose replied, crisply, 'Leicester Scott-Thomas, we're arresting you on suspicion of murder, you do not have to say anything, but what you do say, may be taken in evidence and used in a court of law.'

Leicester sank back down in his chair whilst two uniformed officers moved forward to clap handcuffs onto his wrists.

'My husband hasn't murdered anyone,' Lady Scott-Thomas shouted, losing all dignity, 'you must be lunatics thinking he is guilty of such atrocities.'

'We have strong evidence linking your husband to the murders of Dieanna Payne, Malcolm Frobisher, Liam and Sonia Mercer,' Rose replied, indicating for the officers to escort Leicester from the house.

Rosemary followed them to the front door, a petrified Nancy close behind. 'You are not to talk to anyone without our lawyer present,' Rosemary instructed Leicester, 'no one, you understand.'

****

'Is something troubling you?' Katie enquired of James, watching him read through a simple coroner's report several times over. A task he didn't normally do.

'Aspects of this investigation aren't adding up,' James replied casually, pushing the report aside, 'for some reason I have serious doubts Leicester's our murderer. I would have liked more solid forensic evidence before an arrest was made. Mick should have held back on this one, it's out of character for him to jump to conclusions without real proof.'

'Leicester certainly has motive for killing Liam and Frobisher,' Katie reminded her brother, 'after all, he didn't like either of them very much.'

'Yes, but you don't kill someone just because you don't like them. If that were the case, nearly half the world's population would be deceased, probably in a very short space of time.'

Katie laughed, 'Yes, you're right it's not a very strong case, is it?'

'Even if Leicester didn't like those two very much there would be no reason for him to randomly kill Dieanna Payne,' James continued, 'no, we've got this all wrong. Leicester Scott-Thomas is not our killer.'

'This fax has just come through for you,' Fiona announced, interrupting the conversation between her siblings and dropping the sheet onto her brother's desk, 'It's from Mick, guess who paid for Dieanna Payne's funeral, none other than a company by the name of P.R. Eastly Holdings, now why would they do that?'

'No idea, but we need to find out. Can I take the TVR?' James replied, catching her car keys in mid-air at the same time his mobile started to ring.

'Did you get my fax?' Rose's voice echoing through cyberspace.

'Sure did, I was heading over to see Preston as we speak. Want to meet me there?'

'I would, but I have a crippling migraine. Here are a few other interesting facts I've turned up. Preston Eastly lived in Warwickshire prior to moving to Devon, sound familiar? Isn't that where you mentioned Rosemary Scott-Thomas originally lived? It's a bit too coincidental, especially as they lived a mere five miles apart. Here's more, Preston was a GP before moving to Devon. He gave his profession away to become a very successful businessman.

Now, I've checked for malpractice suits, but there aren't any. It would appear Preston left the medical profession for a sea change, nothing sinister on that score. However, there's something niggling but I can't put my finger on it. I have a hunch Preston Eastly is somehow linked to all our murders; although, I'm not sure how. See what information you can squeeze out of him, James. Perhaps Preston and Leicester are in on this together.'

James ended the call, dropped into first gear and pushed Fiona's red sports at a savage pace towards Exeter along the B roads. At the motorway merger he redlined it, overtaking everything at well above legal limits, and took another incoming call on his mobile.

'James, Margo here,' her voice came through crisp and clear on loudspeaker, 'sorry it has taken me so long to get in touch. The usual pressures of a busy Uni lab, anyway, I've managed to research the name of Daniel's godfather, a chap by the name of Preston Eastly. Mean anything to you?'

****

'A second visit in rapid succession Sinclair, I should be flattered,' Preston remarked, the handshake firm but with only a semblance of a smile, 'have you had lunch?'

Not expecting the gratuitous offer, James shook his head.

'Good, I pre-booked my favourite trattoria just down the road, adjacent to the Cathedral, we can eat there,' Preston announced, 'If we go now, we'll beat the lunchtime rush.'

James followed Preston out of the building, trying hard to match his lengthy strides as they made it to the imposing Gothic masterpiece in less than ten minutes. Settled at a corner table, James began firing questions at Preston, which he seemed to be expecting.

'Why did you pay for Dieanna Payne's funeral? Is it a habit of yours to go around randomly footing send-off bills for the deceased?'

Preston laughed, craning his neck for the black board wine list, 'I wondered how long it would take you to unearth that little secret. Of course, I'd be more than happy to explain: Dieanna was my goddaughter, it was the least I could do to ensure she had a proper burial. Her biological parents were not about to cough up, so I felt it my duty, quite a simple explanation really.'

'And the same applied for Daniel Mercer I presume. You were also his godfather by all accounts?'

223

Preston checked the label on the wine, allowing the young waitress to pour two glasses.

'Correct. However, I can assure you James I am not randomly everyone's godfather,' Preston laughed.

'Would you care to explain how you happen to be godparent to Daniel Mercer and Dieanna Payne?'

'Perhaps another time,' Preston replied coldly, 'look Sinclair, this really is none of your business. Anyway, where's Rose, shouldn't he be here keeping an eye on things and asking the questions?'

James switched tacks, challenging Preston from another angle. 'How well do you know Lady Scott-Thomas?'

'Rosemary, fairly well I suppose. We first met in Warwickshire, when I ran the local medical practice, Rosemary was a patient of mine. We've remained friends over the years. She helps fund certain areas of Eastly Holdings. I hold her in high regard and trust her financial instinct.'

'Surely there must be a hidden agenda?'

Preston threw back his head and laughed, 'You forensic types are all the same, very pragmatic, invariably cynical. You spend too much of your life in a scientific bubble. I'm sorry Sinclair, you'll gain no more from me today, so I suggest you order something from the menu, my treat. I can highly recommend the duck ravioli.'

****

'How did your meeting with P.R. Eastly go?' Katie asked, watching James drop into the chair behind his desk.

'It didn't,' James grumbled, 'the food was nice, but that's about all I garnered from the meeting. A top eating house if you can afford the exorbitant prices. Preston Eastly is keeping his trap shut when it comes to personal matters and everything else to boot.'

'But he admitted he paid for Dieanna's funeral?'

'Oh yes, he claims to have been Dieanna's godfather, so it was his "duty". You know the one thing I can't fathom Katie, is why Eastly would allow Rosemary Scott-Thomas to financially assist his business. Would you say that's normal practice, to allow someone totally unrelated to throw money your way?'

'I wouldn't say that,' Katie replied, 'actually, it's fairly common practice for a friend or acquaintance to invest venture capital in a private concern, especially if the potential profits are attractive. Let's face it, the old girl has more of the folding stuff than she knows what to do with; besides, what can you earn from the banks and stock market these days, a pittance. Or perhaps she's reciprocating a favour, maybe Rosemary likes helping people out. We already know she does a lot for local charities.'

Before James could comment his mobile vibrated, demanding immediate pick up.

'Son, it's your father here,' the gravelly male voice came down the line, 'as promised, I've gone over my stud records and found something which may be of interest to you.'

James pushed the phone closer to his ear. 'Fire away,' he instructed.

'Well, a little over five months ago I sold a gorgeous bay thoroughbred foal to Leicester Scott-Thomas. At the time, a request was made for the foal to be named *Rosemary's Flare,* only there must have been a typing error, because when I handed over the documentation the name appeared as *Rosemary's Affair.* I found it quite amusing, but apparently Lady Scott-Thomas didn't. She even involved her London lawyer, threatening to sue if we didn't amend things immediately.'

'Any idea as to who made that mistake, could it have been deliberate?'

'Quite possibly, I don't recall the mistake being from our end. Sharon went off the paperwork sent through to us, which in this instance came directly from Leicester himself.'

'Was the name amended, and all parties satisfied?' James asked.

'Oh yes, but it took a few days. In the meantime, without realising a mistake had been made, we sent a notice informing other breeders of the sire and mare of *Rosemary's Affair.* I received some comical emails back from the racing fraternity, it was the talk of the county for a few weeks.'

James gave a low whistle, 'Thanks dad, I have a feeling Leicester might have done all this on purpose, but I need to figure out why. Great work.'

'I'm pleased you're pleased, now you can do me a favour. Bring the girls over to lunch on Sunday. Your mother and I are sick of corresponding with our children via email, phone and vague text messages.'

The phone went dead. James turned back to Katie, 'I've had quite an interesting phone call with Dad, by the way what were we saying before the call?'

Katie tried to recap their conversation, 'As far as I remember, we were discussing why Rosemary Scott-Thomas would fund Preston Eastly's business, I said maybe it was some kind of favour.'

James clapped Katie on the back, before dialling DCI Rose's mobile, 'Mick, see what you can unearth from Preston Eastly's old medical records stored in the Warwickshire surgery. In particular you're looking up the patient files for our dear friend Rosemary Scott-Thomas. I have a feeling Preston was keeping a very big secret and in return Rosemary was paying him large sums of cash.'

'Sure.'

James then dialled another number, 'Eastly, James Sinclair here, how long have you been having an affair with Rosemary Scott-Thomas?'

****

'Not interrupting anything?' Matt enquired, popping his head round the Moorland office door encountering James, Katie and Fiona deep in animated conversation.

James looked up, 'No, we're just going over Wetherill's police interview for the fiftieth time. So far, there's no real evidence linking him to the shooting of Michelle Langham, although, we're pretty sure he's guilty.'

'What about ballistics?' Matt enquired, taking up residence on the reception couch.

Again, James replied in the negative, 'No gun, no cartridges, felon long gone.'

'All right, but surely they have been able to implicate Wetherill in something after the paintings bust? For Christ's sake, haven't they got testimony from the yacht crew who were nabbed?'

'Funny you should mention that. Can't get a word out of either of them after two days heavy questioning. Mick says they have clammed up completely, reckons Wetherill has them on a big bonus if they act ignorant.'

'What?'

'Due out on bail today and best guess is they'll skip the country first chance. As for "Fool's Paradise" there's no immediate connection there with either Wetherill or the Judge. It's registered out of home port Nantes. Rose says it could take ages to unravel true ownership seeing the French authorities don't appear too enthused about chasing down leads.'

'Typical.'

'This case is leading us down a lot of dead ends,' Katie acknowledged, joining in the conversation, 'whoever the perpetrator is, they are managing to outsmart us in so many ways and always one step ahead. I can't believe Rose had to let Leicester go in the end, perhaps his team didn't tighten the screws enough.'

'He can hardly be detained if there's no concrete evidence,' James reminded her, 'mind you, it gets worse. I've been handed an official warning by the Chief Constable for accusing Preston Eastly of having an affair with Rosemary Scott-Thomas. His solicitor has threatened legal action if I don't retract my statement.'

'You've clearly read things wrong,' Fiona informed her brother, 'a high-profile individual such as Rosemary Scott-Thomas wouldn't bother having an affair. She's too protective of her social standing.'

'I wouldn't be so hasty with those assumptions,' James replied earnestly, 'Rosemary had an affair all right, my mistake is: I've accused the wrong man. What's more, I believe Leicester Scott-Thomas deliberately tried to name his new foal *Rosemary's Affair* to send his wife an unequivocal message as a way of teaching her a lesson. I think he knew about Rosemary's romantic indiscretions and wanted the world to know about it.'

'Interesting theory,' Katie hypothesised.

'To find out who she was bonking perhaps requires a common denominator,' Matt remarked coarsely, never one for diplomacy, 'it should be easy for you to decipher Katie, common happens to be your middle name.' A twinkle shone in his eyes as he made this statement.

Katie reached over to deliver an unyielding pinch on the forearm. 'There's nothing common about me, Matthew Tyler. I'm made of quality material, with a touch of elegance and class. I wouldn't be surprised if there's also a drop of royal blood running through my blue veins.'

James, gazing through the rear window watching children play on Bovey Heath suddenly swivelled around in his chair, 'Katie, what did you just say?'

'I politely reminded Matt that I am not a commoner, I happen to be the…'

'Yes of course,' James slammed his hand firmly onto the desk, cutting his sister off in mid-sentence, 'now it all makes sense, if Rosemary Scott-Thomas was having an affair, her hard-earned socialite status would vanish overnight. She would literally go from A list to Z list. Katie, get Mick Rose on the phone, he needs to come with me; he's got an arrest to make.'

****

'Where are we going?' Rose demanded, tightly gripping the roll bar as James punted the ageing Land Rover flat chat round a ninety-degree bend. 'Can you at least give me some background,' he shouted above the racket, wishing they had taken his Jag.

'Nope, but if you must know, we're heading for a rather nice manor house set in a rather large estate on the edge of Dartmoor; recently renovated, according to Country Life Magazine.'

'I don't give a shit if we're visiting a semi in Brixton, with half its roof missing,' Rose retorted, a wave of nausea creeping over him, 'just put me out of my misery.'

James gave a sardonic smile, bringing the old 4WD back to the speed limit, not wishing for Rose to throw up over his newly upholstered seats.

'I thought I'd surprise you. Sit back and enjoy the ride, the countryside is lovely this time of the year. By the way, did you manage to dig up the information I was after in relation to Preston Eastly's patient records, from his old medical practice?'

Rose showed dismay. 'I'm sorry friend, how could I forget something so important,' he mumbled, 'These damn migraines have been plaguing me for a while.'

'You've got to get those headaches checked out. You appear to be getting them far too often.'

Rose forced a cheeky grin, 'Right you are Doctor Sinclair. Once we nab our murderer I'll go for a full examination, warts and all.'

'Good, and don't worry too much about the info I asked for. I've pretty much figured it out for myself.'

'Meaning?' A grey faced looking Rose enquired, trying to focus on conversation to distract from the car's motion.

'Let's just say, I believe Preston Eastly compromised his position as a GP by destroying a few patient files. I believe it was carried out at someone's request, and in return that someone paid regular sums of money to Preston funding the capital base of his business.'

'What about this country retreat we're headed to, you've not mentioned it before.'

'Ah, well I happened to stumble upon this by accident. I was having a bite with Angie Fairweather, who owns Fairweather Realty in Plymouth. We got talking properties, and she knows all about "Moorcombe Manor". According to Angie, the owner visits the same time each year for a symbolic anniversary. I've checked my calendar, and assuming my calculations are correct, we're spot on with today's timing.'

****

'I take it you've come to apologise for wrongly accusing my husband of murder?' Rosemary Scott-Thomas remarked as James and DCI Rose approached her in a vast sunken garden, repotting orchids.

'If only it were that simple,' James commented, coming to stand next to her, 'we're actually here to ask a few questions, firstly I'm curious as to why you purchased three headstones all with the same inscriptions? Lucky for us the stone mason who engraved them remembers all the orders being placed.'

'You've obviously got a touch of the sun,' Rosemary retorted sarcastically, heavy handed with her secateurs, cutting off the heads of two splendid specimens, 'I wish you'd stop meddling in other people's affairs.'

'Great choice of words,' James ridiculed, 'I find it remarkable that in order to keep your elevated status in society you decided to resort to murder, interesting. The sad thing is, your first victim was only ten years of age. Did you really feel it necessary to kill Daniel Mercer, what had that young boy ever done to you?'

'He lived, that's what he did wrong,' Rosemary replied, anger etched in her voice, 'I don't expect the likes of you to understand, Sinclair.'

'I take it there was a reason Daniel died on his birthday?' James fired back, 'it appears a lot of careful planning went in to these murders, not just a spur of the moment decision.'

Rosemary's shallow, sharp laugh echoed through the garden, 'You're cleverer than you appear Sinclair, I'll grant you that. You see my Warwick died on his birthday, so it seemed fitting others should do the same.'

James was puzzled, trying to make sense of Rosemary's words. He waited patiently for her to continue.

'Not long after Leicester and I married I had an affair, nine months later I gave birth to a healthy baby girl, when that girl grew up, she also had an affair giving birth to a son.'

Rosemary reached into her jacket pocket for a small notepad and pen, she scribbled frantically before passing the paper to James. 'There you go.'

James read what she'd written, prior to throwing the paper onto the ground in disgust.

'So, you see, the bloodline was contaminated,' Rosemary continued to explain, 'I needed those people to die, in order to stop the poison.'

'You killed for the sake of nobility?' James shot back, 'Where's the sense in that?'

'You're a commoner, with no proper breeding. I don't expect you to understand,' Rosemary replied calmly, 'James, my family has been part of the English aristocracy for centuries, I did everyone a favour by throwing away the dead wood, no one wants hand me downs.'

James was bewildered, wondering if he'd heard correctly. Rosemary Scott-Thomas was insane. 'You murdered innocent people for the sake of vanity?'

Rosemary sighed, 'Oh dear, do I have to keep spelling it out, Daniel was my illegitimate grandson, what purpose would he serve in this world, so I decided, he had to go, murder number one. Then I got thinking about his father Liam and how he had seduced Dieanna Payne, reason for murder number two. I also came to realise Sonia Mercer was as much to blame, if she had kept Liam happy and content he would never have strayed, murder number three. Of course, my own daughter Dieanna, the result from my affair with Malcolm Frobisher was also a problem. Gradually, over a long period I became angry Dieanna was still alive, especially after my dear sweet Warwick was tragically taken from me, so I was left without options, she was a curse on my soul.'

'But you prolonged the poor woman's agony by having Dieanna certified as insane, didn't you?' DCI Rose accused, listening to the macabre story unfold. 'You also initially tried to make us believe Dieanna's death was a suicide? You even made it impossible for us to pinpoint anyone to her death by throwing a mixture of pills into the bottle. Any one of the nursing staff could have been held accountable.'

'Yes, clever, wasn't I?' Rosemary chuckled, 'Now, where was I? Oh yes, that only really left that parasite Malcolm Frobisher, who was probably the guiltiest of the lot, after all, if it had not been for Malcolm forcing himself on me one evening at a London party, none of this would have happened. He was my fifth and final victim.'

'You killed for self-indulgence. What kind of sick person does that?'

'Oh, Jim honestly, you make me sound like an ogre,' Rosemary laughed, 'all I did was put the poor unfortunates out of their misery, they would have ended up on the bottom of a dung heap regardless; yes, you can thank me for rescuing them all from Purgatory.'

****

'Boy, am I pleased this case has finally ended,' James remarked, putting his feet up on the laboratory bench, with little intention of doing anything too taxing for the next half hour. 'DCI Rose did a fantastic job helping grab Scott-Thomas. Totally mad, I reckon she'll spend her last years in a secure women's institution. Hopefully, I can work next time with Mick to nail a few charges on Wetherill.'

Fiona looked at Katie before passing James the early morning edition of the Newton Abbot Star, left open at the death notices. James scanned his eyes halfway down the page,

Michael 'Mick' Rose, died peacefully in his sleep at his home in Exeter during the early hours of Tuesday morning. He is survived by his wife Christine and two children Nathan and Victoria. Mick's funeral will be held at St Stephen's church in Exeter on Friday at eleven – all welcome. Instead of flowers all donations to go to the Neurology Department at Exeter Hospital.

James stared at the notice dumbfounded, reading it several times before the paper was tossed to one side. 'What happened?'

'Cruellest of luck, Mick had an inoperable brain tumour,' Fiona replied softly, 'there was nothing anyone could have done. According to his wife, it was a peaceful end, he just didn't wake up.'

****

'James how lovely to see you,' Lois smiled warmly, 'I've been reading all the local and national papers. Your team did a remarkable job bringing the killer to justice, hopefully we can now all sleep at night. What an evil woman Rosemary Scott-Thomas was.'

'It's been on my mind for a while, I want to ask; can you honestly say you have no idea who draw "Falling Memories"?' James pressed, intrigued if Lois really did know but wasn't prepared to say.

'Why are we put on this earth, James?' Lois conjectured, purposely avoiding the question. She reached for a paintbrush adding a splash of blue to an intimate watercolour. 'Is it to lead our lives to the fullest, or are we here for others? I've never quite worked it out.'

'Does it matter?'

'Oh yes, it matters a great deal. As an artist I strive to reach into the very soul of all creations in order to uncover the truth. Take the painting "Falling Memories", have you not asked yourself what the artist might have seen beyond the canvas? Perhaps they never really saw the five portrayed on the beach, or the lad falling off the cliff. What if they saw the future, long before they witnessed the past?'